SWELLEN'S RECKONING

by
W. HOCK HOCHHEIM

Audio ISBN: 978-1-932113-96-9
Paperback ISBN: 978-1-932113-97-6
Digital Ebook ISBN: BOC3451KHV

Other Titles by W. Hock Hochheim
Fightin' Words
Knife Combatives
Impact Weapon
Combatives Footwork and Maneuvering
My Gun is My Passport
Last of the Gunmen
Rio Grande Black Magic
American Medieval
Blood Rust
The China Alamo
Be Bad Now
Face the Muzak
The Great Escapes of Pancho Villa
Training Mission Series 1-5

Prologue

My name is W. Hock Hochheim and I am the author of the *Renegade General* series. I am also the author of the Gunther western series and book 5 in that Gunther series is ***THE CHINA ALAMO***.

In it, Gunther tries to rescue 3 Shanghaied medical doctors from the Boxer Rebellion in China. In doing so, he and his team get trapped in what is historically called the "55 Days in Peking." About half-way through this book, an American gun runner using an alias, a minor character turns out to be a mysterious AWOL fugitive, once a Lt. General, a Mordecai "Swoop" Swellen. As the China Alamo progresses, Swoop becomes a fierce, action-packed, important character in the book. A fan favorite, if you will.

At the end of THE CHINA ALAMO, Gunther helps the hunted Swoop remain in Peking as a bodyguard to one of American doctors that wishes to remain there and practice. Swoop is far from the U.S. Army, the law and obsessed bounty hunters tracking him. The end of the Swoop story? No.

Sometime later, my publisher staff and I discussed creating a series for this Swoop Swellen and this book is his origin story. A new series was born.

This books starts out at that point in China, post Boxer Rebellion, then rips back in time to the U.S. and his origin story. I can only hope you will enjoy this tale and series.

TABLE OF CONTENTS

Chapter 1: Broken China
Master Lay's Kung Fu School, Peking, China 1903

"Men will kill the doctor," the boy whispered in Chinese into Swellen's ear.

The neighborhood child had charged into Master Lay's Kung Fu class in too noisy clutter of interruption. This annoyed the strict Sifu Lay's school rules. Mordecai "Swoop" Swellen left the wooden class floor and ushered the neighborhood boy near the lobby front door. He took a knee and asked him in Mandarin to repeat the shocking message.

"You must go to the doctor's office." the boy said, "They told me to tell you to come to doctor's office or they will kill him and his wife."

"Who said this?" Swoop asked.

"Two men, Americans like you. They have guns."
Swoop felt a wave of anguish overcome him. His worst nightmare had suddenly come true. They'd found him. Discovered. And as far away as China? How could this be? And his one remaining mission in Peking after the Boxer Rebellion, his one assignment was to protect the American Dr. Bellmont and he had failed. Now the doctor's life and his new family were in danger because of his own secret past.

"They said they are waiting for you at the doctor's office."

"Okay, kid. Go home," he said.

The Kung Fu class continued on behind him. Swoop stood and nodded and bowed at Master Lay from across the room who'd frequently cut his eyes at him and the boy. Swoop had a sinking burn that he would never see Master Lay again. He grabbed his leather bag and shoes. He circled the kwoon floor and after a bow, slipped out the back door, just in case the child messenger was followed.

He scanned the rear alleyways and yards, then jogged across the kwoon's small backyard, through an alley and out onto a narrow, dirt, back street.

Dressed in Chinese clothes, the Scotch-Irish Swoop always walked the streets of Peking like a native, despite being 6 feet tall and having somewhat curly, brown-reddish hair. This anonymity came because the regional streets and avenues bustled with legation-embassy members from numerous European countries, the U.S. and Canada. Post Boxer Rebellion, all the local Chinese were acclimated to a "melting pot" of international pedestrians and lifestyles. This section of Peking looked like western towns or in some areas, bigger western cities in the U.S., except for some of the distinct oriental architecture, or the occasional camel train hauling goods to markets.

Mordecai "Swoop" Swellen had lived there in China for almost three years. Not only was he tasked by an Army Major Johann Gunther in 1901 to protect the young Dr. Bellmont, but he was also considered a respected hero inside the legation communities. Swoop was a champion of the Boxer Rebellion, a wild, warrior protecting the embassies in their darkest of times, those days known by Western historians and newsmen as the "55 Days of Peking" siege. The new American Ambassador Devin Larmes even hired him on for extra security, all under Swoop's accepted alias of one "Robert Small."

Those enduring and early survivors of the Rebellion heard whispers and rumors that Robert Small was once some kind of vicious American officer, possibly even a general! And that "Small" was not his real name. But no one really cared in those dark hours as he was revered as another fearless lifesaver with guns protecting them from the Boxers. As peace developed, the negative rumors slowly disappeared, and he just became…just good ol Robert Small to everyone. Even the Marines stationed there called him Robert Small and told tales of his rebellion-squashing heroics.

Dr. Bellmont and his Chinese wife and their young son required little security this third year of his medical residency as Bellmont welcomed and treated the area Chinese for their ailments. He'd become rather beloved in the community. While the legations paid Bellmont for medical services, the locals could trade eggs, chickens, bread, silks, whatever in exchange for his treatments. Some he treated for free. As a result, Swoop felt less and less concern for Bellmont's safety as the years ticked by.

His days escorting the Bellmont family, his extra job of trolling the embassy grounds, almost with policeman-like status, quickly became uneventful, if not downright boring, the typical curse of so many security jobs. But this monotonous languor was better than being a hunted man, always on the run back in the United States.

He had Major Johann Gunther and a hefty salary from Bellmont's rich, California father to thank for these calm times and easy job.

So, Swoop studied the books in the British Legation library and attended Kung Fu classes four days a week out in the city, learning Chinese hand, sword and knife fighting.

One positive thing about serving on embassy security was, he was a legal man of arms in China. Pistols, knives and rifles. In the leather bag rested his two-gun, pistol belt with two Colt .38, double-action revolvers. The bullet belt loops were full, and he had a box of rounds in the bag's side pocket. The gun belt also held a ubiquitous, large, double-edge, fighting knife with an ornate handle in an artistic sheath, one he once confiscated from a dead Boxer he killed, like so many, with his bare hands. Back in his quarters at Bellmont's residence were many other weapons. Would he, could he ever return to those rooms again?

He's been visiting a Chinese woman named Ya-tang for some time. Her polished quiet, matched her solemn wisdom. He was, he felt, falling in love with her, a dare he could heretofore never dream of as a federal fugitive. Would he ever see her again?

Who could have found him in China? But, whomever, however, now some hunters had. And now they'd captured his friends to use as bait. Dr. Bellmont's office was just outside the official multi-embassy grounds on Legation Street, a site of horrible battles just three years earlier. It was once again full of shops, houses and normal China life.

The neighborhood boy warned him of two men, but Swoop knew there would at very least three, the third or even more would be across the street or staked out in the area, perhaps in or atop the two-story stone buildings that lined the avenue. That's where he'd hide and spy, if in their boots. These others would be lookouts or snipers for a quick kill, as Swoop knew well he was wanted alive or dead.

These hunters had to be ex-military to track him here, probably from that Ditch Digger bounty business, and would plan for his reputation of pure violence from those dead Diggers Swoop had escaped from since 1892.

Swoop did not run straight to Bellmont's office. Instead, there was section of various stores a few blocks away, and he was bound for the largest department store in the neighborhood. Once inside the store, Swoop purchased the common, large conical, Oriental, straw hat. And in the women's department, he purchased a long, black-haired wig.

Once again on the outside steps of the store, he pulled the wig over his reddish-brown hair and shoved the big hat atop his head. The lengthy black hair covered his shoulders. With this disguise, along with his customary Chinese outfit he already wore, he hoped to sneak close to Bellmont's office unnoticed. He hoped the Americans would expect him to look like his wanted posters, dress like a Westerner and appear to be his old Scottish-Yankee, "cowboy" self.

He walked toward an alley next to the store and once a few steps inside the passageway, pulled his two-gun belt from his bag and buckled it on under the long loose, colorful, silk jacket.

He quickly arrived on the corner of Legation Street and peeked all around and up too. Chinese rooftop eaves were turned upward to prevent evil spirits from above looking down at them. And this time evil surely lurked above. He immediately spotted the upper half of a man atop the building right across from the Bellmont's office. The man wore a dark Stetson-like hat.

Swoop shuffled across the street and down the side of that building. He knew the three-story edifice was a cramped series of decrepit apartments. He'd reconned the building once before to evaluate the safety of the Bellmont office location. The rooftop was a natural surveillance and attack point.

Swoop crossed the street and shuffled inside the building through a back door. He climbed the filthy steps to the closed rooftop door and silently dropped his leather bag just inside the roof door. He took off his jacket and draped it on his shoulders like a long cape, his arms free and hidden inside. He pulled one of his pistols and held it "boot-legged," as in pointed down beside his thigh, yet still concealed beneath the long coat. Hat and head down, he pushed the worn, wooden door open and entered the roof.

"Hello, how are you," he said in Chinese to the tall man in Western clothes about 12 feet away, who peered over a wall at the street below.

The man turned and looked him over. He was indeed an Anglo.

"Scat! Geet, Chinaman!" The man growled, waving his hand as a signal for him to leave.

"Oh?" Swoop said.

"I said go. This ain't none of your business, Chinaman!"

"I think it is," Swoop said in slow, perfect English, raising his head all the way up, his face now in full view from under the big hat.

Eyes-wide, the surprised man recognized Swoop and he began that telltale leg crouch, the bend at the knees, the beginnings of a gun draw. Swoop lifted his pistol and shot him in the stomach area, into his right side near his holster and gun. He shot low hoping the man would not fall over the wall to the street below, but rather double over forward.

The man didn't fall over the wall. He had no time to. As the man doubled over forward a few inches, Swoop was in a mad charge, holstering the handgun and pulling his China knife. Swoop was on him in a second, his left hand swept off the Anglo's hat and grabbed the man's long head hair. Swoop yanked his head up, back and to the left. With that China knife in his right hand, Swoop plunged the blade into the man's exposed neck and pulled it inward and on through the windpipe. The westerner was down and dead in 30 seconds or so, a bloody mess.

"Ditch Digger," Swoop said, looking him over. Yes, a white man in his 40s. Scarred face. Decent clothes. Nice gun rig. Worn boots. He had to be one of the Ditch Digger's Bail Company of ex-military, bounty hunters.

"I'll be back for you shortly, sidewinder," Swoop muttered.

He took off his conical hat, grabbed the dead man's hat and made for the corner of the roof. On his knees, he peeked at the Bellmont office and the street below. No one below seemed to care about the single, rooftop gunshot. There were always occasional gunshots from training sessions at the Legations just up the avenue. No one had burst out of the Bellmont office, looking skyward.

What was going on in there? He wondered staring at the office. Were they beating Bellmont? Raping his wife? What? And he couldn't wait, he simply had to…swoop in. Swooping, that was how he got his old Army nickname. Swooping in.

He left the roof with his big, conical hat back on and the long coat still draped on his shoulders. He grabbed his bag by the door and dashed down the steps, ran out the back, up the alleyway and out to the avenue. All the while, he ran memories of the medical office layout in his mind. The front door had a bell on it, then the big lobby, then the door to the big medical office. There was a bathroom off the lobby, a luxury for this part of town. Where would the Ditch Diggers sit? Wait? Hide? Ambush? No entry to the office would be safe. He decided against any suicidal entry.

He decided to go with the mythology of the classic street showdown, made famous in the Blood and Thunder books by Eastern writers.

Once on the cobblestone street, Swoop set his bag down on the sidewalk, and tore off his hat and wig. He pulled both pistols and kept them boot-legged, concealed under his long jacket. He walked into the middle of the avenue, right in front of Bellmont's office.

"Ditch Diggers!" Swoop yelled out. "Ditch Diggers!"

The nearby people on the street were a bit shocked at this audacious display.

"Everybody get back! Leave!" Swoop yelled in Chinese and in English.

They did, confused and hustling off in all directions. The front door opened. The bell rang. An American stepped out holding the Chinese, Mrs. Bellmont in front of him. He held a pistol to her head. A second American stepped out alone. The three, two gunmen and the trembling hostage, remained on the sidewalk in front of the office.

"Pat Weeps," Swoop said, recognizing the solo man.

"The renegade general! Mordecai 'Swoop' Swellen. In… the…flesh," the solo man said. "Looks like you have turned all Chinese."

Swoop stood still and silent.

"If you don't want to see this little lady's head blowed off," Pat Weeps said, "if you got any guns on under that jacket, you'd best drop them to the stones. You are surrounded."

Swoop stood still and silent.

"General, there's a man on the roof behind you with guns."

"Not anymore," Swoop said. "He's dead."

Swoop could see the ever-so-slight, set-back in their faces. He could see their eyes dart up to the roof and back.

"Will-ARD!" Pat Weeps cried out.

No answer.

"Well, we could just shoot you right now," Weeps added, "bounty is the same."

"Do you really think you'd survive that? Because I will kill you both. We'll all die."

"Ahh…this little lady…"

"Will die too," Swoop said, "we'll all die here today. If I'm going to die anyway, we'll all die."

"This ain't no stand-off, Swellen, it's two against one and…"

Swoop raised his right arm at the elbow, from under the jacket and through the silk, shot Weeps three times. Face. Chest. Hip. Weeps folded and fell against, and then crashed into the Bellmont front window, breaking half the glass, and there in the ragged hole, Weeps hung, framed and quivering.

The hostage holder took the gun away from Mrs. Bellmont's head to aim at Swoop, and with his grip on her distracted, and loosened, she screamed as she dove flat to the sidewalk.

Swoop took off to his right, both pistols angled at the man, blazing away. Hip high at first, but then he lifted the .38s up to eye level. That hunter too, absorbed bullets up and down his chest and hips, and he fell back against the stone office front.

Swoop marched up to the office, eyeing both men, his right gun on the right-side man, Pat Weeps, suspended in the window, and with his left gun on the left side man.

Dr. Bellmont burst from the front door, collapsing on his downed wife, gasping, he turned her over. She was unharmed. He looked up at Swoop, speechless. Shocked. Confused.

"Nice move, Mei Zhen," Swoop said to Mrs. Bellmont. Her name meant "beautiful pearl," in Chinese and she still was, even down on the sidewalk and exhausted.

"Are you two alright? Did they hurt you?"

"No," the doctor said. "They just made us sit, under their guns. Waiting for you. What is going on Robert?"

"There were only three?" Swoop asked.

"Only three," Bellmont answered.

Swoop holstered his guns. He walked to Weeps, dead and still suspended in the broken glass window. He grabbed his booted feet and hauled him out of the window. Weep's carcass, especially his lifeless head bounced hard on the stone sidewalk. Swoop leaned in and looked Weeps over. He'd escaped Weeps and his men for years and years, killing many of them.

"How did you find me here" Swoop said to the carcass, looking Pat Weeps over.

Now, finally, Weeps was dead, But, his boss, the bounty hunter company owner and leader, head "Ditch Digger," one Jerry Pickwith was still alive and well back in an office in the USA, and he would still be ravenous for the bounty, still vindictive for all the damage Swoop had wrought upon them through the years.

"I will explain everything shortly, "Swoop said. "But for right now Doc, will you get on the phone to the American Embassy and tell them, I need a horse and two lengths of rope from the stables?"

Dr. Bellmont helped his wife up and in a clutch of arms they stepped back inside the office. Swoop searched both men, removing their gun belts, wallets and travel papers. He jogged across the street, dashed upstairs and onto the roof. The rooftop sniper's body was right where he left him. With grunts and cusses, Swoop hauled the big man over to the wall. He lifted the body limb by limb to torso, over to the wall's top. He peeked over the edge to see if it was clear below and with a huff shoved the corpse over. The deceased hit the sidewalk below headfirst, not that it mattered. He jogged downstairs to the street and waited.

"The stable boy will be right here. I had to tell them all what happened," Bellmont shouted from the office doorway.

Swoop nodded. A German soldier ran up from the Legations front gate.

"What happened, Robert?" He asked in broken English.

"Oh, these three men are from America. They were trying to kill me. An old American vendetta. 'Rache'- revenge."

"Are you okay?"

"I am okay."

"The doctor?"

"Okay. They are okay," Swoop said.

Within 5 minutes a teenager riding atop a horse rounded the Legation gates and galloped toward them. The other German guards, unable to abandon their posts, gathered at the entrance, watching eagerly. A number of Americans from the embassy, to include some U.S. Marine officers and Ambassador Devin Larmes, followed.

The boy jumped off the horse and handed Swoop the ropes.

"Thanks Jeffrey," Swoop said and set about tying the torsos together of the two men by the office. The German soldier helped.

"Robert! What happened?" Ambassador Larmes asked.

"These three men tried to kill me, sir. It's a…it's an old blood vendetta from the U.S. of A."

Larmes looked at the Bellmonts and they both nodded. Dr. Bellmont quickly explained what happened to them while Swoop tied up the chest of the sniper across the street. He and the German tied up the two on the sidewalk to one rope and tied the sniper with the second rope.

"Jeffrey," Swoop said to the stable boy, while hooking the ropes to the saddle horn, "What horse is this?"

"Samson."

"Can you ride Samson and tow this these dead fellers to the Belgium Funeral Home inside? Is the saddle on good and tight, son?"

"It is sir."

"Good."

Jeffrey leaped aboard, testing the horse's saddle and pull, and Samson was able to drag the carcasses in a slow walk, up Legation Street through the main gate, toward the Belgium section.

"Ambassador, I wanted to clean up the street as quickly as possible. I will be in your office to explain the details in just a few minutes, sir, but first I want to speak with the Bellmonts. Make sure they are really, okay."

"Okay, Robert, sure. We'll see you there. It's a relief to see you safe, my friend," Larmes said. He and the others returned to the legations.

Swoop picked up his hat, wig and leather bag from the sidewalk. He motioned for the Bellmonts to walk inside their office with him. The lobby was a mess. All the daily cleaning and settings work of Mei Zhen was in disarray. Tables knocked over, plants smashed, her family heirloom, China broken. They sat in leather chairs in the lobby, and Swoop "Robert Small" Swellen began...

"I have to go back home, Doc. You are safe here in the legations now. The Boxer war is over. People who want to kill me now, know where I am. They will never stop coming for me. You and your wife and child will never be safe if I stay here. I must leave you. I will go back to the States. I will announce my arrival and draw attention away from you all and China. There are things you don't know about me, Doc."

The couple sat in raptured by his words.

"You remember during the Boxer Rebellion, you heard, you learned that my real name is not Robert Small."

"And you were in the Army. Yes, sir. But I don't remember."

"And you never asked. I was in the Army, my friends. I was. My real name is Mordecai Swellen. I was once a Lt. General. They nicknamed me "Swoop." "Swoop" Swellen because they said I would swoop in and kill... massacre...kill all the Indians. Which was true. If I had to and if I was so ordered. I was deserving of that bad reputation and nickname. But folks there and then, didn't know I am about one quarter Ojibwe Indian, or what many call at home, the Chippewa. It was a secret I kept from the Army. My first wife," he looked right at Mei Zhen, "was an Indian. A Chippewa."

"Where is she, Robert?" she asked in amazement.

"She's dead, Mei. Murdered."

"Wǒ hěn bàoqiàn," she said (– I am so sorry.)

"The Chippewa defeated the Sioux and the Iroquois, in vicious battles through the ages. They too 'swooped' in on each other many times. Many battles. When I had a command in the Army, when I was ordered to attack, when it was time to attack? I swooped in too, like the Indians of my ancestry."

Swoop sat back in the chair, sighed and continued.

"The English dictionary defines 'swoop' as 'to move downward quickly and dramatically, like an eagle that swoops down to catch its prey. A swoop is an impressive movement best demonstrated by a hunting bird,' he explained, mostly for Mei Zhen, his gaze at her face.

"There came a point, a time, a situation, where I could no longer remain a general. I left. I am now a deserter. A traitor. Hunted. AWOL. Absent without leave. A bounty on my head."

"Who are the Ditch Diggers?" Bellmont asked.

"Most of the men that hunt me are ex-Army. They were once called 'ditch diggers' because they were all army criminals and condemned to dig cemeteries for dead soldiers and ditches to burn and bury Indians. Ditches for construction jobs. They are ex-army vets, banded together to catch any AWOLs and collect the bounty. I have a…very…high bounty. They and other bounty hunters will never stop hunting me."

"What will you tell the Ambassador?"

"Nothing. Doc. I am going to leave. Leave right now."

"Leave? Right…now?"

"Leave. Right now. Larmes might feel obligated to arrest me.

There are US Army personnel there. They might arrest me."

"Where will you go?" She asked.

"Back to America. Los Angeles. San Francisco? I will get aboard a ship…somehow...I have the travel papers of the men outside. And their money. I will announce to the Ditch Diggers when back that I am no longer in China. I will mail them proof. You will be safe then."

"What about Ya-tang?" Mei Zhen asked.

"I…must go. You must tell her goodbye for me," Swoop said.

"She will have a broken heart?"

"My heart is broken too."

"Can you go find the major? Find Johann Gunther?"

"No, because then he too will be in trouble for covering for me and also in danger, because of me."

"My father, you can go see him and…" Belmont started.

"You know your father hates me for helping you stay here in China. He only pays me because he has to. Because Major Gunther shamed him into paying me to protect you." Mei Zhen stood up and walked into the office. She walked back in with a small black, silk, zipper bag. She handed it to Swoop.

"There is $300, Robert."

"I…I," Swoop stuttered.

"We love you, Robert," Bellmont said, "you have become an uncle to us. A grandfather to our son. You cannot stay, then. You must go. Come on."

He followed them to the back door, with Swoop scooping up his leather bag.

Once out back, Robert led them to their private stables.

"Take Shelton. Saddle up and take Shelton. Get out of here," Robert said. "Now!"

The three started saddling the horse up.

"I'll stable Shelton at the train station," Swoop said. "I'll have the station stable call you. You can pick him up in a day or two. I'll tell them to wait for you."

"In a few hours, we'll tell the ambassador that you feared for your life. And our lives from these killers and just had to leave right away. We won't tell them about your past," Bellmont said.

"What about your clothes? Your..." Mei Zhen asked.

"Mei, I have had to...to flee many, many times since 1891. Many places. Many...people, people I have become very attached to sometimes. Like you two. Like Ya-tang," he said as he climbed into the saddle. "But this is my life. My curse."

"Goodbye Robert," Bellmont said.

Swoop mounted up and trotted the horse out of the yard. He stopped, took a long look at them, waved goodbye, turned and left.

"He has been my friend, my shadow for three years," Bellmont said, holding Mei Zhen, as both watched him leave.

"And now, he must become like a shadow again," she said.

In two days, Swoop stabled Shelton at the Peking train station and had the workers call Dr. Bellmont. He bought a ticket for the next train to Hong Kong, a long trip with many stops. From there, he would buy passage and board the Dollar Steamship Line bound for San Francisco. He had the money from the Bellmont's, and the identification papers from the three bounty hunters, along with their money also in his satchel. He also had a salary collected from Bellmont's father, growing in a San Francisco bank under the name Robert Small.

His further plans to clear the Bellmont's of future problems? Once back in the states he would use the dead men's information to spread the word of his return to the United States to the Ditch Diggers and their ramrod, Jerry Pickwith.

Wearing his black wig under his smaller, yet oriental hat, he sat in a train car. The train slowly left the station. Swoop stared out the window and studied the Oriental scenery that would soon become just another memory. Another war. Another peace. Another place. Another run for his life. Did he really think, finally, he might live out his days in some sort of peace in China? How many times has he thought that? He'd been leaving places, running, escaping, killing for some 12 years.

On the train ride to ocean port, his mind wandered back, back in time to the winter of 1890 and how this curse, this tragedy, all began. He thought back to his first "reckoning." Back to Fort Shannon, South Dakota.

ORIENT~ROUND THE WORLD
SUNSHINE BELT VIA HONOLULU.
FLEET
PRESIDENT CLEVELAND
PRESIDENT LINCOLN
PRESIDENT WILSON
PRESIDENT TAFT
PRESIDENT PIERCE
PRESIDENT HARRISON
PRESIDENT GARFIELD
PRESIDENT VAN BUREN
PRESIDENT MONROE
PRESIDENT HAYES
PRESIDENT ADAMS
PRESIDENT POLK
DOLLAR STEAMSHIP LINE

Chapter 2: Pour the Rye

November,1890, Fort Shannon Headquarters, South Dakota

"We cannot have any of this Ghost Dance horse manure!" General Shanklin said, pounding his fist on the conference table.

Shanklin's aide stepped in from behind him, refilled his thick, monogrammed glass with rye whiskey, then jumped back and well out of the way.

"This Paiute Wovoka," Shanklin said, "and his Ghost Dance religion is scaring hell into all the settlers and…and all the people reading the newspapers coast to coast. Do you know, have you heard that he claims Jesus Christ appeared to him? To him! Out here on the prairie."

"I do. I know him," said Lt. General Mordecai "Swoop" Swellen, the commander of Fort Shannon, as he rubbed his jaw with his left hand. He sat straight across from General Shanklin.

"He preaches that Christ taught him the ghost dance and we whites would all be swallowed up in earthquakes and floods? Well, we will just disarm them all."

Swoop's gaze wandered the table. Six men sat there in the conference room of his rough-hewn headquarters building.

The observant Shanklin aide had placed six glasses upside down in front of each attendee, as was customary of any General Shanklin official meeting. All but Swoop had righted their glasses up for the invitation to pour the rye.

To Shanklin's left, sat regional Indian Agent Adrian Glance, of the Standing Rock Agency, who looked none-too-happy with this new Shanklin edict of disarmament, though he followed company tradition with an upright glass and occasional sips. To Swoop's right sat his own Major Chevalier Share, a French American and trusted friend.

Over to Shanklin's right, sat Shanklin's main and notorious henchman, a Major Frederick "Bare Eyes" Twenty. Twenty reputation was every bit as ruthless as Swoop's own for killing, yet not as well known for his routine deviousness. The Cherokee nicknamed Twenty "Bare Eyes" years ago because he had no eyelashes or eyebrows, to match his youthful baldness.

Down at the two far ends of the table sat Swoop's secretary and Shanklin's secretary, both sergeants, taking fast notes with feather pens, targeting their ink bottles without looking.

"You realize, Sir," Swoop began, "that if we disarm the Lakota there will be trouble. They hunt and shoot and regard themselves as warriors. Taking away their firearms will be…"

"The ghost dance, Swellen!" Shanklin yelled. "It's an omen of trouble. It tells us all we need to know. They dream of, they mean to, fight, fight, fight and kill the white man. Us. They fight the expansion West. You know this Swoop. How many Indian wars have you been in?"

"Wars. Raids. Hunts. Too many to remember, Sir. I can't remember them all," Swoop answered.

"Too many!" Shanklin snorted. "You damn will, may well be in yet another one, and right under your got-damn nose."

"I will not make them sign a disarmament agreement," Swoop said.

General Shanklin looked astonished, "Swoop, this comes

straight from the Department of the Army. From Washington D.C. The White House!"

"This is the wrong thing to do," Swoop said. "It will create a great problem. People will eventually die. They will refuse. A fight will start. They'll die and we'll die. Doesn't Washington…"

"You'll do it."

"I won't."

"Oh? Oh, you won't? If you don't? If you don't?" Shanklin said, "This is not like you. Listen up, you will, or…or I will court martial you for treason. I will have you shot as a traitor. I will see to it myself. And your replacement Swellen? Your replacement will step in and sign and enforce the disarmament anyway. Right…over…your executed body. This is going to happen, with or without you. Smarten up, boy!"

"You enforce that treaty? And within one year, maybe months even Sir, maybe weeks even, you will be killing all the Lakota here," Swoop said calmly.

"Well now, isn't that what you do best, General SWOOP Swellen? Swoop in and kill man, woman and child," Shanklin said sarcastically.

Swoop didn't answer that. He turned his glass upright and the aide jogged a circle around the big table, lunged in and filled it a few inches. Swoop took a swig.

"I say, we'll let them see if those…those Ghost Shirts really do repel bullets," Major Twenty said.

"And we'll lose men, too," Swoop added. "You know that General Colby of the Nebraska National Guard agrees with me about all this."

"The National Guard!" Shanklin repeated skeptically. "Ha! I have got to get back to Minnesota," Shanklin said.

This was a hint for all to finish their glasses of rye. "Agent Glance has copies of the agreement. This fort and others will be enforcing the agreement, forthwith."

"Another treaty," Swoop said.

"An agreement treaty. Your fort will enforce it too. The

7th Cavalry will be all over this."

They all drained their glasses. The aide collected them, as Shanklin and his team stood, followed by Swoop and his men, the wooden chairs screeched against the oak floor as they stood. The visitors gathered their belongings, put on their heavy blue coats, and opened the door to the brisk, Dakota winter winds. The front porch was shoveled free, but thin waves of loose, icy snow still blew in and around. The general's men waited for him to exit first, but at the doorway, he turned and pointed a finger at Swoop with a menacing expression.

"Swoop, you know what a direct order is. This is a direct order. You'll do this. If you ask for a transfer? I won't accept it. If you want a demotion? I won't accept it. This is a do-or-die deal for all of us from Washington itself. For you. Let's get this deal done! You will ride in support of Major General Miles on this. Disarm all of them."

Then the three left, so fast that no salutes were traded, and they ignored shutting the door, allowing the cold to further fill the room.

Swoop, Agent Glance and Share sat back down. The unit secretary shut the door and chunked another two logs into the fireplace. In the dead of winter, an open front door if even for a few seconds turned the front rooms in a quick ice box. Then the secretary left for another office with his papers. Glance pulled the official papers from a satchel and laid them on the table.

"Whoww-wee," Glance sighed, "That was a whole lot worse than finding a hair in your biscuit."

Swoop nodded.

"Okay! Here's what they gave me," Glance said.

"I am not going to do this," Swoop said, shaking his head and refusing to pick up the treaty that Agent Glance dropped nearby.

"I think…really, I know you will face a firing squad," Major Share said. "Remember what he did with that lieutenant? That kid from Florida? He had him shot and buried in a ditch within 48 hours of threatening him with treason. It was a kangaroo court martial. The kid was doomed, and he is saying all the same things again with his threats to you."

"And the next commander will make it happen," Glance added. "Probably be that Bare Eyes Twenty if you won't. You can't stop this from happening, General."

"Probably," Swoop said, "but I…me…I don't have to do it. I will not be part of this stupid, stubborn, process. I can't stop it, but I am not going to do it."

"Can you…resign?" Agent Glance asked.

"Quit? I can't quit, Adrian. When I requested a slot at the war college, I had to sign a five more year commitment. Then I went. I still have two more years left to do," Swoop said. "At the time, I thought nothing of it. I figured I was a lifer anyway.

"Well, come on, you can't quit. What will you do, Sir?" Major Share asked.

"I don't know, Chev," Swoop said. "I may sleep on what I will do next. If I can sleep at all. I sure don't like the smell of the Ghost Dance. I don't want that Ghost Dance movement to… to… expand. No, I don't. I just don't think it's time to light a match to this stick of dynamite right now. The tribe is contained. There is a peace. There hasn't been an outbreak or a war. No citizen in Nebraska or Dakota has been killed, molested, or can even show a scratch, and no property has been destroyed off the reservation. We have workable connections with them. If we do this? They won't listen to us anymore. And…we will wind up killing all of them. I know it. I've seen it all before. I've done it all before."

"What in hells-bells will I tell the Lakota?" Agent Glance asked.

"The bad news, Adrian. All the bad medicine. With or without me, bad is a coming."

Chapter 3: A Frozen, Muddy Road
November 1890, Fort Shannon Headquarters

Lt. General Mordecai "Swoop" Swellen swept his stocking feet off the bed and onto a bearskin rug. He slept about 7 hours despite his dilemma. The front rooms, the offices just outside of his backroom quarters were empty, as it was an hour before the routine cadre would start coming in and out. Just opening the front door, no matter how quickly, would chill the whole office, fire on or not. Swoop decided he would not start a fire, as was his routine each morning. He had other plans in mind.

Swoop wandered into the office and looked out a window to see the east side of Fort Shannon. Shannon was built along the Wounded Knee Creek Territory in 1867. It housed 426 soldiers and a musical band. The officers' quarters provided housing for 22 families in duplexes built of adobe, rocks, and wood. There was an infirmary with one doctor and a nurse. Fort Shannon was noted for its exciting cultural life. Plays and musical events or "theatricals" were performed by the men, wives and children in a large, dirt-floored building with benches for audience seating.

Weekdays this room served as a schoolhouse for dependents, and operated a pretty decent commissary in one corner. Fort Shannon was 39 miles from Sioux Falls. He'd never been stationed, least of all put in charge, of so many troops and their families and he'd never observed so much of "normal" life before, least of all be put in charge of it. He was now bestowed with so much more responsibility. The experiences changed him.

There were some 2,100 officers and 26,000 enlisted men in the Army declared in it's April 1888 consensus, the last official head count to date. Almost 900 officers and 13,000 enlisted men were in the infantry, and another 400 officers and 6,000 enlisted were assigned to the cavalry. The majority of the artillery branch consisted of some 300 officers. Approximately 4,500 enlisted men were stationed at long established fortifications along the nation's coastlines.

Due to its mobility, the cavalry was the Army's primary force for controlling and combating the Indians, and in the 1880s, cavalry troops garrisoned 55 posts throughout "Indian Country." Swoop had risen to his high rank, as a Lt. General strictly from battlefield combat-promotions, one of the youngest men at 42 to do so. He'd specialized in doing the dirty deeds and the nasty assignments from the high command. A lieutenant general such as Swoop was ranked just below a general like Shanklin. All his promotions were field promotions, but his recent attendance at the war college had helped.

It was the third Wednesday of the month, and the supply wagon train would leave for Sioux Falls in 40 minutes. Six wagons with a Company B escort. Swoop got up, dressed but ignored the brushed uniform hung by an aide against the wall. Instead, he put on his dungaree pants and brown boots, and a black, flannel shirt.

He wrapped a civilian, two-gun belt around his waist, which held two dark finish, double-action, 1877 Colt .41 caliber "Thunderers," his private guns, not the Army's. On serious missions he would stow his army pistol and flap holster rig and wear this civilian, two-gun rig instead. He was taught at a young age when still a private by an old pony soldier, war vet, sergeant advised him that "the 'best-est', fastest re-load is pullin yer second gun."

A two-gun rig! In the heat of battle no one complained, even anal-retention superior officers about this violation of uniform policy, as Swoop was known to be 'double-dog,' ruthless with that brace of pistols. Those guns and a non-regulation Bowie knife in a customized sheath were his call to arms. He did wear the cavalry sword of a commanding officer sometimes, and that weapon he would be glad to leave behind.

But what of his stick? His swagger stick? It laid atop a dresser. Many officers swaggered with their swagger sticks, as far back as the Roman army, and Swoop grew accustomed to it. It was a graduation gift from the war college, made of oak, stained, and inscribed, with a formed, textured, handle grip. Military swagger sticks came in all sizes and thicknesses through time, and this tailor made one was thicker than most. The maker, a colonel in the war college was Irish and held night classes for fighting with these swagger sticks and also the infamous Irish cane, the "Shille-lagh," a knotty walking stick that was also used for fighting. But few knew that inside the gifted war college, the swagger stick was a thin short sword! It was too long to be a kosh as in a short club, too short to be a cane. It was about two feet long. The colonel even made short, snap holsters for these swagger sticks for belt carry. He opened and packed a leather bag with some other personal items and stuffed the swagger stick inside, it just fit.

In an unlocked drawer from the spartan dresser, he pulled a thick, large envelope stuffed with money, his life savings. Since he hardly ever purchased anything and spent his entire teenage and adult years in the army, it was of considerable booty. It too went into the bag.

He slipped into a mid-hip length, brown leather jacket with a sheepskin lining and collar, tucked an old brown hat on his head, grabbed the bag. He walked out the back door of the building under the cold, gray cloudy sky. He saw the supply wagon team amassing and headed their way.

"Sgt. Gates, I will be accompanying you to Sioux Falls this morning," Swoop told the NCO atop his horse and in front of the first wagon. The sergeant eyed up Swoop's civilian clothes.

"Yes, Sir. You…want your horse, sir?"

"No, Sir. No. I will ride in one of the wagons. I…have some personal business to attend to there and am dressing down this morning."

"Ahhh…yes Sir!"

Swoop sat on a wooden cargo box for a moment, taking

a last look around. Then he wandered down the lines of wagons, passed the snorting horses and curious drivers. He climbed onto the fourth wagon, tossed his bag in the back, and sat next to a nervous teen-age, private.

"Good morning, Sir!" the surprised, young driver said.

"Good morning, private. Your name is…"

"Henderson, Sir."

"First name?"

"Larry, Sir,"

"Private Larry Henderson, how are you this morning?"

"I…ahh…I…how are you, Sir?"

"Well. Well. You didn't expect to have a post commander ride shotgun with you, huh?"

"No Sir,"

"Well, Private Henderson, think nothing of it."

Sgt. Gates called the men to order, and the wagon crunched across the hard, frozen snow covering Fort Shannon, out the freshly opened gates and on to the old, frozen muddy trail toward the big city. Major Chevalier Share appeared on the front porch of the officer's quarters, pulling his jacket on while juggling a metal cup of steaming coffee. He stopped cold when he saw Swoop dressed in civies on a wagon, leaving the base.

"The crazy bastard. He is going AWOL," Share mumbled in astonishment.

Swoop glanced Share's way, and from the distance Share could see Swoop half-smile at him and then raise two fingers about an inch high from his right thigh as if to wave a very subtle goodbye. Share nodded back at him.

"Shanklin will haunt him, hunt him down and kill him," Share whispered aloud.

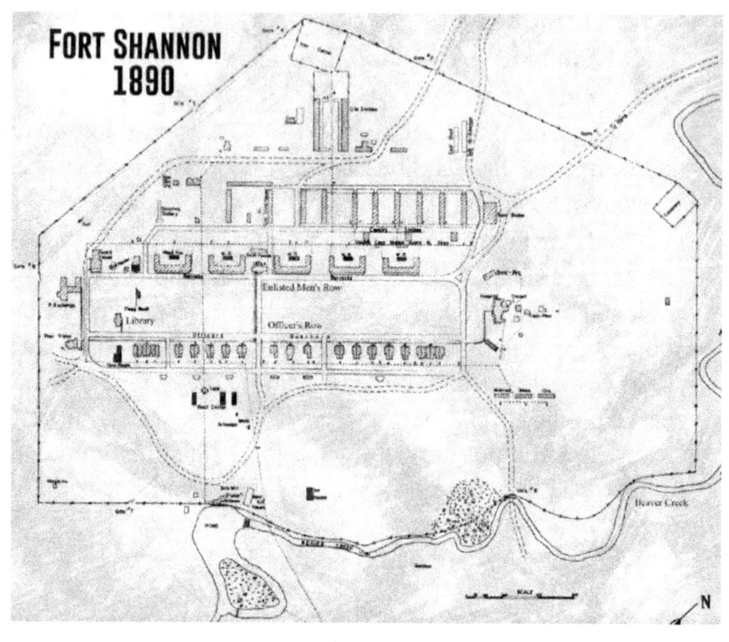

FORT SHANNON
1890
Library
Enlisted Men's Row
Officer's Row
Beaver Creek
SCALE
N

Chapter 4: Kicking the Hornet's Nest
November 1890, Fort Shannon Headquarters

"Well, what did he say?" General Shanklin demanded of Sgt. Gates.

"Well General, he said he had personal business to attend to."

"And didn't it seem odd he was out of uniform?"

"Yes, Sir. He said he was dressing down. I've never seen him out of uniform before. But I thought well, maybe he was taking leave? Doing some private civilian business like he said he was, Sir. I don't know, Sir. I hate to question my superiors. We all wear civies from time to time."

"What exactly was he wearing?" Shanklin asked.

"A brown hat. Not much of a brim. He had a brown

leather jacket with a fur lining. Fur…big fur white collar. About mid-knee length. Levi pants. Just…just boots, Sir. He had a black bag. Like luggage."

Major Twenty sat nearby, taking notes.

"You!" Shanklin pointed at the cowering Private Henderson.

The teen physically shook as if the finger shot a lightning bolt at him.

"What did he say on this long wagon ride?"

"Well, well, well Sir, he…he…he…"

"Gotdammit boy spit it OUT!"

"He asked me about my life, Sir. All about me. He…he said to spread my story out real slow and long, to never mind if it sounded boring to me, because the ride was a long, windy, cold doozy, Sir."

"He didn't say where he was going?" Major Twenty asked.

"He never said anything like that," Henderson said.

"You two get out of here," Shanklin ordered. "If I find out you are lying? I will skin you alive and stick you down in a pile of hungry red ants."

"Yes Sir," Gates said. He grabbed Henderson's arm sleeve and the two left.

Major Share sat in an old chair up against the wall.

"Why'd he leave, Share?" Shanklin asked Share.

"General, all he said was, right after you left, was he would not disarm the Lakota. He said they would eventually, quickly, violate the disarmament, and we would eventually, wind up having to kill them, and he just wasn't going to do that. Again. Another massacre again."

Shanklin sighed and turned to stare at a wall.

"Where do you think he will go?" Major Twenty asked.

"I don't know, Major. He has no…no life. No civilian life. I mean, nowhere to go. He's been in the Army since he was 16 or 17 years old. He is originally from Minnesota. Maybe he'll go there, but he has no reason to go back there that I know of."

Shanklin bolted straight up from his seat, clasped his hands behind his back and paced the office.

"Twenty," Shanklin said to his officer, seated by the big table,

"I want you to gather up a team. I want you to requisition Wilson "Gee" Willikers up here. He's hunting a killer down in Texas. Wire him at Springville, Texas. I want you two, and a platoon to hunt Swoop down. I will initiate traitor charges on him."

"Traitor, charges, Sir?" Major Share asked.

"Traitor charges. Desertion. Cowardice. I warned him. You heard me, Major."

General Shanklin pointed to his secretary with a hand signal as if to get that paperwork started. "It will be…it will be…," he paced, then continued.

"It will be wanted dead or alive cause it's damn-dable treason. Disobeying ME! Bounty $1,000. It's high, it's damn high, but he's a damn general. We can't have top officers like him, wantonly disobeying commands from the White House. Hell, has there ever be a lieutenant general go AWOL before?"

"I don't reckon, Sir," Major Twenty said. "Maybe way back in the ol Civil War? I don't know."

Shanklin walked to a row of cabinets and picked up a wooden picture frame he'd snatched a few moments earlier from Swoop's backroom quarters. He opened the frame and removed the large photo.

"This is a picture of Swoop from two years ago. It's pretty good," the general said. He handed it to Major Twenty.

Twenty looked at it. It was a photo of Swoop, Major Share and another officer taken in front of their Fort Shannon headquarters, just outside on the porch, in warm weather.

"Get a drawing of his face for a wanted poster, then take that picture to Sioux Falls and ask every stable hand, stage-coach charley and train clerk if they remember him. Him…getting tickets for elsewhere. Surely, he's still not there. Be a fool to still be there, but start checking around."

"I'll go to Sioux Falls now," Major Twenty said. "The sheriff there will surely have a wanted poster artist. I'll telegraph Gee Willikers to meet me there in Sioux Falls, unless we quickly find out how and where he has moved on."

"Good."

"We'll hunt that traitor down Sir," Major Twenty said.

"Good. Good. And Twenty? You know, keep an eye on Willikers. Ramrod him. He's about a half-crazy, mountain man. And I hear tell he has gotten worse. He always causes trouble, but in the end he's damn-well, worth it."

"I will, Sir."

"Good. You all are dismissed. Major Share? You wait here."

Everyone left the main office except Shanklin and Share.

"Chev, you've been with Swoop for 5 years now. He's been nothing but a by-the-book, bloody, hound dog. What… why did he do this?" Shanklin asked calmly as he sat back down at the table, void of any command voice and intimidating command presence.

"I don't rightly know, Sir. You boxed him in, and he had no choice but to leave."

"He had the choice to follow his orders."

"That he did sir, but he didn't want to."

"You will take his place here and get that disarmament under way."

"Yes, Sir. Right away, Sir," and Share started to leave, but turned back.

"Sir?"

"Yes?" Shanklin said.

"Sir, I know that Major Twenty and Willikers are some tough hombres. They will have a squad with them?"

"Yes?"

"But there's still a good chance Swoop will kill them all."

"Ahh, you think?"

"I think, Sir. You know of him. I know him. I've been in battles with him. Ever seen or been attacked by hornets from a hornet's nest?"

"No."

"It's like they move…they strike so fast, they seem blurry. Invisible even, can't even tell they're hornets and what's going on. Just pain, and shock. And…and all you feel is a flood, a wave of deep, poison stings that drives your mind crazy in an instant. I have seen Swoop in combat, Sir. Guns. Knives. Fists. Teeth. He's like a horde of hornets afire."

"I know he turns madman. But, there will be a reckoning for what he has done. And anyway, Gee Willikers will probably sneak up on him and shoot him in the back of the head. That'll be all, Major."

Chapter 5: Death of the Lakota Ghosts

Once Swoop arrived by the supply wagon train in Sioux Falls, he quickly commandeered a small coach to the train station. There he bought tickets to Denver, Colorado and caught the last train of the day out. Once in the "Mile High" city, he checked into the Del Norte's Windsor Hotel.

He celebrated a civilian Thanksgiving at the Baur Confectionary restaurant, quite the bountiful feast compared to the U.S. Army's version. There in Denver, he rested and planned. He thought that, of all the military AWOLS at large, he, being a Lt. General, and knowing the wrath of General Shanklin, there would be a somewhat serious effort in chasing him down. But he could just disappear in the vastness of North America and the drive to catch him would eventually dwindle away. A new sense of relief befell him. He was through with it all. He did not know what he would do next, all he saw and felt was…relief.

In the hotel lobby there was a wall of information handouts and pamphlets for tourists. Swoop looked them over. He read one for a somewhat nearby town of Manitou Springs.

"Consider the picturesque location of the springs in a for-
ested box canyon at the base of Pikes Peak, it is no wonder
the Native Americans considered the location sacred. Dr.
Edwin James, a botanist was the first Westerner to "discover"
the health-giving mineral waters. The eruption of bubbles in
the mineral water was considered the breath of the Great
Spirit, and offerings of beads and fetishes were left in grat-
itude. The soothing effects of the soda water on sour stom-
achs and dry skin attracted not only the Mountain Utes, who
wintered here each year, but the Cheyenne, Arapahoe, and
other Plains tribes. This beautiful town boasted of several
grand hotels, including the Cliff House, Barker House, and
the Grandview."

He'd never sat in a hot spring, nor been to those parts of
Colorado. And how many visitors would dare travel to the
Rockies in the winter? The next day, to further disappear
from the mainstream, beaten trails, Swoop took a stagecoach
to this Manitou Springs at the foothills of the famous Pike's
Peak. There was a train system of two trains, Denver south to
Colorado Springs, then Colorado Springs north-westerly to
Manitou Springs, but he decided on the coach as he was in no
great hurry.

Light snowflakes followed him all the way. So, from Fort
Shannon, North Dakota, it all took a few weeks of travel and
overnights to finally find himself ensconced in the expensive
Manitou Cliff House Hotel, a rather famous establishment,
and just before Christmas. This business survived from the
1859 era, area gold rush and subsequent crash, thanks to
Pike's Peak tourism. The hotel managed to retain its early
glory and grandeur. There Swoop hoped to seriously consider
his questionable future for a week or two and make some
plans. He had his life savings with him, but he would eventually run out of money and would have to find some sort of
employment, somehow, somewhere. What? Not there. Not
there too long anyway. He asked a clerk at the service desk to
lock up most of his money in the hotel safe.

The Cliff House was resplendent in holiday decorations with many guests enjoying the festive atmosphere when he wandered into the lobby restaurant for dinner.

"Is there a hot spring nearby?" Swoop asked the hotel clerk.

"Yes, sir, just outside. Have you ever been in one?"

"No sir."

"For some it can be very hot. In the summer some hot springs might burn your skin! One must be careful. At their best, they are comfortably hot, bubbly you know. They seem to come from the center of the earth and have many soothing minerals to calm you and help you. For many people hot springs work well for them. I suggest you try one. Here… here is a map of the seven hot springs around the downtown area."

"Thanks. And I guess someone can change in and out of a bathing suit nearby?"

"Oh yes. Or we provide heavy robes and slippers for your walk to and fro."

"Must be a cold walk back?"

"The heat from the springs lasts on the skin for a bit, sir."

But the winter winds and snow kept Swoop from endeavoring. Each room had hot and cold running water and bathtubs, and that was just a really "short walk."

1891! On New Year's Eve Day morning, Swoop wandered the lobby, then the partially snowy grounds outside. This was his first Christmas and New Year's outside of the army in many decades. Content, he settled in to eat breakfast.

"Good morning, Mr. Turner, Happy New Year!" One of the waiters said.

"Good morning, Ralph, and Happy New Year to you."

"Were you at the party here last night?" Ralph asked.

"No sir, I was fast asleep by midnight."

"Should you wish sir, the weekend Denver Observer came in last night."

"Oh, thank you, Ralph," Swoop said, and he swept up a copy off the big ornate desk on his way to a table.

Once seated and after a waitress took an order of coffee, bacon, and eggs, he unfolded and scanned the front page and saw the shocking headline and story.

"My God!" he said aloud when reading one of the top headlines, almost spitting out his first sip of coffee.

The front page read-

"The Terrible Slaughter at Wounded Knee. The Killed and Wounded up into the Hundreds."

The first paragraph read - "The U.S. Army was conducting disarmament of the Lakota Indians and a skirmish ensued leading into what could be called a massacre…"

"My God, my God," Swoop whispered, "they did it. They killed them."

Chapter 6: A Bounty Killing in Texas
Texas Hill Country, January 1891

Bats. Hundreds of them, if not thousands of them flew just over his head. Wilson "Gee" Willikers remained knee high in the cold, dark cave exit. The thunderous flapping and wing's wind from them filled the cave. It was sunset at Treckston's Cavern in the Texas Hill Country and the mammals were right on time for their nightly escape, hunting spree of bugs, lizards and fruit.

Williker's hat, buckskin jacket and pants were partially covered in bat guano, but for him it was well worth the wait. Some of the feces had even landed on his Uberti 1885 Courteney Stalking Rifle, but the weapon had seen far worse conditions. The acrid smell was overwhelming, like some new clothes-cleaning chemical from a Chicago laundry.

Just outside, sitting on blankets and folding chairs were tens of tourists impatiently waiting on the chilly evening for this one daily, routine, magic moment. And just outside on the hill in the anxious gathering sat a so-called Harry

Holmes, his wife and two kids, on vacation from Lawton, Oklahoma. At least, that was what Gee hoped for, that's what his spies back in Lawton had informed him. And this was the only way Willikers could get close to Harry without Harry spotting him, recognizing him and shooting at him or running away. Willikers and Harry had a past. Willikers still expected both responses, but he felt this element of surprise was in his favor.

Harry, or rather his real name "Horace P. Nerd" was wanted, dead or alive in Ohio for the murder of a military captain. The warrant was five years old. The bounty went up and up each year. It was now $350. Harry-Horace knew Willikers on sight from old military hunts and campaigns.

Crouched over, Willikers started up the slight, elevated walk to the entrance. He could discern the "ooos and ahhs" of the onlookers as waves of bats filled the air. Everyone was looking up and up. Once out, he clung to the rocky side and sneaked closer and closer to the attendees. Then, he ran across the dried winter grass and rocks right at the audience.

Few noticed him at first but the closer he got, the more spotted him in his unusual ground-level, charge up from the bat cave. With a rifle!

Willikers scanned them all for Nerd.

"Jesus, Martha!" Harry-Horace cried out, "It's Gee Willikers!"

"Horace P. NERRRRD!" Willikers shouted, raising his rifle.

Nerd scrambled back to stand up from his seat on the blanket. His wife Martha screamed. Ignorant of their daddy's circumstances, their kids still froze.

"Stand still, you fool!" Willikers shouted, but then whispered, "So's I can kill ya."

Gee Willikers took quick aim and with a snapshot, fired the long gun. The .303 round hit Nerd square in the chest with a thumping, chest bone breaking, wallop. Nerd never stood again. Ever. Onlookers screamed, crawled and ran off. The bounty hunter marched up to the body. Martha Holmes lost control and attacked him with flailing hammer fists. He used the butt of his gun to bash her side, hard enough to probably break some of her ribs. The two kids still remained frozen.

"You too, stand aside or I'll break yer wee little bones like dry branches!" Willikers demanded. The children did.

"You all just go back to watching the bats!" He declared to all the aghast onlookers. "This don't pertain to you. This here man is a federal fugitive. A murderer. I am his justice."

He shouldered his hunting rifle through a sling, grabbed two handfuls of Nerd's long, head hair and behind his back, hauled the dead man up the hill to a parked batch of horses and carriages. He cursed Nerd and his dead weight every single step of the way. He pulled the body up to his army-issue, wooden wagon. He grunted as he lifted Nerd onto the back of the wagon.

Martha tried to stay up with him, clutching her broken side, limping and crying, not really knowing what to do.

"Don't make me smash yer face, woman! Shoo fly, don't bother me!"

He untied his horse from a post and climbed aboard the wagon.

"Let's go Link!" he told his horse.

Link struggled at first with the load. Willikers was an enormous man and the dead Nerd in the back added to even more weight. He turned onto the main road to Springville, leaving the wife with freshly broken ribs crying by Treckston's front gate.

He smiled thinking about the $350 and started singing,

> *"Shoo fly don't bother me,*
> *Shoo fly don't bother me,*
> *Shoo fly don't bother me,*
> *For I belong to somebody..."*

Once in Springville, he steered the wagon up to "Calloway's Photography," shop and he spotted an impatient Mr. Calloway seated on a metal bench outside his shop, waiting, as ordered. Calloway stepped onto the street as the wagon pulled close.

"I told you it would be too dark to take any photogravures, Mr. Willikers. It ain't a gonna work well."

"That dang-blasted lightning flash bar thing you got, lights up the night sky like a gunshot when you pull the trigger," Willikers countered as he jumped off the wagon.

Link the horse snorted.

"Why ain't that bright enough?" Willikers asked.

"Well..."

"Hey! I ain't a lookin fer no Moner Lisa," Willikers said, "just a recognizable replication of this idiot in the back bed of the wagon to mail to Washington. Okay!"

"Okay, okay we'll see what we can do," Calloway said, as he went inside the shop to get his rig.

"Let's see," Willikers wondered aloud, looking at Nerd spread out over in the back of the buckboard, "I guess I'll sit yourself up against the back of the front seat. Yup...yup," he said to the dead man.

He climbed aboard the bed and started hauling the corpse up into a suitable, recognizable position.

"Gee Willikers! Mister Geeeee Willikers!" a teenage girl shouted out, jogging his way.

"Yup. Right chere, little lady! What?"

"We got an important message for you from the United States military," she said as she ran nearby.

"Let's have a look-see, lassie."

She reached up and handed him the paperwork. He took the telegraph. It read-

To: W. Gee Willikers
Message: Major Twenty orders you to meet him in Fort Dakota, South Dakota for a manhunt."

"Bare Eyes Twenty *orders me*, ha," he mumbled, "Twenty orders me. Ah, thank you, young lady. Tap them back and tell them I will take a train henceforth, to wit."

Chapter 7: The Cowboy and the Sicilian
The Cliff House, Manitou Springs, Colorado

Now as the respectable, retired businessman known as "Mr. Archie Turner," Swoop Swellen sat at a table in the busy, holiday, hotel lobby engrossed in a book when a woman appeared in view over the top of his pages.

"May I sit myself down?" She asked.

Swoop's eyebrows shot up and he smiled. "Ah yes," he said, just a bit surprised.

She was an attractive lady, brunette hair piled atop her head, in her late 30s and well-enough dressed. She had a winter coat draped over her arm.

"I see that you are here almost every day this week. Reading a book."

He shut his book and laid it on the table.

"Yes, I have been, but I will be leaving soon."

"Vacation? Christmas and New Year's week?"

"You might say."

"Uh-huh. My name is Catty Corners."

"Catty…Corners," Swoop repeated. He smiled again, "and, that is your real name?"

Her mouth contorted to one side, pulling her nose in the same direction. She said, "Well, my full name is Catherine. 'Catty' for short and my full last name is Cornerwall."

"I see. So, you just shortened it all, for the sake of brevity."

"I did. What is your name?"

"Archie Turner."

"And I reckon Archie is short for Archibald."

"Ah, yes, it is."

"So, we are both running our names a little on the short sheet. And I see that your hand is bare. Bare in that, there is no wedding ring thereabouts."

"Not there, thereabouts or anywhere," Swoop said.

"And you are here, vacationing alone?"

"That I am."

"Whatever are you a pondering?" She asked and tapped a finger on the table near his book.

"Emperor Marcus Aurelius, Stoic," he said.

"Stoic. Is that some kind of wood?"

"No, well, yes it sounds like it's a tree, but it is some kind of philosophy. But…it is solid like a tree."

"What do you do for a living, Mr. Archie?"

"I am retired."

"And you're tired from doing what?" She asked.

"I got real tired of making rules. Following rules. What do you do, Miss Catty Corners?" He asked.

"I am a dancer."

"A professional dancer?"

"Yes. Well, no. I…"

"Catty?" said a man who suddenly appeared beside the table.

The man was in his 50s, well-dressed, with greased back, black hair and a thick waxed moustache. He was dressed in an impeccable three-piece suit, overcoat and bowler hat. Plus, atop all that get-up…he wore a black cape!

"Oh, Zappy, this is Archibald. This is…"

"Arturo Zapello," he interrupted her introduction. In just

two words, he already had a European accent of some sort. His eyes dropped down to the book on the table. He spun it around to him and read the title aloud.

"Emperor Marcus Aurelius, Stoic." You are reading a book about a prestigious Italian. I sir, am Italian. Well, Sicilian."

Swoop half stood and shook his hand.

"I, and my company, my men and I, are all from Italy. Sicily. You must know where that is, eh? We are building the new train line all the way up to the top of Pikes Peak."

"That's a mighty steep climb," Swoop said.

"That it is, sir. At parts. Some sections are flat-a, others very steep. It is what we call a 'cog railway,' different from other rails, a train and rail system that grips the rails on steep angles." He put out his hands and curled his fingers inward. "It's a new engineering science. Like having…how do you say here…teeth…that bite. Tell me sir, how did you learn of our Marcus Aurelius?"

"Army college," Swoop blurted out, realizing he must not be so quick to blurt such things about his past, in the future. "I am really just a beginner-stoic. Trying to understand it all."

"Yessss-a. Simple but still complicated. Yes. Ahhh then, ohhh, an officer then?" Zapello said, eyeing him up.

"Yes," Swoop said, the fact already revealed.

"Well, Miss Catty and I have a dinner date reservation. We must go. It was nice to meet you, signore."

"Yes, sir, the feeling is mutual."

As the Italian turned and Catty Corners rose from her chair, her eyes affixed in Swoop's face as she rose. A man ran into the lobby seeking Zapello out.

"Mr. Zapello!" he yelled. "Mr. Zapello!"

"What is it now, Fernando?" Zapello met the man mid-lobby, away from them.

Fernando seemed worried. He shared his worry with Zapello. Zapello cursed aloud as he listened to this bearer of some bad news. Something apparently was amiss in his new train track world?

Catty leaned in on the table near Swoop, spreading a mixed smell of stout perfume and too much shampoo. She said, "He…has a ring on his finger," in a tone of disgust, clearly suggesting she was available to Swoop. She grimaced, shook her head and walked very "expressively" away and over to Zapello's side.

He watched her cross the lobby and he eyed her up, down and moving, considering he might someday want to get catty-cornered to Miss Catty Corner. They left the lobby, but not before Catty glanced his way one more time and winked.

The manager Howard Holden strolled around the lobby and restaurant in his brushed and pressed black suit, hands held behind his back. He came to a standstill, by Swoop.

"I see you've met our Catherine, or "Catty.""

"Yes, I have."

"She's a local girl. She's very friendly with the tourists."

"Uh-huh."

"Not, oh…not always in such a bad way, mind you, as one might think. She has certainly picked up with Mr. Zapello, a more permanent tourist. Happy New Year, sir."

"And Happy New Year to you too, Mr. Holden."

Chapter 8: A Duel to Die Twice For

That winter's evening the sun set at about 5:30 p.m. Swoop slipped on his jacket and wandered out onto the spacious front balcony, interspersed with several roaring, topless fire pits he thought to be great places to sit nearby.

At 6 p.m. Swoop heard the hooting and hollering of a gathering crowd out on the main street, and across a small field beyond the Cliff House front yards. He could see men, women and a few children converging on the avenue. The streets were dark but from some streetlights and many storefront Christmas lights.

People were even leaving the Cliff House to walk over there. So, also curious, Swoop followed a few of them across a short field of frosty snow. Once near the gathering, he stood on one of the somewhat elevated, shoveled sidewalks. Nothing seemed to be happening.

Then, a well-dressed man stepped up on the sidewalk across the street, slipped off his top hat and shouted out,

"In the honor match of Signore Carlo Greco and a Mr. March Bowden, we begin this honor duel to the death."

"To the death?" Swoop whispered in amused, light astonishment. Surely not. He wondered if this was some kind of New Year's show?

People cheered and clapped. A stout, tall man with black hair greased back and waxed moustache not unlike the man he'd met earlier in the lobby, appeared from a barroom front door of an establishment named Rumy's. He was jacketless and garbed in a puffy-sleeved white shirt and tight, black dress pants. In one of his gloved hands, he brandished an official-looking rapier, a European dueling sword, with an elaborate metal handguard resembling a steel skeleton which protected the hand grip.

Apparently, his opponent was already amid the crowd, but it scattered suddenly, as though he had a sudden case of rabies.

"You come on out here then, you prissy son of a loudmouth bitch!" The man cried out.

People clapped at his words. A few cheered, as this Mr. March Bowden stood fast in the street-lined, patches of snow. He was dressed in the ragged clothes of an itinerant cowboy, about 50 years old, with a wild, head of hair and an enormous beard, long enough to blow in the cold wind like a sheet of cotton batting. His old hat hung on his upper back from a hat string. In his hand, down at his side was a military cavalry sword.

Several cowboys egged Bowden on, even shoving him forward. Some pulled him back, begging him to leave. Greco walked toward him, closer and closer, the rapier tip pointed down at his side. Swoop watched intently as the man slowly moved mere inches from Bowden's face. Bowden's jaw jutted eyes wide, and he did not, would not speak or step back.

Then Greco surprisingly lunged his head forward and kissed Bowden right on the left cheek! Bowden shoved him away.

"You sickly piece of shit!" Bowden yelled.

"You are lucky it was just a kiss you illiterate fool. In my country, Sicily! We bite the ear of a challenger," Greco declared.

"Your country is like the moon from here!"

Like Zapello whom Swoop met earlier, this swordsman must have been a Sicilian too, and not just from accent, but also from his look and the obvious remark.

"That was the kiss of death. For you!" Greco said.
People laughed and cheered. Swoop looked around for some local law to interrupt this scheduled event, but no marshal, county sheriff or constable appeared. This had the look of the rare street gunfight challenge, but with…swords?

On the sidewalk across the street Zapello, arm-in-arm with Catty Corners strolled into view and then stopped to take in the spectacle.

Greco smiled, stepped back, raised his sword and said quietly, "en guarde."

Then Greco, his face emotionless, dropped into a classical fencing position that Swoop recognized from mandatory fencing classes at the war college. Greco's rear hand raised up and back like that of a dancer. The cowboy raised his sword in no such stance, his face full of rage.

Watching this, Swoop lost his place in space and time. He contemplated the differing swords as the men squared off. The European rapier was thinner while the military sword of the cavalry horseman was thicker, wider, and slightly curved. It looked like a light cavalry saber, 1860 model, a beast of a weapon.

Swoop knew these things because not only was there fencing instruction at the war college, the army-school also conducted much cavalry sword training, a lot from on horseback. It was not wise to stab into an enemy while riding because such a penetration might snag, capture and stop you atop your horse's advance, ripping you right from your horse or the sword from your hand! Better to slash with a curved blade than stab on horseback. Thus, the curved blade of a cavalry sword. The stabbing problem with the curved sword was that it was curved upward a bit, and a really good stab might require turning the weapon upside-down for the best tip-entry. Either that or the top inches just below the tip must be razor sharp to help the stab's entry. This curve-for-cutting was a challenge also for the Japanese Katana, their Samurai sword and even their smaller tanto-knife. Whereas the European rapier was straight, not curved. The meager thin sword hidden inside Swellen's swagger stick was no match for either of these weapons.

Swoop reckoned that to survive the bigger sword, Greco would need a lot of fast, evasive footwork because his thinner sword might not parry or block powerful blows from a bit thicker, heavier sword. But the rapier was longer, perhaps 4 feet, while the cowboy's weapon was shorter at about 3 and ½ feet.

Swoop also reckoned that the cowboy knew none of these things that both he and Greco knew about longer, edged weapons. He thought this cowboy…was doomed, if indeed it was as advertised, as a fight to the death?

The cowboy screamed and charged, cutting sloppy, inexperienced Xs in the air with angled, downward strikes from the right, then the left. Greco danced away, his rapier barely "tinging" against the sword. Greco, looking and moving like a dancer, suddenly stepped to the side and sliced the cowboy's right jacket shoulder open with a slash, then he bounced back. The onlookers danced around too, straining their necks to watch and again, some even clapped at this first blood.

Greco chuckled. He hit the cavalry sword with his rapier three or four times in quick hits and retractions, moving like a ballerina.

"Come on, buffoon-animal!" He dared.

The cowboy stabbed forward, not knowing the curved sword tip was a bit of a hinderance for thrusting. The Sicilian dodged and with a low slash cut open the top of the man's thigh. This cut was deeper than just pant material as it ripped open flesh too.

This caused the cowboy's leg to jerk back, then for him to stumble, but he regained his balance and escaped another follow-up slash. He regrouped but now handicapped with a considerable limp. When he glanced down at his leg, he spotted the blood. Greco leapt in and out like a circus acrobat and cut the top of his head open, this along with a jarring impact. He could have moved in for a kill at that moment, but he skipped back, laughing.

"Kill him off!" a well-dressed man yelled from the audience.

"*Uccidilo!*" fellow Sicilians in attendance yelled.

"Now give it up, March!" A cowboy yelled.

"He drew blood, March! You have lost! Back off now!" Another one said.

"This ain't about just drawing blood," March Bowden said.

Swoop wondered just how badly this was going to end up?

He looked around, still no lawmen to be seen. This was no show. The cowboy tried one more stab and Greco smashed his rapier down on the wrangler's forearm. Coat? Cut! Flesh? Cut! The cowboy's cavalry sword hit the icy street from this impact and deep muscle cut. Half his arm was cut open now.

"Now, you kneel!" Greco ordered, "you scoundrel. Kneel before me and maybe I will let you live."

Swoop looked over noticing that Zapello's expression was one of disappointment as he and Catty Corners watched from across the street. Catty on the other hand, seemed excited.

"Kneel!"

The wounded cowboy knelt from dizziness. He couldn't catch his breath. His jaw hung low.

"Do you believe in God?" Greco asked.

The cowboy numb, confused and bleeding said, "Yes."

"I see. If you renounce God, I will let you live."

"Ahhh..."

"Say it!" Greco demanded, "Say it and live!"

"I...renounce him. I renounce God."

Greco didn't smile. He shook his head side-to-side. Then he ran the rapier into and through the man's throat. The onlookers gasped, moaned and some clapped yet again. He pulled the sword back out as the gurgling cowboy collapsed.

The man's few friends stood shocked. Greco glared at them, as if waiting for, hoping, wanting and seeking their revenge and yet another challenge. Then he slowly walked away, back into the bar. At the door he turned, grinned and raised his sword, the tip pointing to the dark skies above to the applause of onlookers.

The man standing next to Swoop said, "There's that again."

"That happen often?" Swoop asked.

"Oh, about every week or so. Week and a half. That guy picks a fight with a fool, claims he's being dishonored. Slaps the guy in the face, even with one of those gloves..."

"Very European," Swoop said.

"Yup. Most people won't fight but once in a while a stupid son of a bitch like this gets mad. Meets him with swords at an appointed time."

"And the law around here lets that happen?"

"Yup. It's a duel. A consensual duel and while it ain't with guns, its still a consensual duel. And the law don't care one bit. Duels of the west. Code of the West."

"I see. Are there any gunfight duels around here too?" Swoop asked.

"No."

Swoop nodded.

"See, yeah. That Greco guy is a supervisor of the Eye-talians working on the train track here. It all started when they came. Bout a hunnerd, hunnerd and fifty of em? They're a different breed. Best stay clear of them. Best stay clear of that Greco, I'll tell ya. He is always at Rumy's."

"I see. And do people come and watch the duels all the time. Like this?"

"Not at first. Of course, that Eye-talians started it when he came. I hear tell such is normal for their country. Dueling. And Europe. England. Challenges and duels and such. Lots of sword duels going on. That Greco feller is an international sword master."

"Does anyone ever gamble on the winner?" Swoop asked.

"Noooo, no, because everyone knows Greco will win. I'll bet there are a few secret fools who bet on the other guy once in a while, hoping to win big."

"I see. Well, some people still do duel here in the states. Flintlock pistols," Swoop said, "come to think of it. Knife fight duels once in a while, too. There's some kind of fighting all the time here and there. Spur of the moment."

"But this here is not spur of the moment. This sword dueling is different. A set-up agreed to time to meet and settle a score. Enough time for a crowd to hear about it and gather round. After a while the word gets out there will be a duel and people come out and watch. Yeah."

"Yeah. Like...like you. And me," Swoop added, smiling at the man.

"Yeah like me. Like us. Ain't it terrible? It's boring round here. We don't have much actors come through for theater. No circus shows. No singing. Use to. Gold Rush days. We do still have Pike's Peak though. Tourists."

"Like me," Swoop said.

"Yeah, anyway, something to see."

Swoop said. "Well, Happy New Years, sir."

Everyone walked off. The cowboy's three friends pulled the corpse off the street, presumably in route to a city caretaker. The raking pulled a boot off, and one stopped and stooped over to retrieve it.

When everyone was gone, one thing remained, bright, shiny and bloodless on the frozen street. The dead man's military saber. Swoop walked over to it, looked at it and picked it up by the handle. It looked fairly new. He looked at the stamp. Sure enough an 1860 model. Just like the ones he'd handled...and killed with before.

"Are you a swordsman?" Came a voice.

Swoop looked up to see by the bar's doorway, Greco again, still holding his rapier. His chin arrogantly held up.

"Oh...oh no," Swoop said, with a fake smile.

"That sword should be mine."

"Huh? Yeah. Yeah," Swoop said. "But I reckon it might best go the man's kinfolk? His family. I think he was in the military. This is an Army sword."

They stared at each other for a moment. And Swoop's blood started to boil, but he knew he should and could do nothing, given his fugitive circumstances. He thought of turning it upside down so the point would be better assessable and throwing it at the man's chest. He'd never done such a toss before, but he so wanted to.

Off to the left still stood Zapello and Catty Corners, watching the two men stare at each other.

"Perhaps," Greco said.

"I might just take it down to the caretakers and see what his friends say," Swoop said.

He turned and walked away, sword in hand, feeling the hot eyes burning into his back. He listened for any rushing attack. But none came. He'd heard all the gunfighter legends, tales and stories and he knew just a few of them. All dead now. This man was a sword fighter, a skilled man in an un-skilled category. The odds were always in his favor. Swoop realized he'd been trained...he'd...no. No, he mustn't. No

Swoop followed the fresh ruts of the dead man's drag in the snow. In many towns in the west, doctors and even furni-ture makers did double-duty as undertakers or caretakers. Doctors because they knew fresh death when it happened, and woodworkers because a coffin was involved. Street signs for this ugly job alone of handling dead bodies...caretaking were rare to find. But this city had a gold rush once, rough living and plenty of tourism thanks to nearby Pikes Peak that helped civilize the location. He saw an actual sign up ahead read:

"Funerals for the Young, the Old, and the Dearly De-parted."

Sure enough the recently departed March Bowden's trail led there. Swoop walked into the large lobby that resembled a nice hotel, to see March's body stretched out on the tile floor and his three friends talking to a pale salesman dressed in black clothes.

"Men, here's his sword. Do you want it? Does anyone want it?"

"No. Damn thing," one said.

"Was he in the Army?" Swoop asked.

"No, his pappy was. That sword was March's father's sword. Officer, Illinois. Civil War. March carried it around mostly to cut brush for our boss. We run cattle east of here for the William Brothers."

"Now we have to go back and tell his son, his father's dead. The kid works with us."

"How old's his kid?" Swoop asked.

"Owen is seventeen. Yup, he works with us back at the ranch. Imagine this starting your year off."

"If the boy Owen gets that sword back, he'll probably ride out here and try to kill that sommabitch with it. Best it all end right here..."

"I understand."

"He died with a full head a hair," one said, staring down at the body.

"But thanks for thinking about the sword," the second friend said.

Swoop nodded and said, "Well then, I might just keep it."

"You can have it. That Greek..."

"Eye-talian," the third corrected.

"...Eye-talian somabitch saw the sword and scabbard on March's horse day before yesterday, then later that night he picked a fight with him at Rumy's Bar. March, may Jesus-Mother-Mary-bless-em, was a bit hot-headed and he was drunk. The Eye-talian said he looked stupid, didn't know what to do with that sword and didn't deserve having it. March said 'oh yeah? I'll cut you down to size with it.' The Eye-talian slapped his face silly with a glove. The challenge was on. Hey, what's with all that believing in Jesus stuff? God. All that renouncement stuff? He kept with Jesus and the Eye-talian still kilt him."

"I don't know," Swoop said.

"Well, March got kilt anyway. March had em a Bible, but he wasn't the religious type. But who says they don't need God?"

"We got a scabbard for it, if-in you want it, sir," the third man said.

"I do," Swoop said.

"You been in the Army?"

"No, sir," Swoop lied, having learned that admission-lesson.

"But I do want a scabbard. Yes. And to keep it from the boy. A naked sword is a dangerous sword."

"More dangerous in the hand of damn fool," one said with a sigh, watching two funeral men drag March's body into the back room.

"I am at the Manitou Cliff House..."

"Yup. Know it."

"Just leave it there for Room 12, Archie Turner's room."

"Will do, Mr. Turner."

"Whenever you can get around to it," Swoop said, motioning to the back room, "no hurry."

"Thanks fer asking though."

"If that Eye-talian sees you with that sword, he'll be gunning for you next," the first friend warned.
Swoop half-smiled, half-winked and said, "Good luck with you, men. My condolences."

Swoop left the building.

"Reckon that man was in the Army after all? He's got Army all over em like a tattoo," the first man said.

"Reckon so," the second man said. "If he stood any straighter, he'd crack his back."

Chapter 9: A Spider Web of Travel
February 1891, Sioux Falls, South Dakota

The pen and pencil drawing was like a photograph and truly resembled Swoop Swellen's face as rendered by the photo from Swoop's office. His brown hair was covered by the drab Army hat he wore in the picture. As requested, rank was removed from the hat. Major "Bare Eyes" Twenty was quite pleased with the rendition. He paid the artist a full dollar coin for his artwork, which included a healthy tip.

His next visit would be to the Washington Steam Press printing company to submit the drawing and layout the wording for the first stack of newly minted, dead or alive, $1000 bounty, wanted posters with replications of Swellen's face in the middle of the sheets. Meanwhile, Major Twenty retained in his close possession the original Swellen photograph to immediately show around town in person to potential witnesses.

The Washington Steam Press salesman insisted they wait a few hours, and he would rush the production of the wanted posters, after all it was to capture a real, low-down traitor to the United States of America!

Then, Major Twenty and his assistant, a Lt. Bernes made their way to the first of five stagecoach lines in the city. They both wore their full Class A, blue uniforms to further officially press their cause. And then, the walk around search-and-questioning began.

"Hello sir," Major Twenty identified himself and pulled the actual photo of Swellen from his file. He asked the man at the front counter of Blusters Stage and Delivery,

"Have you seen this man? Within the last two to three weeks, he came into town and left again. He's about 6 foot tall, brown hat and a brown leather, jacket with white fur trim. About early 40s in age. You might remember a big white fur trim collar."

The clerk studied the picture and chatted while Lt. Bernes scrutinized a schedule hanging on a wall and wrote down a list of all the cities the business line ran to. Given the local access to trains, this list was small and what was left ran only to nearby towns.

"I can't say that I have sir," the clerk said.

"Okay. May I leave some wanted posters with you? Will you post one and make sure all your employees look at it? There's a $1,000 reward for him."

"My God, did he kill the President? A thousand dollars!"

Major Twenty smiled and said, "No sir. Treason, sir. The man was once a lieutenant general, and he must be taken to task for cowardice, desertion and treason."

Lt. Bernes pulled 10 posters from his leather satchel and laid them on the desk.

"We are currently staying at the Crescent Hotel should

anyone remember anything.”

With the same line of questioning and poster distribution, they visited:

Christopher Stage Lines.
Amid Fields Coaches.
Travelers.
Greater North Carriers.
Sioux Falls train station (they felt most hopeful).

Nothing substantial was gained. Much later, tired, the two men whipped off their caps, tugged off their gloves, took off their heavy uniform jackets, and plopped into velvet chairs near the roaring lobby fire at the Crescent Hotel. Major Twenty stuck a hand in the air, a signal, and a waitress quickly arrived. He ordered two Schmidt beers.

“The stages all run to 11 cities nearby in total,” Lt. Bernes said, “The train runs direct to four major cities. He could have taken any stages or trains once in any of those cities. From there, Swellen could have jumped on any stages or trains in those places.”

“Quite the spider web of travel,” Major Twenty said.

“Yes, Sir.”

The beers arrived and then a bellboy approached and handed Major Twenty a note. He read the message aloud.

“Gee Willikers will be here in three days by train. I sure hope we have a lead on Swoop before he gets here. He’s an impatient cuss.”

“I’ve never met him, is he as...as colorful as stories go?” Lt. Bernes asked.

“Let me put it to you this way Bernes, if he’s stuck here with us with no leads? In about two days, he’ll start taking the town apart brick-by-brick, plank-by-plank.”

“Searching?”

“No. Just ornery,” Twenty said.

“Major Twenty! Major Twenty!” a man at the hotel counter called out.

“Yes?”

"Telephone!"

Major Twenty got up with a tired grunt and walked to the side of the counter to stand beside the wall phone. He put the receiver to his ear and spoke into the mouthpiece, "This is Major Twenty."

"Mister, er, I mean Major, my name is Elton Willbarger. I work at the rail lines. I punch the tickets on the trains, ya know. And I have seen that man you are looking for. I eyeballed yer poster when I came in the office this afternoon from the St. Paul run. I especially remember his furry white collar and that face. And I spoke with him. He asked me how I was, which no one ever does. We spoke a bit."

"Where was he going Mr. Willbarger? Do you remember?"

"Denver, Sir. Denver, Colorado. I know it. I remember."

"What is your home address, Mr. Willbarger? If this helps us find him there will be some reward for you. It won't be a $1,000, that will be reserved for the man who lays hands upon him, but there will be something for you. I will see to it that you get something for your help."

As Major Twenty spoke to the man, he gave Lt. Bernes a thumbs-up signal from across the room. He hung up and sat back down with Lt. Bernes.

"A ticket puncher positively identified our man, on a train to Denver. I will leave in the morning for Denver and Fort Logan. You stay here and wait for Gee Willikers. Then the two of you train on down to Denver and meet me at Fort Logan."

Chapter 10: You Should Not Know My Name

"Mr. Archie! Signore Archie."

Knock, knock, knock.

"Yes. Who is it?" Swoop asked.

"Mr. Zapello wishes to have lunch with you."

"Mister...," Swoop opened the door half-way to see a swarthy man in a black suit and a well-dressed Catty Corners standing behind him. She strolled right past the man and right into the room with her hands clasped behind her back. The man stepped in next.

"It's too early for lunch," Swoop said.

"Lunch will be served at the Zapello base camp office of Pike's Peak," the man said. "It will take almost an hour by carriage to get there."

"Less," Catty added.

"I see," Swoop said, watching Catty with a curious eye as she paced and studied every corner of his room.

"You won't find anything interesting in here in any corner, Miss Corners."

"A stoic has such few possessions," she added.

"Well, come to think of it, yes. Few," he said.

She sat on the bed, palms flat on each side of her, her fingers stroked the blanket's material. Swoop watched her fingers move.

"Sir?" the man said, getting back Swoop's attention.

"Oh, ahhh, yes. I think I will go. Yes, of course. I will meet you downstairs?"

"Yes."

"Ahh, Mr. Zapello asked..." the man said sheepishly, "for you to wear your guns if you have any?"

"My guns."

"Yes sir, I see you have guns," the man pointed to the gun belt with two pistols, hanging on the back of the desk chair.

"Rough country out there, I guess, huh?" Swoop said.

"Rough, sir."

"Well, okay," Swoop said with a sigh.

He walked to the room door and opened it all the way for both their exits. "I will change, and I will meet you downstairs."

"I think I will stay," Catty said, "I need a change today."

"Ahh, oh, well, very well!" The man said.

He backed up, nodded with a bow, and walked down the hall.

Swoop shut the door.

"You know, a lady alone in a hotel room might have her reputation ruined," Swoop said unbuttoning his shirt.

"Well then...since my reputation has already been ruined by me just being here..."

About an hour later, Swoop and Catty appeared on the stairs and in the lobby, dressed for a cold ride to the foothills of Pike's Peak. Under his long jacket, he wore his guns and even snapped his swagger stick into his belt, to punctuate the "armed" request.

"Got something for you, Mr. Turner," the hotel manager Mr.
Holden told Swoop.

"Oh?"

Holden handed him the long, heavy scabbard of the dead duelist's cavalry sword.

"Some fellows, cowboys, came by last night. Dropped it off for you."

"Thank you," Swoop said, admiring it up and down in his hands. "Can you keep it here until I get back? Or maybe have a maid leave it up there?"

"Certainly, sir."

Outside in the cold, the Zapello's man paced around a very nice enclosed, European-style, two-horse coach. He seemed relieved at their arrival.

"We will be late," he said in a frustrated whine, opening the coach's side door.

Once inside, the ornate coach took off for Pike's Peak.

"Ever been to Pike's Peak?" Catty asked.

"Never have."

"I have lived here since the Gold Rush. 1859," she said.

"You were but a child," he said.

"I was. My parents came here for Kansas. There wasn't much mining right here, but all over the mountains there was. The news is that there will be gold found in Pike's Peak soon again though, especially after Zappy's train is complete. Easy up and down. It's part of the Rocky Mountains. It's about 13 miles to the top on very skinny mountain roads. Rugged roads. Too narrow at times. But not narrow other times. It's beautiful at the top..."

"You've been to the top?" Swoop asked.

"Oh! Yeah. Many times. The state of Colorado has hired Zappy to build this special mountain-climbing train so everyone can get up there easily and see it all. It's too hard now. You see the poles and telephone wires?"

"I do."

"Zappy has it all wired, and now half-way up the mountain where there is the Half Way Hotel."

"Does everyone call him Zappy?"

"Oh, pretty much. Or Zap. Don't ask me what I call him."

"I can only imagine. Why do you think he wants to talk with me?"

"You're an interesting fellow, Archie. I'll say that. But he's having some serious troubles. Best he tell you. I don't know the whole story and I don't want to know the whole story. I'll still be here long after he's gone back to Sicily. AND...back to his wife. Or he'll stay over here and build trains on all the mountains and his wife will come here. Where does that leave little ol me?"

"I understand."

Within some 45 minutes, the coach reached the base camp. From the compartment windows Swoop could see the area under a cold, crystal clear blue sky. It was Colorado-Rocky Mountain beautiful, with a spectacular view, even at that lower elevation than the Peak's official climb. Pine trees, rolling hills, a distant river surrounded tents, buildings, train engines and train cars stacked side-by-side, ready to be placed on future tracks, storage yards, horses and stables, a large, two-story, square-shaped, log cabin near piles of rails and equipment. It was a work yard for a large project and men were moving everywhere as busy as bees or ants in the snow.

"Happy New Year! Welcome! Welcome. I see that Catty has delivered you successfully," Zapello shouted from the cabin porch.

"I have been delivered," Swoop said softly, and Catty gave him a short, sharp elbow to the ribs.

This time Zapello was dressed in alpine clothes, boots, baggy pants, wide suspenders and a red flannel shirt, not a man prepped for a European opera like the evenings before. He beckoned Swoop and Catty onto the wide balcony encircling the log cabin.

Once inside, Swoop cast his eyes upon a long table loaded with food.

"Come. Come. Hungry?"

"Yes," Swoop said while the driver collected their jackets and hats. This exposed Swoop's guns and stick, of which Zapello took note. No less than six cats of various colors roamed the big front rooms.

"Yes! I like-a the cats!" Zapello said, "And I see you have the Roman, Centurion stick at your side. I like that."

"Habit," Swoop said. "We call it a swagger stick here. And if I am told I need my guns. I probably need my stick too."

They sat with Swoop shifting the guns and his army stick around, guns parallel to his thighs, stick hanging down. They proceeded to eat a heavy lunch of steak and vegetables, supported by Italian wine. Zapello explained his train-mountain-climbing, construction mission. Swoop asked questions a few questions about Sicily.

"Miss Corners, might I have a word with Mr. Archie alone? I don't want to bore you my dearest."

"Sure, sweetie," she said, and stood. She meandered off to another room.

"Archie..." Zapello started, lighting a pipe, "I noticed that you watched Carlos Greco's duel with that most ignorant cowboy the other day."

Swoop nodded.

"Greco as you might guess, works for me. Here for me. With-a me from Sicily. He is a supervisor. He is also a master swordsman. He has studied with many great masters of Europe. Anyone who duels with him is an ignorant fool. He has killed many men. Reminiscent of the American gun-fighter? Eh?"

"Gunfight duels are mostly in the pulps, Mr. Zapello."

"Oh, oh call me Zap!"

"There are not a whole lot of real, gunfighting duels in the West like the Eastern magazines print. Just maybe sudden gunfights spurred up inside fist fights, bushwhacks..."

"I see."

"...ambushes. Not many standoff duels. Do all his sword fights end up in a death?"

"Yes-a. Now. But in his years of fighting in competitions of course no. Those were controlled sports. He had challenges to the death in Italy and Austria. France. He now enjoys the true sword fight that ends in death-a. In Europe the laws of the sword fighting, the duel, come and go, here in America, the consensual duel, specially in the...wild, wild West...is okay."

"The wild, wild West. I have a question. What...why did Greco ask that man about God? Renouncing God? Then kill him like that?" Swoop asked.

"A sad story. You see in the European traditions of some bad men, the...the evil side of history of the sword in Europe...for some, to kill a man, to really, really KILL a man, some think that they must also kill his soul. They must totally win. Kill. By that, they must stop the soul from rising to heaven. So-a, they trick the wounded. They suggest the wounded man renounce Jesus to live. Renounce God to live. Of course, the wounded man wants to live in the scary moment, the sword tip at his neck. So at that moment, scared, he declares this renouncement of the savior. And at that one Godless moment, men like Greco stab and kill them. Men like Greco think they have really killed an opponent. Killing their soul too. Or you might say...you might say...killed him twice. Heart and soul."

Zapello inhaled on his pipe.

"That's some very evil thinking," Swoop said.

"Yes, it is. Very. The Bible says, 'They will face a reckoning before Jesus Christ-a who stands ready to judge the living and the dead.' Are you a religious man, Archie?"

"Rather not."

"Seen-a too much? Too much in the Army?"

"Perhaps," Swoop said, "did too much. Seen too much."

The tobacco aroma of the pipe lingered around the table. The coach driver, now in white, who had transformed into the food butler and dish remover, appeared with some coffee.

"Italiano coffee," Zapello said with a sweeping hand and a big smile.

"Thanks," Swoop said, spotting how small the cups were.

"Italian style coffee. The essence of the coffee," Zappy said. He downed the hot stuff in one gulp, like a shot of whiskey.

Swoop sipped his.

"After the duel the other day," Zapello continued after the butler left. "I saw you speak with Greco. Then I saw you on the street. You stare him down. Unafraid. Right into his eyes you stared. Right after you saw him kill a man, right before your eyes. I saw your blood a turning, burn hot. I could tell. I saw...I saw...what I think was a certain 'maschilismo.' The Spanish here call it "machismo.""

"I might be one of those ignorant fools," Swoop said.

"I don't think so, Archie. Archie is not your real name is it, Mr. Archie?"

"No."

"What is your real name?"

"You should not know. I should not burden you."

"I should not. You should not. I have enough burdens already. I have a problem." He sat back in his chair. "There are many opportunities in the Rockies for the trains I have designed. The United State wants many of them. All the other states with mountains too. I am associated with an American businessman Ralph Englemen who visited Pikes Peak once. He said it was a miserable, two-day pack mule trip to the top. He'd visited Europe in the past and he knew I had built these mountain-climbing trains in Switzerland. He contacted me and we created a very good business deal. A partnership."

Swoop nodded and sipped his coffee.

"We own...what your country calls...patents on the train system. Now, we do here too in the United States. The papers are on file in Denver and Washington. For the law-abiding citizens, Engleman and I own it all. Everything. But, people here, my people...some of them? They have a curse. A burden. Have you heard of the Mafie? The curse of mafie? Have you heard of the American version? The Black Hand? Or the Mafia? On your east coast?"

"No."

"I see. By the 1800s my Sicily was very disorganized.

The government was a stupid mess. So, small private armies, like clans or families, known as "mafie" took advantage, took control over the chaotic conditions. They extorted protection money from landowners. They threatened, they destroyed and killed. They steal."

"Mafie," Swoop repeated.

"Yes, they are like a disease for some of my people. For them? No rules. Back in Sicily, one day, the mafie walked into my office. They wanted half my company. For nothing in return. Just they say, my...my safety. Money from me, or I will start to have all kinds of problems. Maybe problems like deaths in my family. Explosions. So! So I moved. I agreed to this business deal with the American and I moved over here to escape these threats. Soon my wife and children will come. I hope to build many trains in the Rockies. And any-where there are mountains."

"Uh-huh."

"But some mafie," he pointed through the big windows to the workers on the grounds and then up to Pikes Peak, "they are here with me now. Just the curse of them. The curse is here with me. When I first came to your country, I had 151 Sicilians. Now I have 132. The rest are...missing. Gone," he snapped his fingers.

"Dead?"

"The workers claim they quit. Went back home. But I am told though in the whispers, that they have been killed. Ven-dettas. Coltello! Knife! Some sword fights, but mostly knife fights. You say here, arguments over who knows? Eh? In-sults? The dead? They are buried away on the Pikes Peak somewhere. Out in the woods? I cannot tell what really hap-pened to them. But, most of my men are good men. They keep secrets from me. Many have wives and children and al-ready live in the town. But they have these secrets from me. And some have the curse of the criminal."

"Greco?"

"Greco. He is a gang leader. A trickster. He has some of my men right under him, listening to him and working for him, not me. Some, once my men, now his. They are stealing my equipment, Archie, as I am told. In whispers. They are going to other cities like Denver and showing the equipment to metal factories. To copy! With copies of my plans. To builders to make the engines and train cars. My secrets. My patents. This is all underway as we speak here right now at this table. Soon, Greco and his men will leave me here and start their own mountain train companies, cog trains, all with my business secrets, all over the Rockies."

"And that is why you asked me here?" Swoop said.

"I now need to hire some men with... maschilismo. I want you to kill Greco."

At that instant, Swoop noticed for a second, the brunette-colored, hair bangs of a woman, Catty's hair bangs, protruding from the very doorway she'd disappeared into moments earlier. He also saw the tiptoe of her boot on the doorstep, accidentally visible. Back in 1875, Swoop once shot a man in the foot in St. Paul, Minnesota who was waiting to ambush him when he walked by. Exposing the front of your foot around a corner for balance, while "hiding-leaning-waiting...or spying...like this was a common and natural, ignorant mistake. Catty was spying.

"You want me to do the reckoning of which you speak of ...but killing him is not going to solve your problem." Swoop said returning his attention to Zapello, "He could be replaced by someone in his gang. And it sounds like a lot of the damage to your patents has already been done."

"Fare i conti. Reckoning. I guess. But if I lose the confidence of Mr. Engleman. I will lose everything."

"Where does Englemen live?" Swoop asked.

"Cleveland, Ohio."

"Is there a marshal here? A county sheriff?"

"Worthless," Zapello said with a growl. "His name is Gene Martins. The sheriff won't stop the sword duels in town. He is never seen. And my problems are not down there in town, or in Denver, not in the city limits. The county sheriff is elected and only worries about places where there are lots of people, lots of votes, lots of businesses and money. We will be gone from here after the job is complete, leaving only a few caretakers. No voters for him. The man is also a half-wit. He doesn't care about thefts out here in the country. He is from your deep south and thinks of me as a rich carpetbagger. Worse than a Yankee. A foreign carpetbagger from overseas."

"You have a lawyer?" Swoop asked.

"I do. In Denver. I wanted to...."

While Zapello droned on, Swoop thought about his own money problems and how he really needed more money. A lot. Fast.

"Hmmm. What you need is a guard here. Security." Swoop said. "A picket."

"Aaaa...picket? What is this?"

"Yes, in English, military, for a guard. Someone to investigate this problem." He leaned in, putting both elbows on the table.

"When I was in the Army, at one post, we lost a lot of supplies. I took over operations and I decided to investigate the problem. Soldiers were stealing goods and selling them to Indians and a nearby wagon train trail when the wagons passed near the tribe's reservation every month. I caught them all."

"Can you do this here? Such an investigation?"

"I can. I need $25 a week. A horse and tack. A shotgun and a rifle. Binoculars. Shackles. You must have rope here already. I need 'No Trespassing' signs made. I need dark clothes. I need a sturdy small, one-horse wagon. I need to sleep out here a lot. But I need to maintain my hotel room in town too. I also need the right to fire people."

"Fire people?"

"Yes. I need to meet with one of your top bosses here that you trust and...as you say 'whispers.' I need to meet with the man who whispers a lot to you."

"That would be my man, Fernando Bosco. Hmmm, but $25 dollars a week. That is $100 a month," Zapello complained.

"I will save you thousands," Swoop said confidently, "maybe even save your whole business."

"Okay then, you can pick out a horse here in the stable. I have 33 work wagons also in the stable. You can also go to the outfitter in town. Pick out what you want. What you need. Make the signs. Tell them to put it on my bill."

"I want you to write a letter to your lawyer this afternoon," Swoop said. "Tell him, we want him to write a letter warning anyone that steals your patents will suffer the consequences."

"That they'll be sued?" Zapello said.

"No. No, he must just say they will 'suffer the consequences.' Make sure he words it just like that. Consequences might just mean a lawsuit, or... something else. Far worse."

"Catty!" Zapello yelled.

Swoop looked back at the doorway. She had really been leaning in and listening. Lots of foot and hair accidentally protruding, but with her beckoning, her bangs and toe tip disappeared back from the door frame. There was a pause, as though she was deep inside the room, and then about 10 seconds later, Catty fully appeared in a full stride and a charming smile.

"Yes?" she said.

"Come join us again my dear. Get some wine please-a. It is late and we are all staying the night up here."

"Okay, Zappy," she said.

"What about Greco?" Zapello asked Swoop quietly as Catty walked to the kitchen for the wine.

Swoop sipped the last of his coffee and said back in the same low volume, "I'll kill him if I have to."

"You will have to. I warn you Mr. Turner, or whoever you really are, you must always wear your guns and that Roman swagger stick of yours, now in Manitou Springs and out here too."

Chapter 11: Half Way and Back from Hell

Swoop was guided upstairs to his guest bedroom by the butler who explained that the indoor bathroom was down the hallway. Swoop closed the door and began to undress, but heard some tugging on the door? Catty Corners? Surely not here. No, he discovered, a gray actual "cat," as in kitty was the culprit. The cat dashed in when he cracked the door open and jumped on the bed.

"Good evening," Swoop said.

The cat meowed.

Sometime after midnight, Swoop awoke. He rested on his right side and the guest cat was folded up "in a loaf," towering up on his left side, sound asleep. He didn't know why he awoke. He grabbed his pocket watch from the nightstand and twisted it over in his hand to see the time, but it was just too dark.

"Gettin-up, geeet, gettin-up, cat," Swoop warned the feline and it leapt off of him. He took a deep breath, and watch in hand, barefoot, he walked to a window and partially opened the curtain. The light of the starry night revealed it was 1:50 a.m. But something caught his eye out on the grounds. Movement. He zeroed in. Running from the house, wrapped in a long coat over a nightgown, heading for piles of supplies and gear...well...it had to be Catty Corners!

"What the..." Swoop whispered and leaned in.

She disappeared into the factory warehouse landscape. She had to be meeting someone. An affair with a worker? Perhaps, someone less prestigious than the married Zapello, but one that offered more of a future? After all, he thought about their late morning "meeting" in his hotel room. She was certainly...more than available. But he also remembered her the prior evening, hovering in the doorway, spying, listening in while he and Zapello pow-wowed. Swoop swore in the future, he would keep all his clothes on while in this room and make ready to exit the next night, or any night he stayed in the cabin, to investigate this or other surprises.

The next morning was bitter cold. Zapello insisted that his new employee Archie Turner, be given a tour of the cog railway construction operation, which Archie agreed to, especially when he was to be guided by Zapello's chief "whisperer," team boss Fernando Bosco. The crew boss met Swoop in front of the cabin on the frigid, cloudy morning. Fernando was a tall Sicilian, dressed in work clothes with a closely trimmed beard and moustache, about 45 years old. He seemed happy to meet Swoop.
They started walking across the yard.

"The grounds here-a...are our main operating area," Fernando began, "Over there are our train engines we use and the ones that are in storage. We work with Baldwin Locomotive in America. Steam of course. We only use two engines a day to deliver men and supplies to the end of the line and back."

"The engines sure look different than regular train engines," Swoop said.

"Yess-a, because they must sit higher and...tilted. It looks funny, yes? Si. Si. Si. The teeth that collect the special line of track in the middle of the regular railroad tracks make them look different. Different than other trains. The engine must-a bear down on the track in the middle.

You see, over there are our piles of special rails. As you can-a see, Signore Turner, we must cut down some trees. Sometimes, the new track runs into trees. Many times, just rock, big and small, but many times, we have many trees in our way. We bring the cut-down trees down-a here, take them over to that wood shop over there..."

Swoop saw and heard the men in the wood shop grinding away. The cutting saws were massive, like those in the lumberjack business, which the railroad business was also in the business of cutting down and ripping up trees.

"...and they cut the trees into the...the...'sleepers.' These are planks of wood that runs across the track, between the rails. We use all the wood. And we still have to buy more wood than we cut down.

You can see-a, way back over there, we have cattle and pigs and some cowboys, local Colorado cowboy men, to take care of them. Mr. Zapello likes his piglets and we have to have a lot of food for the workers. Mr. Zapello brought his chef all the way from Sicily. All the other food we buy in Manitou Springs."

"His chef is very good," Swoop added.

"And those two big buildings over there, are our caserma, barracks – you would call them that in America. Most of the men eat and sleep there, but many live in Manitou Springs, by themselves or with family. We offer two stagecoaches a day to the city to haul them back and forth. Most of the families are back in Sicily, waiting for news of more jobs. But some families came over with us."

"Does this Mr. Greco live in the barracks or in the city?" Swoop asked.

"In the city, most of the time. He spends his evenings and weekends in Rumy's Bar. Where he sleeps in Manitou, this-a I do not know."

Fernando guided Swoop over to the 7 a.m. morning run of workers boarding the work train. There waiting, was one of the odd-shaped, tilted steam engines and two cars. The first passenger car held the workers, the second car was a flatbed and carried supplies. The two men boarded the worker's car. Some ignored Swoop. A few others stared at him. There were only two rows of seats running down the sides of the car, the rest made do with standing room only with high wooden rails to grab for stability. Most of the men stood.

But in a last minute, none other than Greco the infamous swordsman himself, along with 12 more men, all boisterous, laughing and arguing with each other, piled into the car. Greco's expression froze when he spotted Swoop.

"We have already constructed the rail past the Ruxton Half Way Hotel, which has been up there for years. You and I will stop there. We will have some coffee and bread. Years ago, the Palsgrove family built the Half Way Hotel for the tired travelers riding the mules up Pikes Peak. To rest-a, and to eat. Once this train is done, rich people will have houses at Ruxton Park. They are buying and selling the land already. The view is magnifica! Is good for business."

"The steepness of the mountain is...is very steep-a, you know? At parts. A regular train can work at 10 degrees." He held his hand up flat. "BUT, Pikes Peak, is a 25% grade at parts. Grade is what they call it. Grade. The teeth of the engine on the center rail can climb this grade, but also, also control going down. The descent. In the end-a, we are building two tracks. One for going up, one for going down. We are building two tracks for two trains. These trains run up and down-a all workday. They carry workers and supplies. We have the two tracks done three-fourths of the way up."

"I see that. Yes. When will you be done?"

"Maybe one year? More? The climb up was *tortuosa*, aah, circuitous, not one steep, straight line up. And the views even in this dark, foggy morning are still spectacular. Almost heavenly. The elevation climb was slow and at times, even when the land appeared quite flat, but still, indeed...some climbing."

Soon the train stopped not far from the Ruxton Half Way Hotel. It was an old wooden structure, quite big, located down in a slight, small valley from the track lines. Only Fernando and Swoop exited.

"Look! Look-a. The Garden of the Gods over there. You been?"

"No," Swoop said, squinting as though such might pierce the fog. He could only spy glimpses of cliffs.

"She's-a beautiful. A small mountain range of rock over there in the mist. Very unusual shapes. You must visit. Very popular."

They made there way to and through the big, ornate, front door of the Half Way Hotel.

"Good morning gentlemen!" An elderly man roared.

"Coffee, bacon and eggs, Mr. Ralfmussen," Fernando said, and the pair took seats in the restaurant area.

"I understand you have told Zapello of a lot of problems you have heard about. What is going on?" Swoop asked.

Fernando grimaced and said, "Yes-a. Most of the men are good men. Loyal. But some? No."

"Greco."

"Si. Si. Si. Greco. All of the men in his working crew, they are too close to each other. If you do not join into the 'blood,' 'la mia famiglia' the family of Greco, they make you leave. They have already killed one man on his crew that they could not trust."

"They have?"

"Yes-a. A very nice man, with a nice family back in Italy. He would not listen to their crime plans. There have been several men killed-a. We think from Greco, and, and some feuds of all kinds? Some in the sword fights with Greco, not all of the fights are in the city, but some up here too."

"How many has Greco killed in duels?" Swoop asked.

"I think Twelve."

"Twelve!" Swoop said." How does he trick 12 people to sword fight with him? Such a master?"

"Greco has a special way with words. He pushes and tricks them into an anger. But some of the missing-a, the dead, are not in these open, sword fights. Some-a just were jumped and killed. Beaten to death. Up here? The bodies are buried everywhere we think," Fernando said, spreading his arms.

"What crime plans does he have?" Swoop asked.

"Zapello knows of these plans. They want to take over the company. Or copy the company and move away with it to make their own jobs. Their own company. Takeover or copy, they will do whatever is the easiest."

"And they take over this company by..."

"Killing Signor Zapello. If that becomes the easiest way. I understand they make such plans all the time. Kill or not to kill?"

After breakfast, they strolled back outside and up the small hill to the railroad tracks.

"I must report up to the front line now, my friend. It is only a short walk up ahead. If you wait at this platform for 5 minutes, the return train will be here. The engineer will see you, but...but, good idea, you wave your hands at him any-way. It will take you back down to the camp. Bon jornu, Bona sira."

Fernando left and Swoop alighted upon a wooden bench on the wooden platform, to wait. The sun was breaking through the clouds and each new minute of light changed this and the nearby, mountain landscapes.

He contemplated his situation. This was a crime-business problem. New to him. So different than the world of the mili-tary, fighting with Indians, hunting people, being a pawn in a chain of command. But how different really? There were many insidious people plotting "coups" in the military chain of command all the time. Evil unions. Political plots. Crazy, ambitious leaders. Death from mistakes. Enough to drive any real stoic crazy, and now this Zapello plot, to include a mur-

derous, assassination if need be. It was all really the same in
the Roman Empire, their own military, their own businesses,
but the same wicked schemes found in all human nature and
history.

He heard it coming. The unique, tilted, broad train engine
appeared from around a bend. Swoop stood, then waved a
hand as the train approached. The engineer waved back and
stopped. Swoop climbed into the front of the passenger car.
He saw four men far in the back and he decided to take a seat
in the front end. Like on the ride up, the car only had two
rows of bench seats, one on each side.

The four men, two seated, and the two standing gawked
at him. The train started its slow descent. One could feel the
teeth clench underneath. The slip and catch. Slip and catch.
Open and close.

The two seated men stood. The four men slowly walked
toward Swoop, their grim faces advertising trouble.

Swoop unbuttoned his leather jacket and scratched his
ear, his face expressionless.

"Who are you? What are you doing here?" One man
asked.

"The same as you," Swoop said calmly. "I'm going down
the mountain."

They started to get closer, but a strange look befell Swellen's face, a flare, a wide eye, and a show of teeth, with a slight snort and move to a nostril. It was as if, he became a different person. They stopped. He stood.

"Have you idiots been riding this train up and down waiting for me to get back on?" Swoop asked calmly.

"You will regret-a you ever coming here..." the closest man said as his lip twitched and...

Swoop unsnapped the swagger stick with his left hand and in a split-second, it was out and up. Swoop's toes clutched the insides of his boots like the teeth of the engine. He made a fist with his right hand, and it flew up and hit that closest man's jaw in much of an uppercut angle. Both of Swoop's boots left the floor about half an inch with the impact adding extra dynamite to the head blast. Before the man could fall completely back, Swoop cracked him in the head with the stick. He was instantly brain-splash-uncon-scious while airborne, curling backward. Swoop lunged for-ward to hit him more times, but the man flipped away fast, down and out of his reach.

A second man at Swoop's side, lunged in, poorly, and clipped Swoop on the face with a punch. This sudden pain caused such a rush of energetic anger in Swoop that he knew he might be unlikely to remember details about this encounter afterward. Swoop's face was knocked to the right and since turned there, looking there now, he saw and shoved the third man hard on the chest with a two-handed grip on the stick, a tip end forward near the throat in a stab-bing thrust. The man crashed back on the bench and even slid further away on the slick wood of the long seat.

Swoop spun back to the man who struck him, but the man was fast after him like a lion within the close, two feet of distance. Tackle! They both hit the bench hard with Swoop on the bottom. The man grabbed Swoop's throat with both hands and started choking him. Swoop let go with one hand of his two-handed stick grip, swung the stick out and over the arms of the choker. In the pass over, the free end of the stick struck the man's face. He regained the two-hand grip, this time with both hands and stick above the choking arms, and he crashed the stick down on the man's arms, bending the arms, breaking the choke. Breathing again! This caused the man's face to drop closer to Swoop's. Swoop then forcefully hit his face with the center of the stick, three, four times about the nose and mouth. The last blow broke the nose and some teeth. Then he put the stick on the stunned man's throat and thrust. Swoop sat up along with the movement, driving the man off of him and onto the floor.

Swoop rolled up to stand, the fourth man, furthest away yet still pretty close, crouched a few inches at the knees, giving the first look of a weapon draw as he made a twisted face, and his right hand plunged into a pants pocket.

Instantly, Swoop pulled a revolver, holding the Thunderer hip high and aimed at his chest.

"Oh, go ahead. Knife. Gun. Or a peppermint stick. You pull it out? I kill ya," Swoop growled.

And oh, he *so* wanted to shoot. To shoot him in the face. The throat. Shoot! Two or three times. But the fourth man froze. He put his left palm up. He slowly retracted his right hand, empty.

"Sit down. All a ya," he ordered and pointed to the right-side bench halfway down the car.

The one man missing a few teeth grabbed the coughing, wheezing man now flat out on the floorboards. He lifted him up. They limped and gasped and gathered on the bench as ordered.

Oh, Swoop thought, could he at least shoot all four of them in their kneecaps? Or a foot each? He quivered with excitement. That one man he hit in the throat with his stick was still having serious trouble breathing. Maybe that was enough for now. Calm down! No! He thought. He just couldn't kill four men on the train. What would Zapello think?

"SIT!"

The four did.

"You four are dumb idiots. You underestimate the enemy. Me. What's in that pocket?"

"A switch-a blade," the fourth man said.

"A switchblade. Well, I have some bad news for all of you. I now work for Mr. Zapello. He has hired me. Security. Who told you to take this ride with me?"

Silence.

"Huh?"

"No one. We just don't like-a you. The looks of you," the knife man said.

"Uh-huh," Swoop said, glaring at them. "I wonder if I shot one of you in the ankle, what would you say?"

"Bafongool!" one said with a disgusted expression.

Swoop needed only to imagine what that word translated to, so he continued, "I am now security around here. But...I'll bet you know that already, somehow, you know that. Mr. Zapello has also granted me special powers. You see, I can fire people. And you four skunk-fucks are now fired."

"Skunk..." one mumbled.

"F..f..fired?" Another declared.

"Yeah. Fired. If I see you tonight or tomorrow on the compound, I will whip you with my stick. Whip you and hope I can kill you with it. The new signs on the gates will read 'trespassers will be shot.' Shooting is fast and a swagger stick is...slower. I like the slower."

"You can't..."

"Try me."

Swoop sat down about 10 feet away, and said, "Right now, I am contemplating shooting each one of ya, in one foot each. Just cause. Just so you get a lesson in life to remember how stupid you were. Look down at your foot for the rest of your life. Limping. One foot all mangled and bones blasted. You'll limp forever from this stupid moment. We'll see how the rest of the ride down the mountain goes...maybe it will calm me down."

He rested the handgun on his leg, the barrel still pointed generally at all four. He watched their faces go through emotions, accompanied by their raging thoughts.

"We could-a just rush you. You cannot-a shoot all of us," one finally growled.

"Ohhh yes, I could. But, how about you all give it try? How about on three! Get ready. Ready? One. Two. Three. THREE! Come on."

They just stared at him.

"Ohhh, well."

As they neared the bottom land, Swoop saw four men loitering on the platform, waiting for the next ascending train. The train reached the compound and came to a stop. Swoop realized that it took two teams running up and down to try and catch him alone on the train. Organization! The four-in-waiting were this group's relief, taking turns until they could catch a vengeance ride with him.

"Out. Get yer pay. Then get."

"You have not seen the last of us," one said. "You will see us again!"

"When I see you again? That will be the last of you. You can thank Mr. Zapello that you are alive now, as I am doing the best I can to behave for the sake of his reputation. If it were just up to me? Mountain wolves would be pickin at bones off the side of this mountain right now."

The awaiting group of four replacements watched a healthy Swoop strut out of the car and were shocked to see their four co-workers limp out, bleeding, one with an arm wrapped around the shoulder of another needing help to walk. The four onlookers glared at them, not knowing what to do.

"They're fired. You're lucky. Go back to work," Swoop shouted to the new four, "this stupid idea did not work."

Chapter 12: Vulgar Latin
Sioux Falls Train Station, South Dakota

Gee Willikers bounded off the train and was greeted by Lt. Bernes, who recognized him by Willikers enormous size, wild beard, tan, and fringe jacket. Lt. Bernes noted that people waiting on the platform couldn't help but gawk at the man for several seconds, a few appeared taken aback by his mountain man presence. Willikers wore a rifle bag on his back and handled one large suitcase which in comparison to him, appeared small.

Willikers saw the soldier approach and assumed the uniformed man was there for him.

"Well now, who the heller you?" Gee said when Lt. Bernes stepped close.

"Lt. Bernes, sir. Major Twenty is not here. He is already in Denver sir."

"Already?"

"Yes, sir. We received solid information that our AWOL took a train from here to Denver. I have two tickets in my hand right now for Denver. Train leaves in two hours."

"Well, shit-fire and save matches," Gee said, looking

around the station. "More days on a dang train. We, I reckon then, we're going to Denver."

Once aboard and once departed on the train ride to Denver, and once alone in a private cabin, Lt. Bernes opened his suitcase and pulled out some papers, to include the newly minted, wanted poster.

"Here is Mordecai "Swoop" Swellen. This is what he looks like," Lt. Bernes said, handing Gee the wanted poster. "He is about 6 foot tall. Stocky. Irish, or Scottish-Irish."

"He's a mick-bastard, yeah," Gee said, eyeing up the drawing,
"Yeah. I know em from years ago. We chased some Apache in Arizona a loooong time ago. He was a lieutenant. He's a little part hinjun, you know, which makes him rougher than most pale faces."

"Part...what?" Lt. Bernes said, astonished.

"Yeah. Small part, Minnesota hinjin," Willikers said. He looked up at Lt. Bernes. "You don't know that? Huh? Where you from?"

"Well...ahh...New Hampshire," Lt. Bernes replied, trying to recoup from the claim that Swellen was of an Indian heritage.

Gee Willikers sneered at him and then returned to his study of the wanted poster.

"But, the man...hates Indians," Lt. Bernes said.

"He don't hate no hinjins. Not all of em. Just some. Don't you know that hinjins hate other hinjins? Tell you more, he was once married to squaw. She was murdered. Let me tell you something even more, Lt. New Hampshire, it twas other hingins what killt his squaw wife."

Lt. Bernes was flabbergasted.

"I know this because his men told me. Fellers in his platoon. Look here," Willikers pointed to parts of the facial drawing, "part hinjin. This part hingin," he said pointing to parts of Swoop's face.

"I didn't know about this Indian history. I don't think Major Twenty knows anything about..."

"General Shanklin don't know either," Willikers interrupted.

"It's a secret Swellen keeps like cards close to his chest."

Lt. Bernes studied the poster and said, "Well, I see...I see what you are suggesting. Yes. But, he has reddish-brown hair. A little curly."

"Yeah, yeah, mick-curly. Mick momma. Hinjin granddaddy or grandma in the woodshed."

"Major Twenty wants you to know that Swellen is a very calm, quiet person, ordinarily. But in a scrap, he is a wild man animal. Like two different people. The major calls him a "Dr. Jekyll and Mr. Hyde.""

"And just who in hell are those two pilgrims? Am I supposed to know?" Willikers asked.

"Well, it's just a book, sir. A newer book. Novel. About a man like Swellen, I'd say. A very calm man that's a doctor that turns into a crazy, monster, by drinking a potion of some sort. That's Hyde."

"A potion. Like a whiskey of some sort?"

"Ah, no sir, a chemical, a doctor's potion."

Gee Willikers grunted and said, "Ain't they all chemicals?"

"Yes. I guess they are, sir."

"Don't catch me drunk on a bad booze, I'll be bad monster man too."

"Swellen has enormous fists, and he studies fighting," Lt. Bernes continued. "Close-up fighting. Knives. Swords. The Irish stick - the Shillelagh."

"I have seen him kill." Willikers said, "Years ago, we was ambushed in a rocky pass, and...and I have seen him kill. Shilly-ailly you say?"

"An Irish cane."

"He need a cane?"

"No, sir. Just for fighting. People carry a cane but do not need one."

"Why did they start calling him Swoop?" Willikers asked.

"Mid 1880s. When so ordered, Mr. Willikers, Swoop will

swoop in and kill. Kill everything in sight. You might say when the Mr. Hyde monster takes over. He has killed many an Indian tribe or encampment when so ordered. And that includes all of them. The braves, the squaws...and the children too."

"Swoops in. So, the Army used Swoop Swellen the same way that the army uses me, only for bigger people killin."

"I guess that is one way of looking at it, sir. Swoops. Yes."

"Swoop," Willikers contemplated the nickname, new to him. "Swoop, huh. On that Apache hunt years ago...we was a hunting, a raiding party that were burnin and a killin, led by an Apach' they called 'Blue Ricardo.' It was one evening, sun setting, we set up camp. Spread out on dry yeller dirt and rock. A war party and Blue Ricardo sneaked up behind a ridge of rock before we could post pickets. They started a shootin at us. Swellen was already way off to the right, he and some pony soldier were doing something. Afoot. And Swellen...he was wearing a two-gun belt, out of uniform, he didn't wear that single toy shooter he was issued when he left the fort on a mission. He circled the ambush far to the right and got up and behind those hunjins."

Lt. Bernes was engrossed.

"Okay so, he had em 12 shots in them two six guns, right? There was eight in the war party. He came a runnin in at em, shootin at em. I guess...I guess the party, what with all the gunfire noise in the air, didn't tell, couldn't tell right away, there was gunfire a runnin up behind them? Swellen shot EVERY one of them, eight of them with 10 shots. ON THE RUN, mind you. The last two rounds he shot the friskiest wounded ones again, what needed killin. Then he faced the sky and let out a war whoop wail when he saw Blue Ricardo was amongst em."

"Wow, that...that flanking should be in a training manual."

"Swellen kneeled, reloaded while the rest of us ran up to the rock ridge. We kilt off the ones still breathin. All of them from Swellen were good shots. Shot up real good. Swellen then, walked up to each one and he spit on em."

"Why?"

"Hinjin thing of some sort, I...then he kicked every one of em in the leg."

"Kicked them in the leg? Indian thing?" Lt. Bernes asked.

"No. Just seeing if theys dead."

"Oh."

"I asked his troopers about the spittin and the war whoopen myself. That's when they told me they knew he was partial hinjin. He swooped in that evening all right. I can still see him runnin, firing those two pistolas. I got me the full bounty again, since I led them there, I got the full bounty and my regular scout pay too. Yer evil Swellen, he saw to it."

"He was once a good man."

"Might still be. So, why'd he run off AWOL on y'all? The army musta drove him crazy over something."

"We don't know exactly why he left. We have reason to believe he refused to enforce the new disarmament rules on the Lakota. His underlings said that Swellen argued it would lead to big trouble. The massacre of the Lakota."

"HA! Then you all kilt the Lakota anyway. Wounded Knee," Willikers said. "So, he ain't so crazy anyway, is he."

"We did. I was there."

"You were?"

"I was. It was a mess. It just escalated from a small argument about collecting a gun, then a small fight...then..."

"Then it all went ca-razy mad, huh," Willikers said.

"Yes sir. It did."

"You shoot anybody?"

"I did, sir. I...I remember well the day. It was insanely cold. Colder than usual. Everyone was on edge. The fight started. Then it came down to surviving, we thought. I thought."

"Then it went way past that. Came down to...sompin else," Willikers said.

"That it did, sir."

"You can quit callin me sir."

"Why did he leave?" Lt. Bernes said, "we can only assume Swoop grew tired of all the killing? Knew there would be more. One morning he just put on his civies and rode off his fort in a supply wagon."

"And now, he's wanted dead or alive? Just fer leavin? Fer predicting a mess. Fer leavin a mess before it happened?"

"That's right sir. General Shanklin has officially declared him a traitor. Disobeying direct and important orders to collect all the Lakota weapons."

"General Shanklin!" Willikers said with a scoff, shaking his head, "God o mighty."

"If we find him, you get the full bounty," Lt. Bernes said. "We are paid by the Army, so we are rewarded nothing. If he's still in the Denver area, we will garner some support from Fort Logan to help us."

"Yup he's part hinjin. My momma and pappy come from the Netherlands. Direct. Directly from Vikings," Willikers added, eyeing up his new traveling companion from New Hampshire.

"My grandparents were the last of the Vikings. I am a straight-line-arrow from the Vikings. You know about the Vikings?"

"Ahhh, yes. Pillagers," Lt. Bernes said.

"Pillow what?"

"Pill-a-gers, sir. The Vikings were pillagers. Looting and plundering. The word comes from vulgar Latin."

"Vulgar…they learn ya that in New Hampshire? Vulgar Latin? So, there's Latin and then now there's vulgar Latin?"

"Well, yes, it's a description."

"HA! Must include a lot of cussin to be so vulgar," Willikers said, his eyes dropping down to the poster again. "One thousand dollars to pillage," he said slowly. "Maybe they'll write a Viking book in vulgar Latin about all this someday? Call it, 'Dr. Gee Willikers and Mr. Hyde Swellen.'"

"Yes, sir. Maybe someday they will, sir. Though I am not sure who would be Jekyll or who would be Hyde. They tell me," Lt. Bernes said, "that Swellen can act like a madman. His long-serving major informed me that should Swoop accidentally, oh say, bump his head on a cabinet door? Or stub his toe? Best get back away from him for the next 20 seconds or so, because Swoop would want to kill everyone around him."

Willikers listened and grunted.

"He has a...big, anger, sir," Lt. Bernes added.

"And you can give up callin me sir," Willikers said. "I ain't no kind a sir."

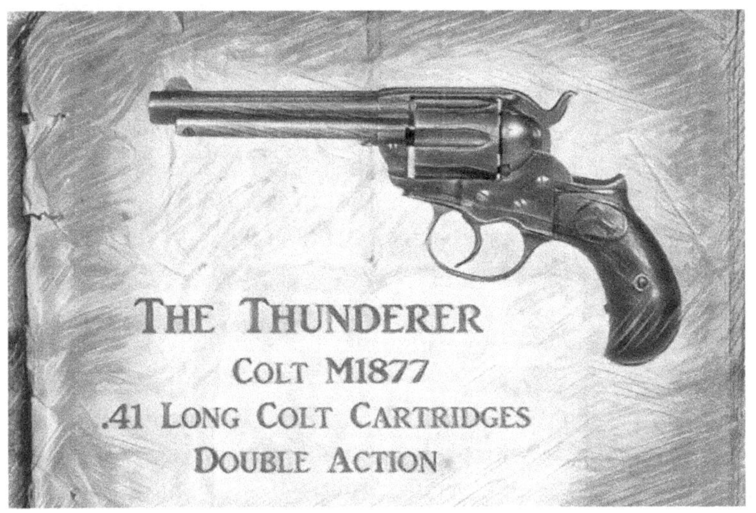

Chapter 13: More Lost Teeth

Zapello Headquarters Cabin

"I fired four of your men this morning," Swoop told Zapello when he entered the office-cabin.

"Ahh, ohhh? What?"

"They jumped me on the train ride down the mountain."

"They what? Who?" Zapello asked.

"These four men waited for me to head back down here on the train, and they came after me. I beat them. I sent them packin. They went in for their last paychecks, so you'll have their names. There were four more waiting for me at the bottom. They were taking turns, just riding up and down the train trying to catch me."

"Why they do this-a?"

"Greco saw me and Bosco ride the train up and get off at the hotel. They obviously have identified me as the enemy, hired by you," Swoop said.

"How-a?" the baffled Zapello said. "So soon?"

"I'm working on that. Spies in this house maybe."

Zapello approached Swoop and looked at his reddened, left cheek.

"They hit-a you?"

"They...hit-a me, yeah. But I hit them back."

"Did you have a nice conversation with Fernando, then?"

"I did. And you probably already know everything he told me," Swoop said while scanning the room for others to steal more intelligence info. Alone, but for three cats, he continued, "if their business replacement plan fails, they will try to kill you."

"And now, you too," Zapello said.

"And me too," Swoop said.

Later that night, as he had planned, Swoop remained dressed and armed, with his jacket hooked by the door of the guest bedroom. He sat in a chair right by the second story window. The same cat remained posted on the made bed, watching him, then finally giving up falling asleep.

"Gave up the goat, have ya, pussy?" Swoop whispered.

Swoop lifted the window several inches to better hear the sounds from the outside. The light winds drifted from the south, and they did not leak their chills much into the room. The curtains didn't even budge. Still, he carried a quilt from the foot of the bed and threw it over himself.

He knew he would doze but counted on any noise outside to wake him up. It was late, 2 a.m. by his pocket watch when Swoop heard a horse whinny and snort, then some low, scraping noises sounded outside his window from out on the yard. He leaned forward and peeked outside. The three-quarter moon revealed some secrets across the snow patched ground. Two men were hauling metal train tracks, one at a time over to a wagon. No torches, just work in the dark. It seemed they were trying to do so quietly. This was not Catty Corners sneaking around in her night gown, this looked like sheer theft.

Swoop stood, slipped on his jacket, and stepped quietly down the hall and stairs. He pulled his Bowie knife and walked to a front window, finding, and feeling for the rope-draw strings of the curtains.

The cords were substantially thick and ornate, almost rope. He cut a string from high up near the rod. Then he cut that in two pieces. He shoved the two pieces into his pockets and eased outside the front door.

Crouched over, he tip-toed across the yard and out onto the supply grounds, getting near the two working men. They were whispering in what sounded to him like the Italian language he'd heard lately. Swoop got to the corner of the pile where they were scavenging and pulled a pistol.

"Working late boys?" He said, while cocking the revolver.

The two men froze, hearing the hammer cocking noise and looked at the gun.

"Who are you?" One said.

"I work for Mr. Zapello. Security."

"Working security? We...he..."

"We are delivering some rails to the city," the second man quickly said.

"At 2 a.m.? Where in the city?" Swoop asked.

"We...ahh...to..."

"Drop all your knives and guns," Swoop ordered.

"We don't..."

"Drop em or I'll drop you."

The two men looked at each other. Each had small pistols and big knives on their belts. The weapons hit the frozen grounds.

"Turn around and put your hands behind your back."

"What do you think..."

"Turn around! Hands on your spine."

"Spine-a?"

"Back. On your back," Swoop corrected. "You on the right, you step back here. Backwards."

"Indietro," one translated for the other.

This way the one on the left could not easily see what was happening behind him and to the man on the right.

The man followed orders. Swoop holstered the pistol and pulled a cord from his pocket. He approached the closest man on the right and wrapped and tied his wrists. Despite the positioning, the second man on the left craned his neck to watch. Then that man suddenly sprang like a panther at Swoop, covering some 8 feet in seconds. And he was reaching into a jacket pocket as he burst forth.

"Get him Diego!" the freshly tied-up man yelled.

Swoop sprinted "indietro" too! And quickly pulled his pistol back out and kept it tight by his right ribs, maintaining weapon protective distance.

"Drop *IT*!" Swoop ordered. He could see that the man had pulled a small knife.

The man stopped with a stagger, considered the pistol and dropped the second knife he carried. Swoop walked up to him, slugged him with the barrel of his Thunderer pistol with a strike so hard the man fell like he was shot on the head, not hit by a gun. But he still wasn't unconscious because he was whimpering and mumbling.

"Cagacazzo!" The disappointed, captured man barked, obviously a disappointment curse in Italian.

Swoop walked up to the first man, got behind him and

stomp-kicked him behind a knee so that he too fell down, face first. Then he stepped back over to the head-wounded man, this Diego, and rolled him over face down and tied his hands off. Now both were tied by the curtain cords.

He stood the conscious man up then hauled the stunned man to his feet.

"To the cabin," Swoop ordered.

He shoved the two across the yard and up the front porch of the cabin. Swoop opened the big double doors and shoved the duo through them. Once inside he kicked and pushed both men so hard, they fell down face first onto the wooden floor. Both groaned and coughed.

"HeeEEEY! Hey!" Swoop's shouts carried through the whole two story, cabin. "Wake up! Wake up!"

Zapello, Catty and every house worker appeared in their night clothes on the second story balcony. Meanwhile, Swoop gathered up two wicker chairs, pulling them to the living room's middle and picked each man up off the floor and shoved them in the seats.

"What....is...?" Zapello said descending the stairs.

A butler lit lamps.

"Just now, these two men were loading up rails on a horse and wagon outside. Get their boss," Swoop said.

"Arturo, get Fernando Bosco," Zapello ordered.

"WHAT...were you doing out there?" Swoop asked the man on his right. Diego, the one who charged him with the knife.

"We work! Working."

"On what!" demanded Zapello in Italian, now standing beside Swoop.

"Ahhh. Loading a shipment."

"At this-a hour? To where?" Zapello asked. "Rail ship-ments only go up the mountain. By train. Why do you have a horse and wagon?"

"Ahhh, I will say a no more. I do not know. I follow or-ders. Fongol!" The man said with a sneer. "I only speak-a to my boss and..."

"He just tried to stab me, outside," Swoop calmly told Zapello.

"Stab!" Zapello said in astonishment.

"I do not know who you! are! Who are you? A thief?" Diego said to Swoop.

"You're the thief," Swoop said and hit the man on the jaw with a closed fist, penetrating with such force that the man and chair toppled over, pitching him rolling and sprawling onto a rug.

"You!" Swoop now said to the man still up and in a chair. "What were you doing out there?

"This is Tony Facillo, my cousin's best friend," Zapello said staring at Tony with such disappointment.

"I was just-a following orders from Diego," Tony said.

The crew boss Fernando Bosco walked in with Arturo, freshly awakened, hair disheveled, with a jacket covering sleep clothes, his shoe laces untied.

"Have you told these men to work?" Zapello asked in Italian.

"Now? For a shipment somewhere to be sent with a horse and wagon?"

"No, sir. Of course not. Of course not. What? Diego, what in God's name were you doing?"

Diego, still on the floor, looked away from his crew boss, his body wriggling and snaking in the fallen chair.

"Tony!" Fernando said to the second man, "What?"

But Diego suddenly got free! He'd squirmed and worked his hands free from the curtain cord and jumped up, glaring at Swoop.

"You a big-a man! Huh? You hit a man that is tied up!" Diego growled, raising his hands to fight.

Swoop sneer-smiled at him, delighted with this new opportunity to hit Diego yet again. Perhaps several more times. The man made his move, a big distance-closing step and a right-hand swing. Swoop stepped right and in a blurry, flurry of violence, in a second or two, he crashed his big fists multiple times into Diego as he marched forward into him. It was such a blur of speed and pounding that the onlookers were in a jaw-dropping, shock.

Diego collapsed to the floor again. Out. Done. Down. Broken. He had some spastic shakes. Face down, drool tinged red, dribbled and bubbled out of his mouth. In the saliva, a tooth slimed out along with a short, spastic cough.

Swoop started to charge in even further, wanting so to stomp kick and break both of Diego's ankles, but with a frustrated grimace, he stopped himself short. Instead, he moved right back in front of an aghast Tony and took a deep, deep frustrated breath.

"I will bash you to bits next," Swoop growled. "What were you doing out there?"

"We were taking rails to town. To meet with a wagon from Denver. Some company..."

"What company?" Zapello asked.

"I don't know. I don't know! I was told-a to meet a wagon."

"Who told you to do this?" Fernando asked.

"I...a..."

"WHO?" Swoop repeated, raising a fist.

"MATTEO!" Tony cried out.

"Matteo," Zapello repeated.

"Matteo?" Fernando repeated.

"Where will you meet this wagon?" Swoop asked.

"Behind Rumy's Bar. I was just a following orders. Orders from Matteo."

"When?" Swoop asked.

"Four? Five a.m. Whenever we got there."

"Was he paying you extra?" Zapello said.

"Yes."

"Then Matteo was not working for us. You were not working for us. You were working for him."

Swoop backed away and Zapello followed him to a corner of the big room. Fernando joined them. Swoop asked Zapello to translate the Italian parts of their inquisition. He did.

"What we do now?" Zapello asked.

"I will take Tony with me to town in the wagon. We'll meet the men at Rumy's and I'll find out who in Denver is buying the equipment."

"Good idea. This is all Greco's plan you know," Zapello said in a hiss. "Rumy's. That is his favorite bar. His hangout. Matteo is one of his best amicos."

"Keep Diego here. Tie him up again. Better with better rope. We'll figure out what to do with him in the morning. Where's Matteo?"

"He is asleep-a in the barracks," Fernando said. "I can only guess, but he is there. I saw him."

"Let Matteo sleep on at the camp," Swoop said. "By the morning we will know a great deal. We have to fire Diego. Run him out of town."

"Si," Zapello said and nodded.

Swoop walked back to Tony.

"Stand up Tony."

Tony stood, his face distorted, expecting to be blasted in the jaw.

"Turn around," Swoop said as he undid the rope around Tony's wrists. You and me are going to ride that wagon to Manitou Springs and you can introduce me to your friends waiting for you."

"I don't know-a they're names. I really don't. They are not my friends."

"Then I will introduce myself."

Catty Corners watched all the drama from the balcony above, biting a few nails from a nervous hunger, wondering what would happen next in her world with this underground revolution.

About an hour and a half later, now 4:30 am, the Zapello wagon slid, shook and rattled its way across the frozen ground and into the outskirts of Manitou Springs, with Swoop and Tony riding up in the front. Tony ran the reins.

"This is all Greco's idea?" Swoop asked Tony.

"Si. Yes. He is selling the train idea and train parts to a

company in Denver."

"Zapello told me he has about 130 Sicilians working with him now. How many are really working for Greco?"

"He has-a, maybe thirty? He make his own gang from making promises."

"Thirty!"

"Si."

"So, will he start a new train company?"

"I think so," Tony said. "It is not like a mafia gang. No criminali. He has just promised to pay us more, the men more, if they go with him. Most of them want a better job. Better pay. He promise us. He promise me this!"

"But first, some of you have to do this stealing. To get it all set up."

"Si. But many don't know this whole plan. No criminali. They just think they will work for a new business-a, make a new business. With the same skills. Same jobs. More money. Just business ideas."

They turned right down a side street and into open gusts of frigid wind, then a quick left to the dirt road behind main street.

Ahead, about where Swoop assumed the rear doors of Rumy's Bar would be, they spotted another open bed wagon in wait and three men shuffling nearby, afoot to keep warm from the cold.

Once closer, they saw that each man held a cup of coffee and the two back doors of Rumy's stood wide open, despite the frigid air. An older man stood just inside the doorway smiling, with a white apron tied around his winter clothes.

"That's Mr. Rumy," Tony said to Swoop.

They stopped the wagon.

"Coffee, boys?" Rumy shouted.

"Well, yeah!" Swoop said with a smile, as they jumped down from the driver's seat.

"That don't look to me like a full load of rails ya got back there," one of the men said, the oldest by far of the trio.

Swoop circled the empty wagon before them, looking for a business sign on the craft somewhere. None.

"No sir, it ain't," Swoop said as he searched their wagon.

"So, who's he?" The man asked Tony.

"Oh, I'm new," Swoop quickly answered for Tony.

Rumy walked out with two cups, "Black, I presume."

"That's fine," Swoop said, "okay for you, Tony?"

Tony nodded.

Swoop and Tony took the cups in their gloved hands.

"Yeah, I am new. I am here this morning," Swoop stated between careful, hot sips, "representing Mr. Zapello."

"Za-whaaa?"

"And you don't even know who that is, do you?" Swoop said. "Anyway, this business deal...whatever it is...what is it?"

"I reckon it's none too much of your bidness, that's what it is," the man said.

"Uh-huh. Well, whatever it is then, it's over," Swoop said.

"Over?"

"Over," Swoop said. "Who do you fellers work for anyway?   Whose wagon is this?"

"That man there said it is none of your interest," a second man said stepping forward.

"We are all a bit pissy," Swoop said, "given it's the middle of the damn night." Swoop grinned with a bit of chuckle, eyeing the two up and said, "You know," he ran a gloved hand over his face which popped his hat back a bit, "I have broken one too many a tooth tonight, way I figure. The older I get, I just hate to see a feller loose teeth. Over nothing much really. It's...it's such a permanent thing. Ya know? Tooth. Gone. Now, a punch, a punch ain't permanent, it hurts. Sure. Maybe the feller falls down. Maybe takes a nap. I have! But a tooth! That's a lifetime hole. A hole for good. I never mean for that to happen. Only if I decide to graduate things, it will well surpass teeth."

"Listen-a to the man," Tony warned in a low, slow sentence.

The two eyed up Tony after his response, then looked back at Swoop.

"It's a, it's a real simple question, who do you fellers work for? Who is supposed to get this delivery?" Swoop continued.

The first two men just stared at him.

"Portland Mechanics," the third man leaning against the wagon bed shouted out from the rear of the wagon. Then he stepped forward.

"Thank you, sir. Wellll. Can you tell the boss man of Portland Mechanics that an Archie Turner. That be me. Will be in to see him late tomorrow...oh well now, I don't know about that...maybe, maybe early the next day would be best, and talk with him about...about all this mess we have here. This shipment was stolen, as are all the train ideas. I'll straighten all this out. For now, I am truly sorry you fellers had to ride out here, middle of the damn night, in this cold, for nothing. I did too, Tony here too. We did. And we don't like it either. You're just doing your job and we are too. Jobs."

The three grimaced, handed off their coffee cups to Rumy and boarded the empty flat wagon. Tony and Swoop watched as they backed it up a bit then led the team around Swoop's wagon.

"You ahhh...you always up working at this ungodly hour?" Swoop asked Rumy, after drinking the last of his coffee.

"Depends. Depends. Late night or early delivery," Rumy said still maintaining that big grin.

"Or a favor from a friend?"

"Huh?"

"Nothing, Mr. Rumy. It's so damn late, it's early. Here's your cup and thanks for the coffee. It got cold real fast out here."

Tony handed off his cup too, and they both jumped up on their Zapello wagon. With the path clear ahead, Tony led the team to the next corner, and turned for the main avenue, then west.

"What will happen-a to me?" Tony asked, turning onto the main street.

"Tony, pull over there, stop there by that hotel. The Beaver Station."

He did. Inside the Beaver Station lobby, some of the lights were still burning. Not a soul could be seen moving in there, through the glass doors and windows.

"Tony, you're fired. Get a room here at the Beaver. Someone will bring all your belongings to you and your last paycheck tomorrow. You are fired."

Tony made a face full of resignation, staring at Swoop.

"You were caught stealing, Tony. Plotting against your boss, the company you work for."

Tony's shoulders slumped. Resigned, he stared ahead and shook his head. Swoop reached into his back pocket and pulled out his wallet.

"Heeeerre, here is 7 dollars. Get a room here. But, if I were you, I would leave town as fast as you can, once you get your money, Tony. I would not talk with any of your friends back at the mountain. Go back to Sicily. Go. Go anywhere but leave hereabouts. There's nothing but trouble coming hereabout in the next few days."

"You can-a fire me?"

"I can fire you."

Tony nodded, jumped off the wagon. Swoop took the reins and rolled them over the horses' backs in a wave. He left town with the echoing sounds of Tony yelling and pounding on the Beaver's Station locked, front doors behind him.

"Come on, wake up in there. Wake up!"

Chapter 14: Thorny Bounties

Gee Willikers. Lt. Bernes. Train to Denver. Coach to Fort Logan, a fort built a few years earlier on a treeless plateau located about eight miles southwest of the city. Field Officers Quarters. Conference room.

"Gentlemen this is Lt. Tembers," Major Twenty introduced. "This is our veteran scout Gee Willikers and Lt. Bernes."

Three men sat at the big table. An active fire in the fireplace struggled to warm the cold room. Lt. Tembers placed another log on the fire and sat down with them.

"In the last three days I have been distributing the Swellen wanted posters everywhere I can," Major Twenty said. "Police departments. Post offices. Train and coach stations. Restaurants. Respondents will contact Lt. Tembers because he is local and established here."

"We've set up ads in the local newspapers to be run in the next Sunday papers," Lt. Tembers added, "that will be our most far-reaching attempt to spread the word."

"We have little to do now but sit back and wait for anyone to call," Major Twenty said. "And we have four days until Sunday."

"So, yer thinkin he is not here in Denver?" Willikers asked.

"I would think he is gone. Or maybe in the area? I don't know. We'll see what the newspaper ads gleans," Major Twenty said.

"And it will take several days for the newspaper to get around the mountains," Lt. Tembers reminded.

"In that case," Gee said, "I will lay an egg at the officer's bar. You got one here, right?"

"We do," Lt. Tembers said, "while we have a lot under construction here, but we always take care of our officers first."

Gee bolted up, which scooted his chair back about 5 feet.

"Try to stay out of trouble, Gee?" Major Twenty said.

Gee ignored him and strutted off.

"It's over on..." Tembers started.

"I'll find it. I'm a... veteran scout, remember? I'll smell it out." And he was gone.

"Bernes," Major Twenty said, "watch him."

Bernes shook his head, sighed, slowly stood and walked out of the room.

"Willikers trouble?" Lt. Tembers asked.

"Like a canker sore," Major Twenty said. "But when he gets a tooth into someone, he eventually eats them alive. We call him in on big AWOLS, and for military 'hunting' problems. When someone is wanted dead or alive, he usually finds them and just kills them. Finds a way to kill them. He says it saves time and prisoner transportation problems."

"I see."

"If the word 'dead' isn't involved, he usually does not get involved in a hunt. Lieutenant, here's the real play. We...we hire Willikers for certain thorny problems. If we find where the bounty is? We...we send Willikers in a day or two early. To scout it all out. He is a scout, after all. We then gather the troops, gather, gather, gather. Make ready to go out. He either reaches us and confirms or we wait a bit. Usually, by the time we get there? A day? Maybe two days later? Willikers has already killed off our problem. You see? The United States Army...officially...has done nothing. The hired hand scout has done the deed. We pay him the bounty."

"I really see. Uh-huh. I see. I am optimistic about the newspaper ads," Lt. Tembers said. "The Denver papers go out to the whole region east of the Rockies and a bit into the Rockies. If he is still anywhere near here? We should find out."

"Swoop Swellen is a special problem, Tembers," Major Twenty explained, "we can't have a court martial for him. He predicted the Wounded Knee Massacre and refused to participate. The Army is getting into more and more trouble every day over Wounded Knee..."

"Every day," Lt. Tembers added.

"Yup. If the public finds out about Swellen's story, he'll be a sympathetic hero. So, for many reasons we cannot have a trial, have him present a defense, have him testify."

"I understand, Sir. I understand." Lt. Tembers said.

"Yup. Dead or Alive. Dead, not alive."

Chapter 15: Dead Man's Contract

Swoop Swellen had himself quite a shopping spree in Manitou Springs stores, amassing gear and clothes on the Zapello tab.

Diego was fired and removed from the job site by Fernando Bosco, uneventfully. Zapello gave the old friend of the family a thick envelope of cash. They decided to leave Matteo and Greco alone and ignorant about what had happened with the midnight delivery. Would the four train attackers leave Manitou Springs as suggested? Swoop thought it unlikely. Gossip down in Rumy's might reveal all their whereabouts and the failed tales against Swoop anyway.

Swoop loaded up the open-back, single-horse Zapello buckboard wagon with purchases and made the short trip to the Cliff House. Not expecting any immediate trouble at the campsite, he spent the night in his hotel room, so that he might leave on the first train to Denver the next morning.

At sunrise, Swoop caught the first train to Colorado

Springs then the second to Denver, wearing a new, modern business suit, but still packing a single newer, smaller revolver, an 1892 Navy double action, on a smaller "dress belt," under his jacket.

In Denver, his first coach ride stop was to Zapello's lawyer's office, Deblazzio and Sone, for a planned appointment to retrieve copies of the "cease and desist" letters and pow-wow about the company's latest piracy problems. Mr. Deblazzio was not fully aware of the internal strife, and he wanted to fire, arrest and sue the traitorous employees and sue Portland Mechanics.

"Let me see what I can do, first. See what they say?" Swoop advised.

Next, he caught a coach for the visit to Portland Mechanics. As the ride approached, he found a two story, fairly new, brick factory just outside of downtown, in a business district. Once inside a busy lobby of customers and sales crew, he spotted the front service counter.

"My name is Archie Turner from Manitou Springs and I really need to see the owner. I think he may be expecting me," he told the young man there.

The man nodded and disappeared into a series of back offices to emerge again in a moment and beckon Swoop inside with a hand wave. He guided Swoop to a big office and before a well-dressed man in his 60s behind a mess of a paperwork on small, machine parts on a massive desk.

"Mr. Deming," the guide offered, "this is Mr. Turner from the Springs."

"Thank you, Leonard," Deming said.

Swoop did not attempt a handshake. The mood in the room, Deming's expression and sheer breadth of the desk seemed against it. He swept off his new hat and sat in a plush leather chair. Deming, though seated, was apparently a short, wiry man with an oddly narrow head and neck, a face full of freckles, bad teeth and dressed in a pressed, starched white shirt, as far as Swoop could see.

"Okay, Turner, I wonder what in hell is going on with my train company deal?" Deming asked.

"Me too. We are too," Swoop said.

"You are? How can we both be confused?"

"Because of a third-party criminal, sir, victimizing us both."

"You are the man who met with my delivery men the other night, canceling a shipment of rails? Stopping it?"

"I was. Isn't it odd for a shipment to be picked up at 4:30 a.m.?" Swoop asked.

"No, not really. Early bird and all. They would have arrived here at about 6 a.m. Start of a workday."

"Well sir, I think your early birds are dealing with the wrong worm. I am here representing 'Zapello Mountaineering Trains,' and I understand that you have been contacted by a man named Carlos Greco."

"Greco, yes. I have not heard of such a Zapello business."

"And I gather Greco claimed to be a train company owner from Sicily with new equipment for a mountain climbing, rail system."

"Yes," Deming said, "we have a contract with him to copy and reconstruct his equipment from Sicily, right here in my plant, and then be partners in our first project together in the Rockies at a popular skiing area. The start of many such projects."

"What's he call himself?"

"Greco Mountaineering Trains," Deming said.

"Of course. Well, Greco works for Zapello. He is just a crew boss. The plans for all the train equipment are stolen by Greco. The materials you have received are stolen too. Zapello owns the U.S. and international patents on all that Greco has given you, as well as the actual supplies he has already delivered."

Deming sat with a puzzled look on his face. Swoop leaned forward and handed him the several pages of the cease and desist letter from the law office. He scanned the letter.

"I...have to show this to my attorneys," Deming said, trying to speed-read the documents.

"We understand. I understand. Meanwhile, no more materials from Manitou Springs. It will be considered theft."

Deming grunted.

A side door opened. Clanging and machine humming noises filled the office as a large man wearing dirty coveralls filled a side doorway. Deming nodded his head to the left suggesting the man step inside and shut the door.

"Conrad, this here's the redneck that stopped you in the Springs the other night?" Deming asked the man.

Swoop turned to size the worker up. It was indeed the older, uncooperative man from behind Rumy's two nights earlier.

"That's the spoiler," the man said.

Swoop saw he held a big wrench in his right hand. Expressionless, Swoop looked back at Deming.

"I can't tolerate an interloper stepping in my way, interfering with my business," Deming said. "Look, I am on the move. I have already given Greco $5,000 to engage in this project. We have signed contracts, I..."

"He is a con man and a thief. I will deal with him myself, but I am not sure I...we...can get that money back for you. I'll do what I can. But, I'll bet he has spent it already."

Deming grunted again. By this point, Swoop had determined that Deming was just like so many cranky, self-righteous, egotist, military officers, especially the higher-ups. The higher up, the worse. He'd been tap-dancing with them and against them his whole military career.

"I mean that, but the man is a snake, "Swoop said. "Meanwhile, here is the business card of the real train company owner, the man from Sicily, Mr. Zapello, who you can and should go in legal partnership with. There is one more partner involved, a rich man back East. You men can legally build such trains any and everywhere if the three of you can work something out."

Deming accepted the card with a dissatisfied expression.

"And you are?"

"Archie Turner," Swoop said.

"I mean, just who are you? I mean in all this."

"I am...just an employee you might say. A security person."

"Security. Like the Pinkertons?" Deming asked.

"No. No. Nothing like that. Just helping out with problems."

"Problems. Just helping out. And I am...am just to believe...you! A total stranger in a suit who, who wanders into my office one morning with a long story and a scary letter?" Deming said.

"It's a...letter from a local lawyer's office," Swoop said. "You can contact them."

"You know Turner, this city is full of conmen. You ever hear of Soapy Smith? His fleet of trained conmen on every street corner in Denver? How do I know you aren't conning me?"

Swoop smiled, "never heard of Soapy Smith, sir. I am not from around here."

"Not from around here, either. There ya go. Not just a stranger in my office, a stranger to Denver. Colorado too, I'll bet."

"Yes, sir. Not from around these parts."

"Look here, Turner, I have a business to run here. I am going to proceed with what I have and what I can. I have a contract. I am going to proceed 'in good faith' with it. I have already invested time and money in this. A lot. So, you go ahead and sue me, and I'll fight it. You tell this Zapello to sue me, or whatever he wants to do, whatever he thinks he can do."

Swoop just stared at Deming, then said, "I wish I could straighten all that out. Get that $5,000 back for you. I am sure it has been spent."

"This is about way more than the $5,000. This is about the future train mountaineering business. Have you ever been in the military?" Deming asked.

"No," Swoop lied.

"Then you might not understand the definition of the

word, mission. Of winning. I was a Marine captain. I run my business like a Marine."

"My employer Mr. Zapello, has been victimized too by this criminal. I do wish the two of you could work together on this."

"I want my $5,000 back, sure. But I would rather have a future plan with this train too," Deming said.

"And we want Zapello's plans and supplies back too," Swoop said.

"Back? Ha! What I have collected so far? It remains here."

"It remains here if Zapello and his partner work out a deal with you. Otherwise..."

"Otherwise WHAT?"

"Otherwise you'll be sued for starters," Swoop said.

"For starters. You have no idea who you are dealing with," Deming said.

Swoop smiled, then scratched his right eyebrow.

"I am operating and will operate on good faith? The train, the rails, the plans aren't going anywhere but here, and then it will be put to good use. This Zapello, Italian too?"

"Yes. Sicilian."

"Well, I am an American. This is America. I was a Marine. I am a veteran. You a veteran?"

"No sir," Swoop lied.

"And I am an important contributor to the community, this city. This country! I have never known any judge to recognize the patents from some foreign country over American ones. All that is fair game when you leave your country. Business is business. I will proceed as I have planned, in good faith. I don't know you. I don't know Zapello. And this here? This is just three pieces of paper."

"I suggest you do have your lawyers look those three pieces of paper over. Well, I have to get back to Manitou Springs, Mr. Deming," Swoop said and stood. "I appreciate your loss. I appreciate your situation and would hope for any cooperation. We have all been cuckolded by this criminal."

Again, Swoop did not try for a handshake and instead put on his hat. He turned to the worker. His eyes cut from the man's face then down to the wrench-in-hand, then back to the face again and Swoop quick-winked at him.

"Adios, gentlemen," Swoop said and left the office and the building.

"Soooo, that was him?" Deming said to the worker.

"That was him."

"Next time I don't want to be stopped," Deming said. "You understand, Conrad? Next time you bring a wrench...or something...along with you and hit the son of a bitch in the head and complete the delivery. Your mission was to return with those train tracks. We have a business to run here."

"Yes sir."

"Greco. Damnable Italian. Put us in a mess," Deming said. "Speed things up, get all this equipment replicated and made as fast as you can. Fast! While we still can be acting under legal, good faith. I'll let this go to court, fight any injunction they might try. Stall any lawsuit. I don't think I will contact Greco for now and find out one thing more that hurts our good faith, legal stance. Just...just go to work on this damn train. Get!"

"Yes, sir."

"I am going to get somebody on this Zapello, this Greco and this dude that just walked in here. I don't like the looks of him. He plays it calm. He wears a gun and is hard to rile. All smiley faced."

"Yes, sir."

"Leonard!" Deming shouted.

The front counter man peeked in.

"Leonard, get Tabby Stallmouth in my office as soon as possible. I need him for some work."

"Will do, sir. He's right chere in town. I saw him at Consuelo's last night."

"Good." Deming said and scratched his ear lobe, "They don't know who they are dealing with, I'll tell ya that right now," he mumbled to himself, then he looked up at Conrad. "Way I see it.

If Greco is a real four-flusher and were to...to absquatulate off. And Zapello were to dearly depart? And then…and then I guess this Archie Turner too, minced into buzzard chow, that would leave just me, just yours truly, holding this train contract, the train system minus any and all challenges. We don't need no Greco to construct the track. Any idiot can do that. Run track. We got plenty of Chinamen in Denver to run track. Bells of hell they built train lines clear to the Pacific."

"Sounds like a plan, sir."

"Geeet crackin!" Deming said.

Outside, Swoop buttoned up his jacket and pulled up the collar. He walked the stretch of the front of the factory, but at the corner, he did not turn left for downtown. Instead, he walked on a bit and turned right, swinging wide enough to see the whole east side of the Portland edifice. Despite the cold, numerous garage doors stood open, and Swoop passed them from a distance peering in. Sure enough, looking in through the fourth door, he saw it. Portland Manufacturing had almost completed a replica of the Zapello cog train, the mountain climbing engine, unique on sight in tilt and shape, just like the ones working at the Pikes Peak compound.

Swoop about-faced and headed back downtown for the train station. On the two evening trains heading back, Swoop contemplated what he would do next with Matteo and Greco. No doubt Deming got on the phone trying to reach Greco the moment he left the office. Or, would he? What would be Deming's game? Dodge Greco and work on the good faith angle as long as he could? Ignore the lawsuit and plow on? And by now, no doubt Tony or Diego had run straight to Rumy's bar to tell Greco what happened to them.

When the second train from Colorado Springs arrived in Manitou Springs, Fernando Bosco was there to pick Swoop up in a fashionable, enclosed Zapello coach. Swoop did not get inside, but rather climbed aboard the top to sit next to Fernando.

"Ferd, I'll be staying in the Cliff House tonight. Tell Zapello I met with the Portland owner, a man named Deming, and he has been warned. And I don't think he will cooperate with our offer. Deming has to figure out what to do next. But it looks like Zapello will have to sue Portland. I'll explain it all tomorrow."

"What is next-a for us, signor?"

"Has Matteo or Greco complained to Zapello. Showed up and said anything about what has happened?"

"No, signor. They will wait and collect the gossip from many whispers."

"It's all like a slow burn fuse on a stick of dynamite."

"Si."

Fernando stopped the coach at the Cliff House Inn. Swoop dropped down to the sidewalk.

"You reckon that Greco is over there now, across the street at Rumy's tonight?"

"I would think so," Fernando said.

"Goodnight toyou, Mr. Fernando," and Swoop watched the wagon ride away.

He took a long look at Rumy's establishment across the field, on the main street and down a few buildings. It was the sunset of a long, busy day, should be over, but he made yet another plan. He passed through the hotel lobby and went to his room.

Then, he removed his new single holster "city" gun belt and strapped on his old double-gun belt of Thunderers, with knife, all under that citified suit jacket.

He left the Cliff House. He crossed the snowy field and street and entered Rumy's. Once inside, Swoop took stock of the big place. The bar and restaurant were built from alpine tress and decorated with wall-to-wall, Rocky Mountain stuffed animals. It was smoky and smelled of beer, cigars, barbecue, a touch of urine and grilled steaks.

About half full of patrons, mostly men, were engaged in

pool, cards, dart-throwing and talking, and certainly all drinking on this weekday early evening. But the patrons Swoop was really looking for, Greco and Matteo were carousing there with what looked like a group of coworkers. And yes, the newly unemployed four train attackers, Tony and Diego were among them. Swoop walked to the long bar to stand at it, because he knew not to sit and not to be caught sitting on a stool. Some confrontation was inevitable.

"Coffee, he told the female bartender.

"Oh, I'm sorry, we don't have coffee after dinner, sir. After 5 p.m. I'm sorry."

"Okay, let me have a beer then."

"Would you like to eat? We do still have some food left over."

"I don't think I will be remaining here long enough to finish the beer, least of all eat, ma'am," Swoop said with a smile, plunking a nickel down on the worn counter.

He unhooked the buttons on his jacket, and put a boot up on the bar's brass, floor rail. Unlike many bars, there was no mirror ahead to spy on what was happening behind him. Instead, he turned to lean an arm on the bar.

"I see, I see that it is you, who is this Archibald Turner I hear so much about," came a deep male voice behind him. It was the voice of the sword fighter. "You! the man who picked up the dead man's sword in the street. The Army sword that should have been mine, as a souvenir of victory."

Leaving the beer mug on the bar, Swoop turned to see Greco walking toward him, in work clothes, not his fancy, puffy, dueling attire. No visible weapons.

"I am told-a that you are the man who has slandered me and insulted me and not even in my presence," Greco said. "Such is the movement of a coward."

"And who told you that?" Swoop asked, his elbows resting on the bar.

"As you say here in America, a little birdy told me," Greco said.

"More like a little cat."

They stared at each other, faces inches apart.

"That's why I came in here tonight," Swoop said, almost smiling, "I wanted to talk about that slander. Fact is, I've been busy and time is, is just getting away from me. So, I came in here as soon as I could to slander and insult you in person."

"And what is this - a slander and insult?" Greco asked.

"Oh, do you really need one? Specifically, you are a piece of a horseshit. There's one."

Greco pulled a work glove from his beltline and grinned.

"Then I must challenge you to a duel, you...." he raised the glove...and onlookers, eyes widened, quickly oohed and aahhed. There was a clap or two.

"You hit me with that glove, and I'll bust your fuckin head wide open," Swoop growled. "You won't remember hitting the floor."

No glove slap followed, because in just a second, Swoop's knife was out and the tip placed about a 16th of an inch into the skin under Greco's chin. Eyes wide, Greco's head lifted up as far as it could. The tip followed.

"You knock that knife aside and you'll cut your own throat," Swoop warned in a growl. "You think I'll play some fuckin duel, sword game with you? Some duel at high noon, bullshit? I'll chop your head off right now and hang it on an antler here on the wall."

Greco froze. Shocked.

"You...so you are not a man of honor," Greco mumbled above the knife tip, careful that too much enunciation might result in a close shave bleeding.

"And you? You are honorable?" Swoop said. "I know who you are and what you do. And you are done here. You should leave Colorado before you are sued, arrested or killed. Any of which...I am happy to do."

"You have me at a disadvantage at this moment, but I will not always be at the tip of your coltello. Not always," Greco said.

Matteo, back at the table, stood. Swoop glanced at him,

with a sneer and shook his head – no. Matteo sat.

Swoop withdrew the knife and sheathed it.

"There will be no duel. But there will be a reckoning," Swoop said.

Greco backed up and said, "Oh? To me, to my guess-a, you are a man who also likes to duel. You will duel."

Swoop turned back toward the bar, to his frothy beer, but he looked into every shiny object he could find to see before him, for any distorted reflection-clue of the Sicilian and his next move.

Greco returned to the tables of men, all now quiet. Swoop swallowed a few inches of the beer. He half-smiled and winked at the waitress.

"Told ya my visit would be a short one," he said in a whisper.

And he left without looking the work crew's way.

Swoop crossed the street and field, and into the lobby of the hotel. Now, his workday was officially over.

"Back so soon, Mr. Turner?" The clerk said.

"Back this soon."

"Busy day?"

"Very busy day. The cook still here?"

"Cook's still here, sir. He lives in the back, you know. He's always here."

"How's about your classic steak dinner and that fine whiskey you brag on."

"Have they run outta things across the street at Rumy's? Have they?"

"Bout too," Swoop said, loosening his tie and taking a seat, "any Denver newspaper come in yet?"

"No sir, it always takes a couple of days to wander out here you know. More if there's a snow storm."

Chapter 16: Ditch Digger Pat Weeps
Mess Hall, Fort Logan

"I know you," a soldier said to Gee Willikers. "Ain't you some kind of officer? What are you doing in the enlisted man's mess hall."

Gee Willikers turned away from his breakfast and eyed the soldier standing next to him. He was tall, thin, in his thirties and wearing a deeply, dirt-stained uniform.

"Neither enlisted nor an officer," Willikers said.

"Of course. Scout! Yer that scout man."

"Yup."

"Yer Gee Willikers. One and only."

"I be. I am one and I am only. I like it here with the enlisted. Less snooty. You a private?" Willikers leaned back and squinted at him, "but, you're too damn old to be private."

"I am. I have been just about everything once. Up and busted down and up and busted down. I have been a bad boy."

"Ha!" Willikers often had a short laugh like a grunt or a burp.

"I am currently in military prison. Me and my compatriots."

"And yet! Here you are."

Looking beyond the dirty soldier, Willikers spied several men in grungy clothes at a long table. Then his attention returned to his plate and to further slurp up the over-easy eggs.

"You and yours, well then what the hell are y'all doing loose and eatin here? Dig ahhh....tunnel er somethin to escape?"

"We have been sentenced," the man said, "to ditch-digging. Sleep in the jail. Dig eight to 10 hours a day, digging up the ground for funerals. We've moved a whole cemetery of coffins a half a mile east of their original position last three months. Then we dig for any other construction. The Army loans us in town too for jobs. But, they are building a lot here in Logan. We...dig. At least now for somethin. In the past, we done dug trenches and then, and then, just filled them back up. Busy work to keep breakin our backs."

"Ha! Well, I have one parcel of advice for ya, then. Dig slow."

"Name's Pat Weeps," the man said, offering no hand.

"Okay. And you know me already."

"I do. I have been on a hunt with you back in 83, me and my platoon. I was the sergeant at the time." Pat Weeps took a seat.

Willikers took another long look at him, squinting even, then shook his head.

"Don't recall ya."

"You must be huntin somebody now," Pat Weeps said.

"That I am. A feller worth a thouuuuusand dollars."

"A killer? A killer and an AWOL?"

"Just AWOL."

"Wooooo, $1000 bounty? Not a killer."

"Well, he's a killer alright, but fer our side. But that bounty, that ain't as high as has ever been asked. Billy the

Kid was wanted for $1500. Victorio, $1,500. Jessie James? Jessie James at one point was worth $25,000! The Sundance Kid? $6,500. But $1,000 still trades for a lot of turnips."

"You know, we've been thinkin about becoming bounty hunters too, me and the boys in this little chain gang here," Pat Weeps said. "I have heard in and out of military prison that the army always posts high dollar rewards for its criminals. Higher than civilian. Way higher."

"That they do fer a fact."

"And that most civilian bounty hunters don't know about the ones the Army wants."

"That they don't."

"When this little prison term is over, me and some of the losers over there," he pointed back to the long table of dirty soldiers, "are gonna be discharged. We were daydreaming, talking that once we mustered out, we should just bounty hunt military criminals and AWOLS and such. And dead or alive is even better, ya know. Nobody wants to wrangle with a fugitive fer days and weeks and deliver them to a distant post."

Willikers winked and said, "Dead. I hear ya. Bounty huntin always beats digging ditches into the frozen, winter ground. And then fillin them back up for somethin to do."

Weeps watched as Willikers reached up and filtered his fingers through his long hair. He found a strand, a long one and plucked it out. Then he grabbed the single hair with the two hands, opened his mouth and shoved the hair between two teeth, flossing something out, then proceeded to spit out the chunk on the floor.

"Let's go, Weeps!" A sergeant holding a shotgun yelled from the mess hall door."

"Well sir, we gotta go. They let us eat lunch or dinner over here at the NCO mess hall some nights and maybe I'll see ya again. I'd like to talk with you some more about bounty hunting."

"Yeah. Well, yeah. See ya later, ditch digger. Dig slow. You'll never make it to China."

Willikers turned to watch the ditch diggers get up and head out the mess hall doors.

Chapter 17: Tabby Stallmouth
Curtis Park, Colorado

Tabby Stallmouth was a runner. A real runner. He pounded out the miles on the crusty snow trail that ran southwest out of Curtis Park, Colorado. Each blast of breath left smoggy steam in the air. He wore a black skull cap, a short jacket, gloves, thick pants and light shoes. Rarely would he slip on any patch of ice as he'd mastered a tight, careful way to run on the patchy grounds and, or deeper snow. In serious blizzards he'd run for hours at the inside track at the Rocky Gentlemen's Club which contained an indoor gym, pool and track.

The cold didn't bother Tabby much. His resilience to the cold and pain in general was mysterious, which made him an award-winning, marathon athlete. He was on mile eight of his 10-mile run and that distance really wouldn't challenge him, but he had a busy day ahead of him and would cut short his favorite pastime run by half. A lunch at Rocky's with his old Marine Major Charles Deming was pending.

Tabby and his friends and family could never understand why he, as a young boy in Memphis, Tennessee, loved to run, run far and fast for no apparent reason than how natural it felt for him.

When he joined the U.S. Marines in 1870s, he officially ran in their footrace contests, usually winning. He competed in track and field events since and enjoyed the country's various growing interest and support of marathon running.

Tied high and tight in the small of Tabby's back was a holster holding a 2-inch barrel revolver, hidden under that jacket. He always toted a gun because Tabby was more than just a runner, he was trouble incarnate. He made trouble and solved trouble. Tabby feared revenge and ambush even out there in the wilds, but those concerns alone would never interfere with some long distance, daily running.

Tabby Stallmouth and Charles Deming were old Marines and they'd made several official incursions into Panama. Panama was controlled by Columbia, and Panamanians periodically revolted against Columbia for a variety of reasons, but often involving the politics of the failing, French construction of the Panama Canal. For some odd reasons, U.S. Marines were sent down there, on missions to "quell" the riots and violence. Deming was a major and Tabby his sergeant and they became blood brothers surviving combat.

After the Marines, Tabby then had a unique experience in law enforcement, participating in the Pat Garrett posse hunting Billy the Kid in the early 1880s, and Tabby claimed he was present the night Garrett shot twice and killed William Bonny/Henry McCarty. Whenever the rumors came up in conversation that Billy was not killed that night, as such stories persisted, Tabby insisted that he saw Billy shot dead, but the naysayers assumed his arguments were just in furtherance of his "been-there" reputation.

Next, Tabby returned to his home state and attended the Cumberland Law School in Lebanon, Tennessee for three complaint-filled, critical years. Complaint-filled because with each case he and the other potential lawyers studied, Tabby analyzed with them with a free, frustrated mind, recognizing quicker, usually illegal, "outside" solutions to just about every essential legal problem.

"There's a quicker fix to this," he would complain and interrupt his classes and mates, and in the beginning even his teachers. He was so scorned for such questionable and at times, even blatant criminal solutions that he learned to remain quiet in class. But he could not stop concocting illegitimate quick fixes.

Others toiled with debates within the law while Tabby obsessed on ones outside the law. He eventually left Cumberland, declaring the courts, laws and trials as cumbersome, wastes of time.

He did go to work for various lawyers in Arkansas and Oklahoma and some desperate firms resorted to his drastic measures. It took an exchange of Christmas cards one year for Deming to track down his old sergeant and Deming suggested Tabby move to Denver to work for Portland Manufacturing as well as a few of Deming's business associates. Tabby did move there and was paid a retainer by Deming to keep him handy, but he also hired out to others in need.

It was no secret to this cartel of ambitious owners that Tabby's services included threats, severe beatings, a maiming or two and even the occasional murder. Impatient and narrow-minded, the narcissistic Deming held a view of business that was of a "military invasion" approach, often well outside the barriers of civil and criminal law, cementing his relationship with Tabby.

Tabby returned to the Rocky Gentlemen's Club, took a shower, dressed in a swank suit and tie and met Charles Deming in the dining room. Over a lunch of chicken and vegetables, coffee then brandy, Deming detailed the visit from the mysterious Archie Turner and this mess with Carlos Greco and the train company.

"From a legal standpoint, Major," Tabby explained, "those patents filed in the United States do count. Now, if you could influence a judge to ignore them? That would depend on what jurisdiction this Zapello filed the lawsuit in, as to whether you know the judge well enough. Fortune frequently favors the American over the foreigner. You could always challenge the efficacy of the patent. These are all delaying points. Meanwhile, you could build a train from here to Alaska by the time this had a trial."

"I see. But this Turner said that Zapello has a business partner, an American from the East."

"Oh, well, an American. Well. I see. Well, if he is a petitioner that could change the judge's viewpoint."

"It could."

"Major...should any judge declare an emergency injunction in this matter, halt you, halt your production? Then YOU are stuck in the mud, sir. They win. The delay is on you."

"Shit!"

"Have you spoken with this Greco lately? Since?"

"No. I don't want to know any more negative information. No confessions. I want to stay in the dark, stay in 'good faith' for as long as I can."

"Smart, sir. You think he's a crook?"

"Sounds like it," Deming said. "This Turner guy that showed up looks solid..."

"Like an investigator or something?"

"Yeah, or like a soldier. An officer. Tough, Clean cut. Gun under his jacket. He stopped Conrad and the boys from picking up a wagon of track in Manitou Springs. Middle of the night."

"Are you suggesting that Turner is their version of me?" Tabby said with half a smile.

"I don't know. What do you think we should do?"

"I don't like how this sounds, so far. Legally, courtroom

legally. It's probably a mess. An American and Italian have American patents. Their lawyer in that paperwork they gave you, is he a real Denver lawyer?"

"Yes, he is."

"So, a lawsuit is possible. An injunction? Probable. Against you. If there was no Zapello, there would be no quick lawsuit. But this Easterner? I will go down to the Federal courthouse and look over the patents. See who this Yankee is. Greco will still work with you?"

"So far. Until maybe that greedy son of a bitch turns on me? He sounds like a real thief."

"Fair enough to worry. And if Zapello is...gone, no one is paying Turner, and probably Turner is out and on to his next job."

"Unless he's working for the Yankee too," Deming said.

"Right, right. I will search the patents. Handle the Yankee. Handle Zapello. Make a wicked deal. I'll watch out for this Turner dude too. Leave Greco alone for now, until we see what Zapello says."

Chapter 18: Kill Me. Kill You.

Swoop decided to dine at a nearby Manitou Springs, Mexican food restaurant called "La Senora." The establishment was quite crowded, and he took a seat with his Stoic book near the front windows. He ordered and started to read, when suddenly…

"Colonel Swellen!" A man said too loudly as he approached the dining room table.

Swoops eyes shot up to see a man in his 40s, bearing a large grin, come to rest leaning with his hands on the back of an empty chair across from Swoop. He hadn't been a colonel in years, so he had to think back…

"It is good to see you again," the man said. "Gerald Prince. Ahhh, 'Winky' was my nickname? From West Virginia?"

"Winky Prince, yes!" Swoop said, standing up to shake his hand.

"The 5th Cavalry. I thought this was you," Winky said, "My wife and daughter are just over there," and he pointed to another table where a woman smiled back at him. A child played with toys.

"Are you…have you retired?" Swoop asked, waving to Winky's family.

Swoop was a little tongue-tied. What could he say? What would he say if this happened time and time again in the future. It was such a big country, so full of people, all strangers really. He just assumed he would always melt anonymous and right into society as one of the strangers.

"Sit. Sit for a moment," Swoop said, stalling for time and trying to quiet down the situation in a room full of people.

"Surely, sir, are you still a Colonel?"

"Well, no. I…I…I am on a mission here," Swoop quickly spouted, "I am doing something here and I (he smiled) I am not using that name, and…"

"I, ooohhh, Lord be with me, I am sorry," Winky Prince said quietly and with an aghast expression.

"That's…that alright, Winky. No harm done. No harm. What have you been doing since you left the Army?"

And Winky began a dissertation of his post-military life. Swoop nodded and only half-listened. Swoop's mind wandered on how to handle such future predicaments. Did he need a beard? Moustache? Long hair? A demeanor change even? He never considered himself distinctive looking.

"…and we came here on vacation for the springs and to see the Garden of the Gods…and so we now live in Wichita Falls, Texas."

"Great," Swoop said, snapping back to the conversation.

"Well sir, it was great to see you and I will leave you to your reading and dinner."

"It was great to see you too, Winky, and I am very glad you have turned out okay! No one still calls you Winky? Not even Mrs. Prince?"

"No sir."

They both laughed and Winky Prince left.

Swoop did return to his book, trying to concentrate on it. He felt the encounter went unnoticed, but it hadn't. Several men a few tables away and behind him, were workers from Zapello's and they did take…special notice.

Later, it was another night at Rumy's when the Sicilians gathered. They discussed Swoop in Italian. One man at a near table sat and played the zampogna, a torso-sized, Italian instrument that closely resembled and sounded like the Irish bagpipe. He played the music as softly as he could, so as to not interfere with the conversations.

"So, the American walked up to him and said 'hello' and called he him a colonel," one told the group, consisting of Greco, Matteo, Diego, Tony and a few others.

"Colonel? He did?" Greco said. "So, this man is a soldier, or was a soldier, an officer of high ranking. A colonel."

"It would seem so, yes."

"Sooo, Zappy has hired a military expert. Last night, close up - you saw us - I was face to face with him. Centimeters away. He is a man of calm in his eyes! He does not fear. And his teeth, they clamped down tight, like he wants to bite you, but also to protect his mouth from a punch. He pulled his knife…you saw it. Swish! Fast. Like a killer. Look. Look!"

Greco lifted his chin high and pointed to under his jaw, to his new red, sore spot.

"You see? You see the small cut from the very tip of his knife?"

The men leaned in and nodded. They saw the small scab. This began waves of talk and much hand movements.

"He does not stick me hard. Just the tip. He is very good. So fast and just the tip sticks in. I move up. He moves up. He…he may be a soldier, but I think I have killed more men with a sword, and all over the world, than most soldiers."

"Yes, yes," more agreement in waves and gesturing.

"I think I want to fight him. Yes. But…it would be smarter just to kill him. Get him out of the way. Trick him and kill him."

"I agree," Matteo said.

"I have a plan for this, my friend Matteo," Greco said, "an idea."

Greco motioned for Matteo to join him at another table to further escape the Italian musical soundtrack and anyone hearing murderous plans. Their two heads moved in close so Matteo could hear Greco's plot of Swellen's demise.

"Tomorrow!" Greco summarized. "Tonight, I set the stage. And I have just the beautiful actress. Tomorrow, this colonel is laid low."

The next morning...

Swoop Swellen wandered out on the big front porch, balcony of the Cliff House to take in what was left of the morning sunrise. It was too brisk to remain out for long. It had snowed lightly through the night, but the skies were a mix of red, orange, blue and clear. The many American flags surrounding the front of the hotel were flapping in the wind and he thought of all the bases, schools, posts and forts he'd heard those cloth-whipping sounds.

Then there were battlefields. Then...the "missions," not battlefields, where the solo flag hung motionless and low, or rolled in the wind, in between the sounds before, during and after the shots were fired. Moaning. Horses hurt. Men, women and children whimpering. Crying. Then, after a while even those sounds... died off. And one could only hear the flag, flap, flap.

He took a deep breath and shook his head to snap out of the memories.

"There you are!"

He turned to see Catty. She was dressed for the weather, casual, in boots, pants, a colorful jacket and a scarf.

"What are you doing here this morning?" he asked.

"Looking for you, sir."

"For me?" You look very pretty this morning."

"And by the looks, you have new clothes too. Are we both

clothed by Mr. Zapello?” She asked.

“One way or another, yes. Is Mr. Zapello around?” he asked.

“No, the married Mr. Zapello is not around. He spent the night at his base camp cabin.”

“I see. And you did not?”

“I did not. So, the unmarried me has a question. Have you ever been to Garden of the Gods?”

“No. Saw it from a distance. From half-way up Pikes Peak. And I heard its around here, nearby,” he said.

“It is spectacular. Giant, red rocks rising out of the ground, like towers. The Rockies in the background.”

“That’s what I hear,” he said, stepping closer.

“Why don’t you and me, take us a buggy ride, a picnic up there?” She asked. “A lunch.”

“A lunch date. It’s a might cold, isn’t it?”

“It will warm up some by noon. Sun overhead. We could have a little fire? Some folding chairs will keep our bee-hinds off the ground.”

Swoop chuckled at that. “Yes, they would.”

“We can ask the hotel to prepare some food. Some sand-wiches. Nothing that needs heat. Some wine. I have seen them carry baskets of food out of here. I am still on Zapello’s account here.”

“Okay.”

“You know what? I will happily put it all on the married Mr. Zapello’s bill.”

“Okay.”

“I will arrange it. Be out here at noon sharp.”

“I will ma’am. I will look forward to it.”

He remained outside as she stepped inside. He walked the long front porch but continued to peek through the windows and inside at Cat. She spoke with a waiter. He strolled more, peeking more. Then she walked to the telephone on the wall. She cranked the phone and called someone.

He could look away now. He was sure that the Garden of the Gods would be a place of the Devil somewhere. This…

was an ambush.

At noon, he reappeared outside, and it was a bit warmer, but not warm enough yet to remove his burly new dark jacket which covered his two-gun pistol and knife belt. As he jogged down the stairs, she eyed him up and down, with a few extra seconds spent stuck on the exposed gun belt buckle.

"Sandwiches? Wine?" He said, forcing up a big smile, as he climbed onto the buggy.

"Of course, in that wicker basket," she said. "Want the reins?"

"No, you know where we are going. I don't."

The talk was mindless, as a distracted Swoop watched the winding, rocky, rough roads, worried about a sudden attack. There were plenty of places of scrub grass and then groves of trees where someone could hide. Finally, he saw the famous thin, rocky range. The main unique range was also surrounded by many other, thicker, smaller outcroppings. The mountains looked like giant, jagged inverted icicles jutting, straight out of the ground, and it all was an unusual and unforgettable sight.

They were not completely alone as some other tourists, not many, were about, on foot, on horseback, and some were even trying to climb the prehistoric structures. He watched her face as she too saw them. They might be witnesses to any of her evil plans, yet her expressions revealed nothing.

"How did this place get its name? Garden of the Gods? You know?" He asked.

"I do know, since I grew up here. The story is famous around here. Two railroad surveyors in 1859 were looking around and saw the rocks. One said, 'This would be a great place for a beer garden.' The other said, 'Beer garden! Why this is a place fit for the gods to assemble. We shall call it the Garden of the Gods,' and they did when back in the government offices. That's the story."

He listened and watched. He knew any turn, any corner, Greco or a co-conspirator might pounce out at him. He forced a smile or two her way, otherwise he just looked like he was admiring the scenery.

"Okay," she said, "here we are."

She pulled the buggy over by an outcropping. She got the basket out of the back. He lifted out the two folding chairs, sticking both under his left arm keeping his right arm free. She led him up a small hill and into a rather large, naturally carved out, cave opening.

Swoop noticed a back wall with a potential hiding place behind it, like cave entrances. He put the chairs down and made a quick study of the dirt by the wall, keeping his right hand near his pistol. The dusty sand below looked "well-traveled," but could have been made by any investigating tourist or a potential murderer? He stepped closer to peer around the bend of it and he could indeed see there was a darker, deeper cave. Maybe trouble? He was not about to go crawling into that darkness.

"I'll get the wine," Cat said in a singsong.

She left her purse by the food basket. Swoop went for it and rummaged through the cloth carry bag before she turned from the buggy and started back.

He set up the chairs so that he could see that back wall. She poured some wine into cups and said, "Don't you want to sit over here?"

"This is good," he said.

They talked for a bit; all the while Swoop worried about that back wall.

"How about you take off that gun belt and I get comfortable in your lap? Maybe...maybe open up your pants?" She said.

"Maybe a bit later? When it gets warmer," he said.

The view of the rocks and hills was magnificent. She stared outwards. Suddenly she stood and walked out to the sunshine, her back to Swoop. She started to sing. Loudly...

"So, it's good-bye, children,
I will have to go. Whar' de rain don't fall or de wind

That was a message, the cue. Swoop slowly reached for his right-side pistol, sneaking it out of the holster while shifting his hip for clearance. Would they come at him from the front or the back of the cave?

He heard a sound from the back, and he fully drew his revolver. He saw a shotgun barrel appear, inch-by-inch from behind that cave wall. Then he saw the brim of a Sicilian Coppola hat. A man appeared. Before he could turn to the right and spot

Swoop…

BAM!

Swoop shot him in the head. The man dropped the shotgun and collapsed in a lifeless pile. Swoop bolted up, now two guns out to make sure the man was down and out, and he fired several rounds into him for safe measure, cursing and growling as he did.

Click.

He heard behind him. He turned to see Cat holding a derringer aimed at him.

"It's empty, Cat. I just emptied it. I see now, you would have shot me. And now I don't know what to do with you. I would usually get mad, very mad, and anyone who knows me, my anger is very rip-roaring. I should send you to the glue factory here and now. But I can't get that mad. I just get sad. You brought me all the way out here and got me catty-cornered into an ambush."

"Why did you come?" She asked, tossing the small gun at her purse on the ground.

"Oh, I am not at all new to an ambush. I organized many an ambush myself. I thought I could out-maneuver your ambush on me. I have before. I just did again. I came because I needed more playing cards turned face up on the table. Seeing who's-who and what's-what. Now I know for sure. I know who and what you are, for sure."

"How could you know about me?"

"Oh, all the chatty talk. The quick trip to my bed the other day. Spying on my conversations with Zapello. Greco mustn't be married. Has he promised you much?"

"Yes."

"Yes, I thought so. This...was a big step, Cat. Murdering me.

Who is this poor bastard? Is this who I think it is?"

"Matteo."

"Greco must've promised him a lot too." Swoop kneeled and lifted Matteo's left hand and tapped the wedding ring. "We made a widow out of Matteo's wife back in Sicily. You and me. And Greco."

She backed away against a red rock wall, hands splayed, palms against it. Fingers working the rock as she did on his bed's blanket a few days earlier.

"What now, Archie?" She asked.

"I don't know yet, but..." he stood, "I will tell Zapello what you've done. What Greco planned. I would tell you to leave Pike's Peak. Manitou Springs."

"Where would I go? I don't know how to do anything. I am 32 years old. I...all I have left is doing what, Archie? Being a prostitute?"

"Oh, no, you could do many other things. But that would require...work."

"Why are you doing this to me? Why do you care about all this? You don't know any of us. You could just leave us all."

"I don't know, Cat," Swoop said quietly. "I guess...I guess my whole life, I've been on many missions? Missions. And I guess I need to have a mission."

"The damn Army," she said, and shook her head side to side at him. "can you just leave us alone?"

"Alone to do what? Kill Zapello? Take over his train company? You become the train queen, if Greco even fulfills that promise? Because you know, he is liar and crook."

"Are you gonna fetch the Marshal on us?" She asked.

"Nope," Swoop said. Swoop holstered his guns and grabbed Matteo's arms at the wrists and dragged him back into the deep corner of the cave. Then he tried to flatten the drag trails on the dry dirt with his feet. He picked up the Italian, engraved shotgun.

"Why not?"

"I have my reasons. We'll leave Matteo back in there and you and I will return to Manitou Springs. You don't have to see Zapello again. Or Greco. Or me. You need to leave. To go! If you want, I can give you some money to get on a train and stay for a while, wherever you want to go."

"I'll go to Denver, I guess" she said with great resignation as well as relief, realizing he would not kill her.

"Let's get the hell out of here," Swoop said solemnly.

The ride from the Garden of the Gods to the Manitou Springs train station was a speechless one. Swoop dropped the quiet, sullen Cat off at the stop outside the train station among the others bound for Colorado Springs. Swoop and Cat both knew that she was the odd, unique passenger, a wanton, failed murderess surrounded by "normal" people with family visits, vacations or business plans.

He gave her $75 from his wallet and sat back in the buggy to watch her buy the ticket and wait for the train. A woman on the platform noticed the waiting Swoop and his attention on Cat, and she tapped her husband on his arm, saying,

"That man out there must love his wife. He can't bear to leave her, and he is watching her right up until the moment she leaves. He looks so sad. Now, that Harold, is love."

Harold peeked around and nodded, a little frustrated that he needed yet another lesson in love from his wife. They both had no idea it wasn't love, but rather something quite deadly different.

The first stop on the Denver run arrived and Swoop did watch her board and to ensure the train departed with her on it. Seventy-five dollars was money-a-plenty for food, clothes and a hotel for a goodly amount of time.

Then Swoop made his way to the Cliff House. He rounded the building to the back stables and asked the stable boy to park the Zapello buggy and caretake the horse.

"Mr. Turner! You have a message!" The manager Holden shouted out when he spotted Swoop walking through the front doors.

"How are you tonight, sir? Have you had a good day?" Swoop was rather speechless for the moment. Then said with a yet another forced smile,

"Holden, it's been an odd day at best. Trying."

He swept up a message from the hotel counter and carried it outside, taking a seat on the front porch, near one of the welcoming, roaring fires. The message read,

"Firing Matteo and Greco at noon. I need you there," signed Zapello.

Chapter 19: Seeing In One Second
Cliff House Hotel, Swoop's Room

A creak in his hotel room's wooden floor. Ever so slight. Swoop awoke but remained still in bed, his eyes still closed as he heard it. What was that? Then he barely opened one eye...

"Gooood morning!" A man said.

Swoop grunted, and sat partially up, his heart racing from this morning surprise. A well-dressed, thin man in his 40s, odd-looking, sat in chair a few feet from his bed and right at his face. The man smiled. Swoop saw two other men looming by the closed, room door. Last night, that very chair, Swoop had jammed up under the doorknob of the room door and somehow, someway this thin dude and his two accomplices got around the precaution and planted themselves as guards at the door, and this man sat in that very chair!

"My name is Tabby. You can call me Tabby. And I work for Portland Manufacturing. A place you recently visited. I do odd...odd jobs for Portland and Mr. Deming. Not...not regular manufacturing jobs. Legal and illegal jobs. Problem solving. I calculated that we should have a meeting this fine morning, you sir, and me, sir."

"Breakfast might have been better," Swoop said dryly, trying to calm down.

"Well, sometimes it's good to catch a man unawares, you know, surprised. Even stark naked in bed," Tabby said and folded his arms, in a tight squeeze within his tailored overcoat.

"Your name is not really Archie Turner. Who are you?"

"Somebody else," Swoop said.

"Where are you from?"

"Someplace else," Swoop said.

"But it's easier to call me Archie."

"Oh, I see. I see. Archie. Archie Turner. I had an interesting telephone call to a Mr. Englemen in Cleveland, Ohio yesterday afternoon. Took a long time to connect. Do you know how that is? Making these long-distance phone calls. So many operators. Denver to Chicago, Chicago to Cleveland. Very clear line though. Very clear. Federal business paperwork filed in Denver connects your Mr. Zapello to this Mr. Englemen. We had a business conversation in general, about trains. It seems Mr. Englemen has no idea who you are...Mr. Archie Turner. He's not aware of you and he is not paying you. It seems now that only a local, Mr. Zapello knows you and is paying you. This makes you...a loose end. A loose end of a rope. A loose...thread. Less important. Much less. Lessens your position in this overall business affair. Is Mr. Zapello paying you for your advice? Protection?"

"Something else," Swoop said.

"I see. I see. You are almost then..." Tabby waved his open hand in the air between them, "...like...invisible. Invisible. Somebody else. Somewhere else, doing something else."

Tabby waved his hand to the men and one of the two men started going through Swoops' clothes hanging on hooks on the wall and rummaged through his meager possessions in piles in the room's one chest of drawers. Tabby waited.

The man searched through Swoop's leather wallet, finding only money. He shook his head toward Tabby.

"No identification. I see, I see that you must be some sort of a gunman then?" Tabby said, swirling a pointy finger at the two-gun belt, hooked on another chair across the room.

"Somewhat," Swoop said. "I am a gunman, in that, I sleep with a gun."

And Swoop lifted the barrel of his new pistol up, still under the sheet and quilt.

"I see. Now, is that a real gun or your pointy finger?" Tabby asked.

Swoop so wanted to pull the trigger, but instead pulled the covers off and displayed the revolver. He aimed it at Tabby's chest. The searching man stopped searching and the other at the door stood still.

"I halfway expected to see some sort of identification card or perhaps even a badge of some sort," Tabby said, very cool and ignoring the weapon pointed at him. "Pinkerton? But no. Methinks you are hanging here on a delicate thread, 'Mister. Else.' Barely here. Almost threadbare."

He stuck out a pouty bottom lip and continued, "I would suggest that you cut the thread and depart from whatever it is you are doing here, whoever you are and travel somewhere else. Mr. Deming of Portland Manufacturing is a very important, well-connected man. He always remains un-trifled with, and you sir, appear to be a trifler. Events are pending. Legal and...not so legal, which is where I come in. And it would behoove you to truly be elsewhere. Fast. Care... less, not careless. Do you understand?"

"I hear you."

"But do you understand me?"

"I understand what you are saying," Swoop said.

"Hmmm, well think about fully understanding. And then

doing it! And fast."

Tabby stood, walked to the door with the two men tailing behind him. They left. Swoop could see by the hip-bump in his jacket that this Tabby was also wearing a pistol, like the two other henchmen.

Swoop got up and very quickly dressed. Guns on. Boots on. Jacket on. Hat on. He quickly looked at the doorknob, both inside and outside. Not a scratch. How did they get in so quietly? A key? Would the manager Holden or the clerk downstairs just give them a key to his room, even reveal his room number?

He dashed up the hall and down the stairs, slowing down when in view of the large Cliff House lobby of lingerers and breakfast diners in the corner restaurant. The mysterious three invaders were not inside. He walked out onto the expansive front patio where some guests were bundled up in lounge chairs to brave the morning cold. Nor were the trio visible out there or on the parts of Manitou's streets where he could scan from this balcony.

He cut through the inn, out the back doors to see the stable grounds. Then he jogged out to the stable, falling only once in a patch of ice under some fresh snow. One of the regular stable boys, a Bobby Crisp, was at his post.

"Bobby, has anyone, three men, come in and out of here in the last few minutes? Stabled a wagon or horses? Picked up a wagon or horses?"

"No sir. I have been here since 6 a.m. too," Bobby Crisp said.

"Okay, can you get my Zapello wagon ready for me?"

"Sure can, sir."

Swoop leaned against the barn door frame. No doubt Zapello was next on their "visitation" list and the sooner he got out there, the better.

"Ready, Mr. Turner," Bobby Crisp said.

"Thank you," Swoop said, handing him a few pennies.

Swoop took off for the Zapello compound. He noted what appeared to be fresh horse tracks in the snow also heading that way. Could that be them? Could be someone else, too. Seemed like four riders, a fourth added, if indeed this was all of them.

The tracks must have been them. As Swoop entered the front gates he looked toward the cabin. A stranger, a well-dressed man stood outside the front, lingering around four tied-off horses. Swoop guided the small wagon around to the left of the cabin.

He dismounted and walked around the front. This man, this guard was not one of the trio that invaded his room earlier.

Swoop smiled at him as he got closer. The man smiled back. Swoop started with "Say, I..."

And he belted the man in his face with a right power punch. Swoop actually left the ground a bit with the stroke, putting his entire body behind the strike. Where he had led with his left foot forward, now he landed right foot forward. As with many of Swoop's initial punches, he so wanted to follow up with another, but usually the first one often launched the opponent away and dropped anyone beyond the reach of a second blast.

This man flew back, hitting his head on the raised front porch, which was a problem for him. A punch was one thing, hitting his head on something on the way down was something else. In the snow, he sputtered in a short spasm, then laid still, his bloody mouth wide open.

Swoop gathered up the reins of the four houses and walked them off into the yard, among the stack of supplies and tied them off there. Out of sight.

Then he walked to the rear of the cabin and entered a back door. He pulled both his pistols. In the lobby, conference area he saw the situation. Zapello was at the table in his usual seat. Near him sat this Tabby fellow. Overlooking them, standing were the two "guards" he recognized from the hotel room.

"Hey," Swoop said in a guttural grunt.

All looked at him and he raised his pistols.

"Sit," he told the two guards.

They looked at Tabby. Tabby nodded. The pair sat at the giant table.

"Your horses are not where you left them, in case you have some fast plans to do something and leave fast."

"Horse theft is a hanging..." one guard started.

"This is 'horse-moving,' not horse theft," Swoop corrected.

"And my friend?" Tabby asked.

"He's sleeping like a baby," Swoop said.

"Alive?"

"Oh yeah, Alive. But he may still need a doctor. Now, where were we all here?"

Swoop pulled a chair back quite away from the table so he could see all of them. He rested the two handguns on his thighs, barrels aimed in their general direction.

"These gentlemen," Zapello started, "Have explained to me, that if I will pay their boss, Mr. Deming of Portland, $10,000, Mr. Deming-a will let me, allow for me, to work with him and build a train mountain climbing business in Colorado."

"In all of America?" Tabby calmly added.

"Ten thousand dollars. I see," Swoop said, "and what of your friend Mr. Englemen in Ohio?"

"They tell me to forget about him. They will..."

"We will explain to Mr. Englemen that it would be in his best interests to forget about Zapello train idea," Tabby said.

"And then, what of Mr. Greco?" Swoop asked.

"Mr. Greco," Tabby said with a sigh," is our second choice.   We would rather do business with Mr. Zapello as he is so experienced and organized. But if there is some confusion with our discussion? Some...some kind of problem? We will then turn to Mr. Greco, Mr. Deming's first partner in this venture."

"And all that for $10,000," Swoop said.

"Yes. You see, Mr. Deming needs to recover his original investment..."

"Of $5,000," Swoop interrupted.

"Yes, with Mr. Greco. Plus, there's always expenses," Tabby said.

"And you and this cast of characters you have here are part of these expenses, I reckon?" Swoop said.

"Yes. Yes, you might say that."

Swoop stood and walked slowly and wide around the table, guns down at his sides.

"You know Zap? I was thinking. I wouldn't feel too guilty about Italy. About Sicily. And the Mafi, the Mafia you told me about. I wouldn't feel too ashamed about the criminal families and criminal threads of your people from Sicily that you were worried about the other day. As you can see, we Americans can be pretty damn, low down too. Can't we?"

"Si."

"Well!" Swoop nodded and continued, "this meeting has been very productive. Informative. I suggest you men find your horses on the north side of the cabin, pick up sleeping beauty out there and ride off."

"Mr. Deming is an important man, and you will see that I am an important man. We will not stand for trifling. I won't..."

"There's that word trifling again," Swoop said. "We do more than trifle. I do more than trifle. A funny thing about life is this, no matter how damn important you think you are? One bullet in your forehead and you're gone. Gone and done. Importance? Gone. If I see you again?" he stared at Tabby. "I will immediately shoot you right in the fuckin head. In...a...split second. I will not be...trifled...with."

Tabby stared at him. Unemotional.

"Are you interested in knowing how we three got into your room this morning?" Tabby asked Swoop.

"The only thing I am interested in right now? Is blowing the top of your head off, hat and all."

Then Tabby ever-so-slightly chuckled and stood. The other two also stood.

"I hope you will consider Mr. Deming's offer," Tabby

said to Zapello. "When the clock strikes 12 noon tomorrow, we need an answer. You..." he looked at Swoop, "you, I'll see you again."

"And if so? That 'seeing' will be very brief. One second." Swoop said. It took all he could within him not shoot this Tabby right then and there. But he controlled his boiling temper.

The three walked out of the cabin.

"Get your pistol," Swoop warned Zapello.

Zapello dashed to the cabinets on a wall and pulled a revolver. Swoop watched them through the windows disappear into the supply yard looking for their horses. One of the men lingered and kneeled by the downed guard right out front, slapping his face lightly to try and arouse him.

Zapello joined Swoop in his surveillance by another window.

"You think they will come right back-a?"

"Don't know," Swoop said.

The men reappeared around the corner of the cabin with their four horses. Swoop pushed Zapello away from the windows and he backed up also. The men helped the downed man up and onto his horse. They all mounted and started for the gate, but half-way there, the once-downed man slipped off the horse and hit the ground with a big splash of fine powdered snow.

"What did-a you do to him?" Zapello asked.

"I punched him. Knocked him out."

"Must be some big punch-a!"

"His head also hit the porch. Pretty hard." Swoop added.

Two of the three, not including Tabby, dismounted and hung the dizzy man over the saddle, then circling him a few times trying to figure out how to best keep him aboard and balanced for the trek back to Manitou, or was that a straight ride all the way through to Denver?

Still a few feet back, Swoop and Zapello both changed positions in the bay of windows to watch them fully leave.

"Stay ready, they may sneak back," Swoop advised.

"You are a military man. You think-a like one."

"Zap, Matteo and Catty Corners tried to kill me yesterday at the Garden of the Gods," Swoop said, still staring out the window.

Zapello was aghast and speechless.

"She lured me out to the Garden for a picnic, set us up in the mouth of a small cave and then set me up to be shot. She sang a song letting Matteo know it was time to step out from the back and ambush me. He stepped out from the back of the cave with a shotgun. To kill me. I shot him first."

"My friend Matteo is dead?"

"He's dead. I don't know how much of a friend he was. I left his body in the cave. Probably some tourist will eventually find him if they snoop back far enough in the cave. That happens? They will surely call for the sheriff."

"What about my Cat?" Zapello asked.

"I didn't shoot her, Zap. She's not your Cat, Zap. She's Greco's cat. She's been a spy. She's been with him all along. He's promised her a future."

"Greco is married! She..."

"So are you. She knows you are. But I don't think she knew if he was married."

"Oh. Oh, where is she now?" he asked sheepishly.

"Denver. I gave her a lot of money and put her on the train run to Denver. To stay there. I told her not to come back. That things are going to get very bad here."

"Will she come back?"

"I don't know, Zap. I told her not to. But now we have to worry about this Deming guy and this Tabby dude. He's gonna be tricky. Gunning for us. Tell your attorney to sue Deming and Portland. They were officially warned."

"What will they do next?" Zap asked.

"Kill me. Kill you."

Chapter 20: Gravestones As Wind Breaks
Fort Logan Cemetery, Colorado

Lunch. The work crew of prisoners stretched out and sat under a grove of pine trees drinking lemonade and eating cold sandwiches. Four Army prison guards sat near them, doing and eating the same. Both groups situated themselves to where rows and rows of gravestones blocked the chilly wind. These resting spots changed daily with the fickle currents.

"At breakfast, I met an old Army scout I ran a hunt once with years ago in Arizona," Pat Weeps told the six men seated on the ground around him. "His name is Willikers. They call him Gee."

"Gee Willikers! Ha! Well, 'gee willikers,' there's a man named Gee Willikers," one cracked.

"Yeah. 'Gee' is a nickname. He is a mountain man type. A real hunter."

"A hunter of what?" Another asked.

"Men, Pete. He was a hunter of animals, yeah, but the army uses him to run down important AWOLs, renegades, Indian parties, criminals and what-nots. Even missing officers' daughters. He is hunting an AWOL general right now, wanted for $1,000."

"Whhhhhew!" another said, his half-whistle shooting out dry, white breadcrumbs from his mouth.

"Not that much really when you th-th-think of it," Jerry Pickwirth added, struggling with his stuttering. "Billy the Kid and...and the James Gang...and, well others too, the bounties was thousands more on them. But $1,000 is a lot of money."

"Wonder what he's done?" one asked.

"I just saw a wanted poster for a fellow in the office, some general what ran away, for $1,000. It must be him. An AWOL. Dead or alive," another said.

"He p-p-peeved off the wrong Army honcho," Jerry Pickwirth said.

"He leeched under somebody's wig," said another.

"Got me to thinkin," Pat Weeps said," most of us get out from under Uncle Sam's yoke in a few months. Out! We ain't no fools. We are all veterans. Every one of us. Been in wars and skirmishes."

"I've kilt."

"Me too."

"Yup."

"I'm in prison because I'm tired of all that," one said.

"But that's under a full blown fightin, and under some idiot's command," Pat Weeps said.

"Some of us are real hunter-killers," a man said, looking right at former major Jerry Pickwirth.

Jerry remained expressionless under his oversized, dirty hat.

"What if we took up this bounty-huntin business once we got out?" Pat Weeps continued.

"There are already a lot of starvin, half-wit b-b-b-bounty hunters out there," Jerry Pickwirth warned.

"Yeah, but we know about the military criminals. Usually, they don't. The AWOLS and escapees, the raiders on supply houses, posts and forts. These other half-wits out there, they don't know about this source of business," Pat Weeps said, "we do. We know how to find out."

"It's a market. You just visit the headquarters of any military base. They'll have these posters a hanging," one declared.

"They'll even hand them out to ya," another said.

"What do you think, Jerry," a man said, "you use to be a major. You and yer men have kilt many an enemy. Yer a hound dog."

Jerry Pickwirth lit a thin cigar and they all looked at him for a comment, as he was older and seemed to be the unofficial leader. He took a deep breath, pursed his lips to speak.

"I like the idea a little bit," Jerry Pickwirth said. "It does makes sense. Good thinking, Weeps. The Army, hell the whole military, offers up more bounty money than civilian bounty money." He drew in some smoke, lighting up the burning end of his cheroot. "Plus, I hear they pay the bounties right away, whilst cities and counties, even states can be slow, especially if the caught feller is caught out of state. The Army? It's coast to coast qu-qu-quick."

"I think we can do it, and it'll take all of us because there are so many military bounties," Pat Weeps said.

"And Jerry, you could run us, run the group," one said. "You know bidness, Mr. Major.'"

"We'll be the 'Ditch Diggers'!" Pat Weeps said. "We've done dug ditches fer water flow, but we could be diggin ditches for the easy flow of all the bounties.

"You know, I'm in," said one.

"Me too," said another.

"In."

"It's not a b-b-ad idea," former Major Jerry Pickwirth said, "not a bad idea t'all."

Chapter 21: Catty's March on Logan

Denver, Colorado

A despondent, disorganized, Miss Catty Corners stepped off the train in Denver. It was early evening and she stopped on the platform to look around. The station was crowded as usual, and also full of the usual conmen that plagued Denver with rigged games of chance and bad products, all trying to spot and seduce abundant-luggage-bearing, apparent tourists. She had nowhere to go in this big city, but plenty of money from Swoop. She might stay away for a few days, but Manitou Springs was her home!

She had to eventually go back. She followed several of the travelers into the main station lobby. Her only destination of choice this evening was to order a buggy ride and cool her heels in a hotel. She was aware of the nearby Milton Hotel from past trips.

She saw an office inside the station for coach rides. The line of people ran from inside the office out into the big hall. She joined the line and waited to reserve one. Eventually the line ahead shortened until she stepped inside the coach business office. Bored, she scanned the walls and saw a bulletin board of announcements. Her jaw dropped and eyes widened. She turned, put a "wait" finger up in the air to the couple behind her and dashed over to the board, tugging a piece of paper off the wall.

She darted back in line. She read every word, over and over. Her face reddened. Lips pursed. Eyes watered. There was an extra tab glued to the poster, advising people to contact a Lt. Tembers at Fort Logan.

"Ma'am! Ma-am, where ya going?" The clerk said, prodding her to step closer to the counter.

"I was going to the Milton Hotel, sir, but now I need a ride to Fort Logan."

She folded up the $1,000, wanted poster of Mordecai Swellen into her cloth purse as they reserved her ride.

"Someone outside will ride up and call out your name," the clerk said, handing her a ticket.

She strutted outside the station with a new sense of mission about her. Her head held higher. She had an ace in her purse, and the anti was $1,000 dollars. A buggy came for her, the driver called out her name.

"Catty....Corners? Catty Corners?" the man said, more amused by the name than seeking out the fare.

"Right here."

"And you are going to Fort Logan? It's a fur piece, ma'am. And it's 20 cents. You got that much?"

"I do."

"It's brisk and there's a wooly blanket in the back, should you become winter-bit."

The open coach driver settled into his seat and startled the two motionless horses into action.

"Gotcha a husband or son out there at Logan? Gotcha a man there?"

"Well, no husband, but I damn sure gonna get me a man."

"Ooooh," he said, the curse startled the driver.

In about an hour and a half, they rode up to the front gates of Fort Logan. A well adorned soldier approached.

"Good evening, ma'am."

"I am here to see a Lt. Tembers," Cat said to the troop.

He bowed a bit, smartly about-faced and walked to the gate guard shack. He conversed with another guard, and he cranked up the desk phone. In a minute he returned.

"You spy that big building yonder? The flags?" He asked the driver. "That's the headquarters. Head on there."

Off they went.

At the HQ front porch, Cat dismounted the wagon.

"Wait here, driver," she ordered.

She walked inside and looked around.

"I am Lt. Tembers, ma'am. What can the Army do for you this evening?"

She thrust Swoop Swellen's wanted poster in front of his face.

"I know where this son of a bitch is! Manitou Springs! He is working for the Zapello train company at Pike's Peak. And I want all this reward money!"

"What is your name, ma'am?"

"Miss Catty Corners."

"Ahhh, well ma'am, you might get some of the money. A little, but the person who actually captures Swellen usually gets all the money."

"Well then, damn you!"

She turned right around and started to leave.

"Ma'am, where ya going? I…"

"To the Milton Hotel!"

"We…we will send someone out to see you in the morning then," Lt. Tembers said. But he already knew enough.

And she knew she never should have marched in like this

and lost her chance for $1,000.

Chapter 22: A Weapon In Your Hand

Outskirts of Manitou Springs, Zapello Trains Headquarters Cabin, foot of Pike's Peak

Swoop positioned himself in a suede chair near the second story, balcony rail, to overlook the open living room, lobby and dining room below. Zapello sat at the table at his usual workspace. Swoop had the dead Matteo's, ornate shotgun on his lap and a small Italian, expresso coffee on a small round table next to him, and his Thunderers strapped on.

It was 4 o'clock and downstairs, Greco strutted in through the front double doors, dressed in work clothes, looking annoyed. He pounded his boots on an inside door mat, knocking most of the snow off. Despite the cold he wore no jacket but rather a thick, blue plaid, flannel shirt over what looked like a thermal undershirt.

Greco looked around and then up to spot Swoop on the balcony. He glared at Swoop. Swoop was not supposed to be there. Or anywhere by now. Swoop's mere presence, alive and well, meant yet one more of his murderous plans was spoiled by means unknown to him as of yet, as both Catty and Matteo were...unaccounted for.

"You want something?" Greco asked Zapello in Italian and the conversation continued in that language, leaving Swoop but to guess the topic's directions by gestures, facial expressions and tone. Still, he understood the drift.

"Sit."

Greco took a chair at the big table across from Zapello.

"You have been my friend for years," Zapello started in, "we have know each other since we were teenagers. You have worked for me for eight years. I know your mother. You know my mother. They still break bread every Sunday in Sicily together and ask each other have they heard any new, news about their loving sons. And now I hear...I hear from the Portland Company in Denver, and many others here, that you are...are betraying me? You have stolen my plans. My technical drawings. They are rebuilding my train engines. My ideas. You sneak pieces of equipment and supplies out of here in the middle of the night?"

Greco stared at him, then looked down at the table, moving his head and neck as though his collar was too tight.

"Well, you have something to say?" Zapello said, "Because I got you, you caught like this." He squeezed his fists and shook them in the air.

"It's just business," Greco said with a sneer.

"Business!" Zapello cried out.

"Si! Business. It is nothing personal, Zappy. It is an opportunity. A business opportunity. You are slow. Too slow to move. I am faster. Smarter."

"You have dishonored me. You have done all this behind my back. Like the thief. A stiletto in the back," Zapello said.

"And you have ignored me! All this time," Greco said, "I can make men build these trains and tracks. I know how. I have taught each one of them how. You could have started me out leading a crew on the next mountain, right now! While you build this one. You could have two big jobs working at once. We could even have three jobs going. The money,

Zappy! You know I could do this with you, for you. You could have even made me a company manager, a vice-president. You have..."

"I have no vice-presidents. You are supervisor. I have no managers. Just supervisors! Me and four supervisors. You are one of them already. A top boss in the bosses. Anziana!"

Greco said nothing. He just shook his head.

"I cannot start a new job until this one is finished. You don't understand, Carlo. I have an American partner already. We have to prove ourselves first."

"No, we don't. You don't understand, get free of this partner, free of your stubborn idea of waiting, we could..."

"You are fired!" Zapello shouted.

"Fired! You can't fire me. This...I...I run this place."

"You steal this place! You do not run this place. Ladro! A thief!"

Swoop could tell the talk was really firing up.

"I am not fired!" Greco demanded and pounded the table, "you cannot make me fired."

Three cats in the room went from sound asleep to gone in a flash of a second.

"Oh, I cannot? What, why, because your secret plans are not complete yet?" Zapello said.

"You cannot fire me. I will not go."

"I will stop paying you. Listen to me. You are fired."

"You have...ruined me!" Greco said. "My name. My position. My..."

"FIRED! Go back to Sicily. Go somewhere else in America, but without my equipment, my plans, my trains. You hear!"

Zapello stood, fists on the table, "You... break my heart, Carlo!"

Swoop stood.

Greco stood.

"I challenge you to a duel for the disgrace you have caused me!" Greco demanded and he pulled out a knife from a jacket pocket.

"Don't be a fool. Do you think I am an idiot? That I would fight you with...with swords? Over this?" Zapello said.

Swoop slowly descended the stairs, the shotgun half-aimed at the dining room, half to the floor. On the first floor he walked up to face Greco. Greco turned to him and then he eyed the ornate shotgun.

"That's right," Swoop said, "you recognize your old amigo's shotgun? Matteo's. He's gone. Dead. Shot by me as he tried to shoot me. Put the knife away," Swoop said.

He did.

Then Swoop jammed the double barrels of the weapon into Greco's gut.

"SIT!"

He sat down again.

"He...he was with...with Cat...," Greco did not know how to ask about Catty Corners without incriminating himself.

"She's okay. I did not hurt her. I sent her off, Greco. Away," Swoop said.

Greco was breathing heavily.

"And you;\re gone. Gone from here," Swoop said, "I catch you sneaking around? I'll kill you. I catch you messing with Mr. Zapallo, you're dead. The front gate has no tres-passing signs. Don't cross them. You tried to have me killed. And now I will not need any excuse to kill you."

"Kill you? I..."

"It's too late for words," Swoop said.

"Once again you speak very big with a weapon in your hand, when I have none," Greco said.

"Timing is everything. Get your stuff and get out of here. The shift wagon to town is at 5 p.m.," Swoop ordered. "Be on it."

"I challenge you to a duel! Like men! You are not a man without holding a gun!"

"And you send your woman and your friend to ambush me."

"And wait. Here," Zapello interrupted them, speaking

softly. He reached over to and under a stack of paperwork to his left on the table.

Zapello slid a thick envelope over to Greco. Greco sneered at it, but opened it.

"Your last paycheck, to include today. And extra money. Money for trains to the East coast and a one-way ship to Italy. To Sicily. You...you say hello to our mothers."

Greco shoved the envelope in his pants pocket.

"Our mothers! I am NOT leaving Colorado. I have work to do here."

"Not with Portland Mechanics!" Zapello yelled.

Greco turned for the doors, walked out and slammed the doors behind him.

Swoop walked to the windows and watched Greco head for the workmen's dormitory cabins.

"That was-a so very painful," Zapello said.

"Look at this," Swoop said from the window.

Zapello approached the window to see a group of about 20 men outside greeting Greco on the yard. Greco began yelling and waving his arms dramatically, pointing at the cabin every few seconds. The men appeared angry.

"They are his friends." Zapello said.

"His co-conspirators," Swoop said.

"They are...were...all my friends. Once. I thought I treated everyone fairly."

Swoop leaned against the wall by the window, feeling a little exhausted. He said, "it is very hard to weave our way through people."

"Yes, it is. You too seem tired my friend."

"Yes. I guess I am. It's been a bad day. A bad couple of months actually."

Then Swoop stood straight up and looked back out the windows.

"If he stays in town? Remains in Colorado? He has no choice but to kill you and replace you for Deming," Swoop said.

"I know. This is a Sicilian criminal way. Assassination.

Cat? Will Cat stay away?"

"For your sake I hope she won't come back. Don't miss her, Zap. She was a spy for Greco. She used you, like a...a military spy. And, she did try to have me killed and when that failed, she tried to shoot me in the back."

"Yes. Si."

"I'll stay here tonight and the next few nights. They will come for you in the night, I think," Swoop said. "They'll talk it over tonight at Rumy's and maybe even try tonight or maybe tomorrow night. I am up here in my wagon. It is full of supplies. Ammo. I aim to stay here."

"I will help you, help me. I have-a guns. I can shoot. Yes. Back in Sicily I had to kill. I kill those against me. Yes. I am lucky to find you when I did, amico. The army made a big mistake letting you leave."

"That...is...debatable," Swoop said quietly.

At sunset, a butler named Pepino approached Zapello as the worried owner glanced out the front window of the cabin holding a glass of red wine.

"Mr. Zapallo?"

"Yes, Pepino?"

"Mr. Zapello. I must tell you something. One of the men, my friend from home told me secret. He called me aside and told me a secret that he heard."

Swoop heard the whispered tone of this conversation in Italian and saw the facial expressions. He wandered closer. Pepino looked at him, worried.

"Go ahead Pepino," Zapello said, as Zapello motioned for Swoop to step near.

"Santino called me aside when I was outside getting firewood. He told me..." Pepino turned toward Swoop and started back up in broken English, "you and the workers must go home tonight, to town. Santino say, leave the cabin. Leave Zapello and the Yankee. He begga me. Something is going to happen in the cabin tonight."

"What?" Zapello asked.

"I dunno. But trouble for you, eh?"

"Then you all must go, Pepino. Okay? Yes, you must go home tonight. Tell everyone that they have the night off. Okay?" Zapello said. "You make a special wagon and go home to your wives and husbands. Is good."

"Thank you, sir."

"Thank you, Pepino."

Swoop nodded and smiled at Pepino as the butler walked off to issue the orders.

"Oh! Only after dinner! We eat!" Zapello shouted out, checking his watch, "you make the dinner first! Then everyone go," he turned to Swoop, "They have a lamb tonight-a. I don't want to miss! Tonight, huh? You think?" Zapello asked Swoop.

"Tonight. You have any sleeping bags?"

"Oh yes, many for mountain emergencies."

"Okay. I've got a plan," Swoop said, let's get two sleeping bags ready. Dress warm tonight. Bring some food, some jerky. Binoculars. And bring those guns of yours. We're sleeping out back."

Chapter 23: The Evil Eyes

Swoop stood on the porch and watched Greco board the 5 o'clock wagon for Manitou Springs.

At 7:30 p.m., after the meal of roast lamb, Zapello ordered all the cabin staff to go home for the night and report back for a late breakfast the next morning. Swoop and Zapello herded up the six cats, no easy task, and locked them in a storage room off the kitchen along with food, water and the litter boxes full of dirt, sand, ashes and chopped-up paper. The felines were not at all happy about this arrangement.

Swoop and Zapello exited through the cabin back doors at 9 p.m., trudging out into the darkness and the crisp, clear freezing, windy night air, toting their bags of winter gear. The grounds of the cabin and storage area next door were cold, dark and empty. The two scaled the incline behind the residence-office-cabin. Swoop stopped them a ways up, turned and studied the landscape below.

"This will do," Swoop said.

They laid blankets down, then put their sleeping bags above the blankets. They took their jackets off as Swoop instructed and slipped into the bags and pulled the jackets inside the bags with them.

"The jackets will stay warm," Swoop advised. "If we wear them, we will get out of the bags cold. But if we get out and put the warm jackets on? It will be warmer and better."

"Army?" Zapello asked.

"Yes, Army."

"And so here we sit," Zapello said.

"We have to stay awake. Or at least take turns staying awake. The uninvited 'guests' will be arriving, oh, my guess, 2 a.m.? Three?"

They both had three flasks of coffee and shoved them between their legs in their bags.

"You know, this afternoon, Greco? He gave-a me the 'Malocchio.'The evil eye," Zapello said. "It is an easy custom of the world, but in Italy it is a thing of worry."

"The evil eye?"

"Yes. The power of '*Malocchio.*' It is not some power that only chosen people have. You call them witches and warlocks. It is a power that ordinary men-a have, men that are very jealous. When they have a great amount of envy for another man's success, his possessions. His handsome looks - like me! All those things. HA!"

They exchanged smiles.

"That is why you won't hear from an Italian that everything in their life is so perfect you see? Even if it is, they don't want to attract-a, the evil eye. When you look at me, I can see that you do not have this, this evil eye on me. Which is why I trust you. Your eyes. I see only help-a. And hope-a."

Swoop's study remained on the grounds out and below.

Zapello opened the flask and sipped some coffee, and said, "there are healers for this *Malocchio,* to break the spell. Milk, peppers, chants, prayers. The burning of olives. Several things that break the spells."

"I see. They mention a bullet in that list?"

"Ha! I think now, Archie Turner, you are my healer. Now, your bullets too. You came here like magic. You say yes to help me like…like-a magic. You save my business. You save my life."

"Well sir, it ain't over yet," Swoop said.

"Sicilians have other evil eye spells too. One is to wish great misfortune upon someone. The 'evil eye' curse, a…how-you-say *malacheezus*…"

"Malicious."

"Yes-a! A malicious gaze…supernatural! Causing harm to an enemy. The evil eye is mentioned in ancient clay tablets of the old. The Bible mentions an evil eye. The blessed Pope Leo too. You must be careful showing the evil eye, Archie. Jesus warns from the mount that, 'If, however, your eye is evil, your entire body will be full of darkness', so you must watch out! Because the devil, he loves the evil eye, and he comes into your body, maybe."

"Uh-huh," Swoop mumbled.

"You have to worry my friend, because you, YOU! I have seen you shoot out the rays of evil eye lights from your eyes. It makes someone's heart-a…skip a beat or two. Or more. You cannot do this too much, my amico. The devil? He smiles-a when you do this. And he comes into you."

"Un-huh."

"You read the Italian Stoics, do you read the Pope's Bible? Have you been to church-a?"

"When I was a boy. Something like that. In Minnesota," Swoop said. "My parents were very familiar with the Bible and with Indian religions..."

"You are connected to American Indians?"

"Yes. My grandmother, my mother's mother was an Indian," Swoop said. "They believed in the Wakan Tanka for the Dakota, just west of us and related, and gichi-manidoo for the Ojibwe. Both translate to 'great spirit' or 'great mystery.'"

"I see."

"My only wife was an Indian," Swoop said, after some

hesitation.

"Your wife-a? What happened to her?"

"She was killed by other Indians, mostly because she married me. It's a very long story, Zap. Like a Shakespeare story. We were on a rope bridge over a chasm, and they cut the bridge on one side. An ambush. To kill us both. She… fell. I…hung on."

"Dio mio!

"I have this as a nightmare. These moments. The moments of seeing her look at me as she fell. Fell. She could not hang on. Her face. Night and day-mares, still. It…it steals my breath. I scaled up the other side, the connected side of the rope bridge. They shot arrows at me, but they really wanted to kill her more than me. Then and there, I became disconnected to everything. Every church. Every religion. My Indian heritage, everything," he said. "I was once famous in the Army, Zap, for killing. Killing Indians and outlaws. I have a branding iron temper. I recognized after the rope bridge that man is just another animal."

"We are not animals. God has made us in his image."

"Yeah. Image. Some of those images need killing. The advice when I was young was that I should ask the question when in turmoil, 'what would Jesus do?' You know? I did think about that, then one day I realized, Zap, I ain't Jesus."

They stared ahead, with only questions wandering their minds. There were animals coming…

Swoop lay awake, watching. Thinking. This Tabby. Tabby. A very unusual name. Last name? First name? Nickname? Is Tabby officially just Tab? And Tabby is a nickname? Where had he seen that odd name lately. He's done nothing but read the Denver newspapers and the Seneca book. He must have scanned over the name in the newspapers. He made a mental note to look into this. Manitou Springs had a small library, and surely they saved the Denver newspapers.

Then, at 3:30 a.m., it happened...

"There. There, you see?" Swoop whispered.

Zap was asleep, but rather lightly and he startled awake with Swoop's call.

Four men, dark figures each carrying long objects like sticks, like long guns? They appeared in the storage and work areas, bound for the cabin. Zapello and Swoop sat up and pulled up their binoculars for a closer look.

"My God, it's true," Zapello said.

"Yes."

"They are coming to kill us," Zapello said.

"Yes."

"It is...this crazy-a. It is something like the wild, wild West."

"This is the wild, wild West," Swoop said.

The four men, hunched over, spread out, traveling from stockpile to stockpile to lumber stacks, their staccato advance seemed to resemble giant, invading spiders.

It is...Lorenzo. And it is Tommasso and Trey. Even Edourdo! Madre di Dio, they must hate me so," Zapello said.

The four worked their way to the very back door Zapello and Swoop had slipped through hours earlier and then they crept into the unlocked door.

The surveilling duo on the hillside waited, and then came the explosions. Two of them from inside the cabin. Two flashes of red light from inside two, two-story bedroom windows, Zapello's room and the room Swoop stayed in.

"They have killed us," Zapello said.

"Yes. Shotguns," Swoop said.

"Do you think they will look at the lumps in the beds we made? To see they are just piles of pillows and if they shot us?"

They had piled up the beds in both rooms and left a dull candle glowing in each one.

"I don't know. I hope they don't. They don't know that they are alone in there, they must think the crew is in there, and they have to leave right away." Swoop said, "Expecting your house crew to wake up."

"Yes-a."

Within less than a minute the four men burst from the back door and ran full out across the work yards. One fell, but he launched right back up, and all scampered into the workmen's bunk houses.

"Hmmm," Swoop grunted.

"What do we do now?" Zapello said.

Swoop laid back down on the ground.

"For one thing, in the morning we'll have coffee on the front porch. In a bit we'll go back in."

"I hope-a my cats are all okay," Zapello said.

"I bet they are."

6:30 a.m., the next morning...

The two shot-gunned beds were investigated. They were shot up, but it didn't appear that the covers were lifted to see if Zapello and Swoop were inside. The two stepped outside onto the cabin porch with coffee mugs in hand and three of the six cats followed them out. The other three lounged around inside the cabin. Swoop sat at one of the tables, with his lever action rifle on his lap. Zapello slowly wandered the balcony, as was often his way, seen by all the men gathering themselves and their gear for their work day up the mountain. Quite a number ignored him, some waved to him, but quite another number were surprised to see him.

"Fernando," Zapello shouted out.

The crew chief turned from his work and jogged up to the cabin.

"Yes, Zap?"

"Ferdy, I want you to send for Lorenzo, Tommasso, Trey, and Edourdo. Tell them to come see me right here."

"Si, signor."

Within a few minutes the four men, walked abreast into their sight. Zapello turned and looked at Swoop and Swoop nodded.

The four men's faces were expressionless, but Swoop thought he could see the, "Malocchio, evil eye" of some sort, from all of them, or their expressions of disappointment that they were looking at ghosts?

"Have you seen a ghost?" Zapello yelled out. "Well, you have. You *pazullas*! We know what you did. *Assassnis'*! And now? Now this ghost fires you."

Two of the men sneered and almost growled.

Swoop stood and walked to the stairs and down the steps.

"You men are fired," Swoop continued. "You are fired because last night you tried to kill me and Mr. Zapello. Instead, all you killed were a bunch of stacked up pillows."

They looked at Swoop's rifle. It was halfway up. Other co-workers gathered around, still keeping some distance, but very interested.

"This last month..." Swoop continued with a sigh, "I have been trying, really trying not to kill people. Otherwise, you all would be dead. Guts...all…all over this gravel and snow, right here." He waved his left hand over the ground. "Wanted to kill you last night when you rats showed up here with your shotguns, or maybe right now. But, for right now, you're just fired."

"You..." One started to spout off.

"There are signs everywhere now that say, 'No Trespassing,'" Swoop said.

"*Trasgreesoris*," Zapello repeated.

"And trespassers...*trasgreesoris* will be shot. You've seen em these last few days at the front gates. Perfectly legal up here in the mountains and private property. If I see you here, I will kill you, instantly."

They stared at him.

"Get your stuff and start walking," Swoop said.

"What about our paychecks?" Tommasso asked in Italian.

"We're keepin it," Zapello said. "To pay for the pillows. And the beds are all shot up. Mattresses, bed posts. Sheets. Shotguns do that."

"Idiots with shotguns pay for the damages," Swoop

added, getting the drift of the request for 'buste paga.'"

Some of the nearby crowd seemed confused, others were not. The four men turned for the barracks. Swoop backed up the stairs and walked to the north end of the balcony watching them go. There was a wooden chair already there at the end and Swoop sat in it.

"I would go inside," Swoop quietly told Zapello.

"Why, you think..."

"I think..." Swoop said softly.

And Zapello did.

Swoop watched as workers questioned the four as they walked off. Swoop heard one say, "What's that all about?" More or less, in the Italian he was beginning to understand.

The sun started to fully rise, up over the pine tree tops. The four crossed the yard and entered the barracks. Some of the men returned to their morning prep chores to make ready for the mountain climb and work, but some seemed to "scatter away" a bit. Not a good sign. Swoop watched the barracks' doors.

Then a door swung wide open and too fast. Angry fast. Lorenzo appeared in the frame. He marched back toward their cabin, a pistol pointed down at his side. He split the workers apart like Moses at the Red Sea. Swoop stood and went flush against the cabin wall.

Lorenzo raised his pistol and fired at the cabin balcony. At him. Every five or so steps, he fired again. Carelessly. Madly. This time the workers raced away.

Swoop braced his rifle on his left shoulder, and peeked around the cabin's corner, which displayed less of a target for Lorenzo, and Swoop took aim.

"Stupid son of a bitch," he muttered about the bad tactic, angry approach. Suicidal?

He squeezed the trigger and hit Lorenzo in the center of his chest, just below his throat. Though the shot was center mass, the man twisted hard to the left and dropped, pistol still in hand. Swoop stepped further out on the balcony for a better look at all of the barracks. Zapello charged out the cabin's door with a pistol in his hands.

"It's over, I…" Swoop told him. "Oh, wait…no, no it's not."

Swoop spotted Trey run out from the rear of the barracks, slowed by the drifts of snow, holding a shotgun. Trey was headed for the inclines behind the work yard and the cabin, trying to get behind the residence-office and flank them.

"Trey's making a play for around back," Swoop told Zapello.

Zapello dashed inside. Swoop vaulted the balcony rail and turned for the rear of the cabin, rifle up. Trey had already disappeared from his view, dashing to the south. As Swoop ran to the northeast corner of the building…

Gunshots. Shotgun and…pistol.

He turned the corner, stock welded to his left shoulder again, left elbow pointed down, to only expose his left eye and the gun barrel, ready to shoot.

Trey was down on his back, groaning, about 30 feet shy of the back door! Swoop saw Zapello at the back door, his pistol arm and gun arm extended. Zapello looked at Swoop. Swoop nodded, then slowly approached Trey. So did Zapello. Trey was still alive, still gasping.

Swoop kicked the shotgun away.

Zapello knelt beside him, and they started speaking in Italian.

"Lorenzo is dead," they heard a voice from the side of the cabin. It came from the company's resident doctor. He was shivering without a jacket, and carried a black bag. He ran toward them from the work yard.

The doc said while catching his breath, "How is he?" He knelt by the man and Zapello stood.

"It is Trey!" The doctor said.

"Yes," Swoop said.

"What did Trey say?" Swoop asked as he stepped closer to Zapello.

"He said…he said…he was sorry," Zapello said, full of remorse. "He said Greco offered him, them, so much-a money

to come into the train business with him, that they could not refuse. Even if it meant to kill me, if they had to do it."
It started to snow. Heavily.

"I know him for maybe 30 years. Maybe more," Zapello said. "And now, now I have to shoot him like this. Like a thief in my backyard," and Zapello became speechless.

Other workers ran up.

"I need to get this man back to barracks." the doctor said, "He's not dead. Yet."

The cook and butlers had just arrived from town, and they stood on the back deck, watching, shivering, shocked.

Swoop picked up Trey's shotgun.

"Another very fancy European shotgun," he said, "connected to a very unfancy ending."

He saw Fernando in the group nearby, gawking at the scene.

"Make sure the other two leave, will ya Fernando? Before I have to kill them too," Swoop told him.

"Si, *signor.*"

"What say we get on inside, Zap," Swoop said.

They started for the cabin. Swoop put a hand on Zapello's shoulder on the way. Zapello's nose was running, and his eyes were watery. He wiped his nose and took a deep breath.

"Should we call the sheriff about this?" Zapello asked, "because we never have before when other men fought and died or disappeared out here? But we have two attempted murders last night and two shootings today!"

"I would say from what you have told me about the sheriff…I would say no. And, no one wants the law involved, wants the sheriff poking around into any of this. Everyone has something to hide, something to be investigated."

"I don't!"

"I do. And, the sheriff will not solve anything that you need solving, Zap."

"Yes. Yes-a. He considers this out here, 'Little Sicily,' out of his county. Out of his country."

"Let's see how much of this we can clean up, faster,"

Swoop said.

Chapter 24: Scouting for the Scout

Lt. Bernes and Lt. Tembers found Major Twenty eating breakfast at a table.

"Last night a woman named Catty Corners..." Lt. Tembers started.

"Catty what?" Major Twenty said, his mouth half full of runny eggs.

"Corners. Yes. First name Catty. She marched up to me late last night at headquarters, held up a Swellen wanted poster and declared that she knew where Swoop Swellen was and he was in Manitou Springs, out by Pikes Peak."

Major Twenty stopped eating and sat up straight. "That's not too far from here, right?"

"Yes, Sir. She said he is working security for the Zapello Train Company, a company building a special train to climb Pikes Peak. She said he stays either at the Cliff House Hotel, a famous place there, or out on the train job site."

"You tell Gee Willikers yet?" Major Twenty asked Lt. Bernes.

"No, Sir. Can't find him. He wasn't on the Fort last night or this morning in his quarters and he probably was in Denver, getting drunk I imagine. He's still not in his quarters."

"Hookers?"

"Huh?"

"Hookers," Major Twenty repeated with an empty mouth.

"He's probably laid up with a hooker. Well, we need to find Willikers. As I explained our 'mission protocol' the other day, we let him...scout out the bounty first, a day or so, then we organize and ride in with our men. Usually, to pick up the pieces."

"Yes, Sir. This Catty Corners claims she wants the full $1,000 bounty," Lt. Bernes said.

"Oh, ha! She'll have to wrestle it from Willikers. He wants all the money. Even if we all catch Swellen together, he gets all the money. We might give her 10 or 15 bucks, or something, but it will be out of my pocket. What did you tell her? Anything?"

"I told her it would depend on who actually catches Swellen, how many men are involved and so forth," Lt. Tembers said.

"Uh-huh. Where is she now?"

"She said she was staying at the Milton Hotel down-town."

"Where...where do you think...would any of your local soldiers tell Willikers where to go for a good time?" Major Twenty asked.

"There's a few places around, around town."

"Can you send the troops that will be assigned to us out to round him up? To take this on as their first official task? Send them to those good times places and see if they can root out our prodigal mountain man?"

"I can. They are just sitting around waiting for some or-ders."

"You see, Lieutenant," Major Twenty said, "It is more im-portant than ever to dispatch Willikers first, for his 'day.'"

Major Twenty stood and donned his big blue jacket and said,

"Let's get to headquarters and I'll call the Milton Hotel. Meet with this Catty Corners."

The three walked across the frozen grounds and into the

headquarters building.

"Corporal Shawdroff," Lt. Tembers said to a troop at the welcome desk. "Can you get the operator to connect Major Twenty to the Milton Hotel downtown?"

"Yes, Sir. Major, if you will step around Sir, and get closer to our switchboard."

Lt. Tembers left to organize the men for a scouting for the scout. Lt. Bernes strolled over to a table of coffee pots, loaves of Mexican sweet bread and sandwich meats. He smelled a few pots' spouts trying to locate the freshest one. When he looked up, Major Twenty was approaching him.

"That was fast," Lt. Bernes said.

"Yes. We called, and the hotel clerk said she left this morning."

"Oh?" Lt. Bernes said.

"The clerk said she needed a coach to the train station and was going home. Home to Manitou Springs. You...you don't think that..."

"That she'll try to catch Swellen herself? Get the $1,000 for herself?" Lt. Bernes finished for him.

"Yes. Sounds like it."

"Heck, Sir," Lt. Bernes said. "I'll bet she will."

Chapter 25: Kill-a Zapello!

At a back table in the smoky corner of Rumy's bar, two men quietly conspired and drank coffee - Tabby Stallmouth and Carlo Greco. Tabby had one leg tightly crossed over the other and the high, expensive boot swinging back and forth. Greco just leaned in, his forearms on the table.

"You have the support of Mr. Deming," Tabby told him. "You were the first man to make a deal with him, and he does not care about how you obtained the train plans, or the equipment because they all came from Italy. They're from another country. Mr. Deming feels that the laws of a different country do not apply well here in the United States."

"This is true? True law?" Greco asked.

"Welllll," Tabby said with a small grin and an eye wink, "yes, in one sense it is true. Yes. It is complicated Carlo and takes much time and money to make laws and wrestle with these official, legal decisions. Much of this goes on between countries and America wins. I'll bet if all this was happening in Italy, the situation reversed, then Italy would win."

"Yes! I see. I see," Greco said, stirring sugar into his coffee with a butter knife.

"We have determined that in order for us to proceed," Tabby leaned in closer, "we need to get this Mr. Zapello fellow out of the…way."

"Out of the way. You mean, kill-a him?"

"Yes."

"I have tried. I have. We tried last night. It failed." Greco decided to confess.

"You have?"

"No, not me. I, I am an old friend of his. We grew up together," Greco said with an actual certain sadness, shifting in his seat and looking at the floor. "I myself, I cannot do this to him. I have my men try. These decisions are always hard, eh?"

"I understand. But it is business, Carlo."

"Yes! Business. I know this. I take these actions-a, but you know. It can be hard. This…Archie Turner, he protect-a Zapello. He kill my men. And, he beat up my other men. Many of my men, they are afraid of him."

"I see. Well, we will soon turn these chickens into our railroad men…"

"Chickens? Men?"

"Ahh, afraid men. Scared men. They are called 'chicken,' in America," Tabby explained.

"Oh! Yes. Yes-a, I see."

"We'll turn these chicken men into full time, railroad builders and not killers and fighters. Then they will be happy. We need your experienced men to work on all these future jobs."

"I tell you, this Archie…he is like an American gunslinger. He is not scared. No chicken. And I will say, I am not scared of him. I challenge him! To a duel, to his face, face to face, right here at the bar, and he does not accept."

"I see."

"He just wants to shoot me with his guns. No duel. He is a problem-a," Greco said.

"He wants to shoot. Yes. Well then, I will have to take

care of this problem too."

"But now, who will kill Zapello?"

"I will take care of Zapello and Archie Turner," Tabby said. "It would not be good for you, a new businessman in Denver and being a new partner with Mr. Deming, to risk being involved in murders. And listen, compadre, you have to stop killing people in those sword duels," Tabby pounded a finger on the table, several times.

"Ohhh no. But it is a culture of my country. My sport."

"Sports do not kill people, Carlo. Not in America."

"Okay. I have a few duels that are, how you say, scheduled."

Tabby shook his head, "Scheduled?"

"I must-a do!" Greco said, "my honor is…"

"Okay. Okay. Get them over, then they must stop. Make sure they are clean duels, so the sheriff stays clear of you. But leave Zapello to me. Leave Turner to me."

"I have already tried to have Archie killed once. He outsmarts me. He killed my friend. He is very tricky. You must be careful."

"I see."

"Every Monday," Greco continued, "Zappy comes here to Manitou Springs to shop," Greco said. "Food-a. Some supplies. He goes to the Grain's butcher shop. He goes to Betty Wain's grocery store. Maybe to some other stores."

"All downtown? Around here?"

"Yes-a. He does this every Monday morning. Lunch maybe. He comes in and out on the main road. Then he goes on a date with a girlfriend on nights sometimes. But this woman? She is also my good friend. She tells me all his secrets. I will meet with her again soon."

"Ahh, that is a good friend to have. I will make myself available next Monday," Tabby said. "You stay here in Manitou Springs. Make yourself comfortable. Relax. Things will be changing very fast these next few days."

Tabby reached into his jacket pocket and then handed Greco 50 dollars.

Greco's eyes widened and he took the money.

"On Monday morning, try to stay in groups of people. Here maybe. So there are witnesses to testify that you are not involved in any law breaking. Okay?"

"Okay. I will-a."

Chapter 26: Greco's Reckoning

On the Cliff House front porch, Swoop had to stop and stare once again because of the commotion across the field and out on Main Street.

"Oh no," he sighed.

It looked like yet another crowd had gathered for a sword fight. And sure enough, he spotted Greco appearing from the front doors of Rumy's bar, wrapped again in that flamboyant white shirt with ballooning sleeves and tight pants despite the cold, brandishing his classic sword in hand. Who was to be the new pincushion this time?

The Cliff House steps and sidewalks were well shoveled and salted so Swoop jogged down the steps and onto the field, closing in on the pending action.

"In the honor match of Signore Carlo Greco and a Mr. Bowden," declared the same well-dressed, broadcasting man as last week. The announcer whipped off his top hat as he shouted, "we shall momentarily begin this duel to the death."

Bowden? Death? Swoop thought as he stood among the gawkers on the avenue. The Bowden man was already dead from days ago? This a brother? Father? Not the son! He started studying the gathering crowd. On the left side of the onlookers he spotted a young man, a teenager, holding a rusty machete, and before him stood those same three cowboys from weeks ago, apparently begging him to leave and not fight.

The crowd mumbled and shuffled with excitement as Swoop cut through them making his way over to the apparent challenger.

"What's going on?" Swoop asked.

"This is March's kid, Mr. Turner," one of the cowboys turned and said,. "He's been brewing on his daddy's death for days and days now. Fussin, stewin. Cussin. He's got him one of our vaquero's brush machetes, and he's a stormed himself down here last night and threatened Greco. The Greek bastard…"

"Eye-talian! Denny," one impatiently corrected again.

"This eye-talian bastard will kill him too. Kilt his daddy and now the son, and we can't stop him. Can you imagine! Daddy and boy dead from some somabitch with a skinny pigsticker!"

"No, I can't imagine," Swoop said, staring at the teen, while the teen glared at Greco stretching his limbs up on the sidewalk.

Swoop pushed through the three cowboys, marched up to the teenager, reared his arm way back and blasted a long-range punch smack in the face of the kid. The lanky, young man went airborne, both his feet left the ground, and he landed back on the snowy road, instantly dreaming. The crowd, itching to see this next duel, gasped in disappointment.

"Oh, come on!" One shouted.

Greco seemed outraged.

"I, Archie Turner…" Swoop turned to the audience and announced, "will step in, and I will fight for the challenger

Bowden!"

Greco stared at him from the elevated sidewalk, then got a gleam in his eye.

"Yes! This is an honorable possibility by the official rules of dueling," Greco declared. "He is to be, what we call-a, a 'second'."

"And I will be right back in a second with my sword," Swoop declared.

"Use the sap's machete why don't cha?" An elderly woman yelled.

Swoop ignored her. His blood now boiled as he strutted to the Cliff House. The manager Holden was on the front porch and watched Swoop storm nearby.

"Are you sure…" Holden started.

"Sure," Swoop said, not looking his way.

Swoop went to his room and recovered the Bowden cavalry sword. He yanked it from its scabbard and retraced his steps onward to the main street.

"Good luck, Mr. Turner," Holden shouted as he passed.

Swoop made it all the way back to the street and to the front of Rumy's Bar.

The crowd was electrified.

"This is *your* choice of weapon?" Greco demanded, "you are not using one of your pistols or a rifle like the big bully that you are?"

"This is my choice of weapon," Swoop growled. "And do you know why? Why? Why not a gun? Because it's… slower."

"Ha!" Greco said, understanding the intent. He made a longer, dramatic leap from the bar's doors landing on the crunched down snow of the roadway.

When Greco hit the street like an acrobat, the crowd applauded. They opened up and spread out. Greco struck the classical swordsman stance. Sword forward. Rear left hand up.

Swoop peeled off his brown leather jacket, and unhooked his double gun belt, handing both to one of the cowboys. He crouched at the knees, lifted the Army sword and pointed the tip at Greco's face.

"Your sword is heavy and cumbersome!" Greco said, as he swirled his thinner tip in the air. "Like your heart! And your brain."

Greco suddenly lunged. Swoop battered it off to his left, his sword stopped halfway across his body, keeping his cutlass tight in the rectangular, window of combat in front of his body. Over-blocking is always an emotional, tactical mistake.

Greco did the same lunge again. Swoop same-blocked, but this time Greco tried to whip his sword around the block to catch Swoop's right side. Swoop was able to block that new step too.

Greco same lunge yet again. He was building a strategy, and Swoop knew it.

Swoop same block. Greco same whip around…., but it was a fake whip around!

Greco stayed right of Swoop's blocking sword movement, as he deep stepped to his right and lunged again in a curving stab, catching and tearing open the left arm of Swoop's shirt as Swoop saved his chest by jumping to his right away from the strike.

Greco bounced back and laughed along with the delighted onlookers.

"You have shown me nothing, and you…" Greco said.

Like a charging bull, Swoop burst forward, slamming his sword down like an axe on Greco's sword, close to his hand and above the sword's special, ornate, metal protective weave.

Greco's sword and arm dropped several inches from the heavy blow, and Swoop lifted his sword an inch, and got a horizontal glancing blow up on Greco's sword-bearing biceps, ripping into that fluffy white shirt sleeve. In doing so, in route, Swoop peeling some four inches of flesh in a run up off Greco's forearm to the lower biceps strike.

Greco lost the ability to grip his sword! He dropped it! Swoop circled the cutlass around Greco's body and with a dramatic deep step to the left, he smashed the side of the sword into Greco's face, causing more of a stunning smack than any cut. Then, versus the stunned man, Swoop slashed open the back of Greco's right thigh. This time, a deep cut. Pant leg and muscles were torn open and Greco lost height and dropped to his knees. Swoop noted that on that half-moon path to the thigh cut, he inadvertently hit Greco's left hand, chopping off two of his fingers!

Some women in attendance screamed as the two fingers flipped through the air like flipped cigars, and one stabbed into the snow, remaining upright.

Greco, downed, looked at his hand, then looked over at the fingers when they landed. He was in a death-shock, unable to fully process what had happened. Then he raised his head to look up at Swoop both in a confused anguish and anger.

"You bastard," Greco said.

"So, Greco, what about you?" Swoop said in a growl. "You the starter of all these duels."

Greco panted.

"Are YOU religious?" Swoop asked.

"Oh…yes, I am," Greco said defiantly.

"Then you are a hypocrite liar," Swoop said." Religious! Stealing from your best friend and planning many crimes and murders. Killing people in sword fights for fun…fun."

"I…"

"If you renounce your God, I will let you live," Swoop said, re-enacting the infamous, Greco-old-finale-scheme, and Greco recognized the irony.

"I do NOT renounce my God! NO!" Greco declared aloud.

"Well…you're going to Hell, anyway," Swoop said.

Swoop raised the broad, hefty cavalry sword, and with a two-handed grip he swung a mighty blow downward, burying the war sword deep into the top of Greco's skull and completely into Greco's head.

The audience was now further aghast. Horror. They were used to clean skinny sword stabs, not this sort of barbaric debauchery! Greco's eyes were wide open but saw nothing and his jaw dropped and hung open.

Greco's body remained knee-high, probably because Swoop held the sword, which also held the head up. Then, he let go of the weapon and in a few seconds, the body toppled over.

Swoop looked the audience over. He picked up Greco's sword and like someone throwing a knife, he lifted his arm and heaved the sword at the wooden wall beside Rumy's doors. The tip struck first. It… actually… stuck in the wood!

"This, ladies and gentlemen…is your last duel in Manitou Springs! I hope you enjoyed it," Swoop shouted in anger.

Off to the left, there came a high-pitched moaning. It was from the waking kid.

"What…happened?" the bedazzled young Bowden sat up and spoke, spitting out some blood running down and out of his nose.

"What happened, sugar foot? That army feller over there, just killed yer pappy's killer all while you were having a nap," a cowboy said, helping the boy afoot.

"Huuuuh?"

"He busted yer nose, but saved yer got-dang, foolish life," said a second friend.

Swoop walked up to them.

"Sorry about your nose kid, but you needed a fast, serious interruption," Swoop said. "If you want your father's sword? You can pull it free from that son-of-a-bitch's head over there, like…like Arthur pulled Excalibur from the stone. It's all yours."

"Who's Arthur? And what am I ex-calabin?" the teen mumbled.

"I think we will let the sword be where it be. Thank you, sir," one cowboy said. "We'll take the young prince back to the ranch house, with your permission."

"Oh, you have my permission," Swoop said.

Rumy's workers gathered around Greco, trying to figure out what to do next with the body. Could he be buried with a sword in his head like that? At some point, somebody's got to remove that sword. Witnesses also closed in to see the damage up close.

"He about cut that man's head in two like splittin a rail!" An astonished man whispered.

Rumy pulled the swaying European sword from the wall.

"I will keep this here weapon," Rumy declared. "I will hang it upon a wall. I will, with a plaque. 'The sword of Carlo Greco. Master swordsman. Killed by a… by a, what in…what are you sir?"

They all looked to Swoop, who was busy donning his discarded gun belt and jacket.

"I am a damn, fool," Swoop said.

"Well, you are a fool of a second that became a first." Rumy said. "One drink on the house!" He motioned for all to go in. "In the memory of a great European swordman we have seen and lost today. As he is on to his reward!"

"YEAH!" Came the crowd.

"And to the winner, Mr. Turner, a free steak, beans and beer! Will you join us?" Rumy shouted.

Swoop sneered and half-grunted. He wouldn't participate and he was still just a bit concerned the sheriff might show up. He left for the Cliff House, still roaring like a kiln inside, enough to punch through several walls, but enjoying a sense of revenge.

The day of reckoning with Greco had arrived and it was over, with one fell…swoop.

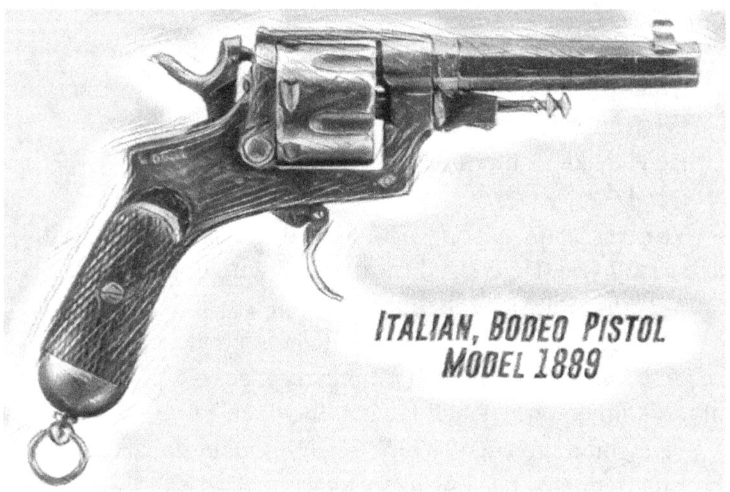

Chapter 27: A Canvas Body Bag

The next day, Catty Corners stepped off the train at the
Manitou Springs station. Still dressed in her hiking clothes
and boots from her fiasco at the Garden of the Gods. She decided to walk home to her boarding house, rather than hire a
coach ride. These last few months she spent many nights at
Zapello's cabin and was rarely seen at her rented room except
for some clandestine overnight meetings with Greco. In her
big purse was the folded, wanted poster for Swoop Swellen,
the Renegade General.
Hiskia, the house owner from Finland, was painting the side
of his two-story, long-term, stay hotel.

"Hellooooo, Catherine!" He yelled out as she got near the
porch. He knew her before she became Miss "Catty."

"Good afternoon, Hiskia," she said.

"You look tired, dear."

"I am tired," she said.

"And are you tired from the bad news?"

"The bad news? What now?"

Hiskia laid his dripping brush carefully down upon a sawhorse.

"This morning I heard, that yesterday…about your friend, Mr. Greco?"

"What? Yes?"

"He is dead, Catherine."

"Dead?"

"Yes. Yes. I am so sorry. But he is dead, and I am sorry to have to tell you. He is dead from a duel with that stranger man working for Mr. Zapello as his policeman."

"Archie? Archie Turner? He killed Greco yesterday?"

"Yes, him. It was a fair fight they say, dear. A sword duel only this time your friend? He lost the duel."

She stood there silently looking at him, but not seeing him. She finally pursed her lips to speak.

"Figures," she said to no one, "monster."

She walked into the narrow lobby and upstairs to her single room. The doors were never locked, and she entered. She opened the bottom drawer of the dresser, moved some clothes and lifted the big, dark, gray pistol that Greco gave her.

It was an Italian, Bodeo Model 1889, a 6 shot, revolver, an ugly thing compared to the pistols her father and her uncles had, or the ones most men carried around these days, or the brace of pistols this fake, Archie Turner brandished. There was no trigger guard on this one, just a naked trigger, exposing the trigger to any and all accidents. Greco had warned her about this feature.

She sat on the room's one rickety chair with the weapon on her lap, next to the bed where she and Greco laid many times, many nights, making their plans and dreams of traveling the Rockies, building trains. While she slept with Zapello, Greco stayed alone in this room. Then she considered plans for the monster Swoop Swellen.

Swoop Swellen, dead or alive. If she shot Swellen with this big Italian gun, Greco's gun, it would be so ironic. Justice. But if she shot him, where would this be. In the street? In his Cliff House room? How would she get his body to Fort Logan? Or to the sheriff's office maybe to collect the bounty?

"That's it!" She thought. The Sheriff's Office would be the best place and he would have to make the news official. But then, could she trust that crooked sheriff not to steal her bounty? Kill her and claim the capture and all the money for himself?

But never mind the sheriff, if anyone helped her move the body, they could steal the body from her, steal the story, kill her, and get the bounty money. One thousand dollars was a lot of money. She'd kill someone over it, why wouldn't someone else kill her over it?

Time! Time was against her. She leaned over and drummed her fingers on the coarse patched quilt on the bed. The army would come later today or maybe tomorrow? She should have never marched into Fort Logan with that wanted poster and given away Swellen's location to that lieutenant. What was she thinking? Did she really believe that simply telling them where Swellen was, was enough to be paid $1,000? The officer told her,

"Oh, thanks, ma'am," he said, and she would only get a tiny portion if it, if it all worked out. Stupid!

She was stupid! That soldier told her she would get "some" money. A little money. If she killed Swellen in the right location, she could figure out a way to drag his body into a rented closed coach? Maybe steer that coach all the way to Fort Logan?

Denver, Colorado…

"I'd say he's best described as lookin like a mountain man," Sgt. Baston offered the bouncer at Heart Stopper Bar.

The bouncer was a young, off-duty, Denver policeman, fresh off of a day shift, half in uniform, drinking a mug of beer, his big moustache full of froth.

Sgt. Baston and three troopers had a long day trying to find this Mr. Wilson Gee Willikers. Most of the bars were closed in the morning and afternoon, opening up after 3 or as late as 6 p.m. But it looked like they might get lucky at the Heart Stoppers and with this moon-lighting, police officer?

The man eyed up the uniforms of the men and decided to

help them, being a uniform-man by trade, himself.

"Beard? Tan, deerskin, fringe shirt, big ol boy? In his 50s?" The bouncer asked.

"That'll be him," Sgt. Baston said.

"Okay. Contain that thought," the bouncer-policeman said and placed the beer on the bar. He walked into what looked like a kitchen at the far end of the long bar.

"Follow me, pony soldiers," he shouted from the doorway and all the men followed in suit, their boots ka-thunking and spurs raking the worn wooden floor. They walked out back to a dirt road and a poverty scene of small, gray shacks. An emaciated dog barked at them.

"Shush up, Lucy," the bouncer ordered.

A small wagon sat in front of one shack, its wheels chocked. No horse to be found. The sides were about three feet tall and hooked over one end, hanging off the back was a pair of lower legs encased in brown pants and deer skin boots.

The off-duty policeman poked a finger in the air at the wagon, then left for his beer. The soldiers surrounded the wagon, all looking in and resting their arms on the sides. Sure enough, a mountain man was asleep inside the bed, covered against the cold air by several blankets. He was snoring and with each breath shooting visible steam out of his mouth into the cold, like a train.

"Mister Gee Willikers?" Sgt. Baston said. "Mr. Willikers!"

"The hell of it! What?" Willikers mumbled when startled awake.

"Mister Willikers, I am Sgt. Baston, D Company, Fort Logan and you are needed back at the fort. Apparently, sir, the man we will all be hunting for? He has been found-out, more or less found-out, and they need your scouting services, pronto."

"Oh, oh yeah. What, where…where am I?"

"You're in Denver, Colorado, sir."

"OHHH, yeah. Yeah. I know that! That sounds right. I

mean where am I exactly in Denver?"

"You are behind a bar, sir."

"Oh yeah, that girl in there...I...," Willikers got up on his elbows.

He was an ugly cuss to the men. He shoved his big, soiled hat on.

"I can't always sleep inside a building, no matter the cold," he explained. "I have to geet outside. Ahh...stars. Under the stars. Okay. Okay. You got some kind of a wagon out front?"

"We do, sir."

"Ohhh boy. I'm too rickety from, from the shine last night to walk too far. Lead me to your caisson, Sergeant."

Once at Fort Logan headquarters, a hung-over Willikers met Major Twenty.

"Not a word! Coffee!" Willikers said. "Milk and sugar."

Lt. Bernes went to the main lobby table and poured a cup. He added a dash of milk and a spoon of Dominos sugar. He returned and handed it to the scout. He sipped it, allowing for the conversation to begin with an approval hand wave.

"A woman walked in here last night and told us that Swoop Swellen was working for the Zapello Railroad outside of Manitou Springs by Pikes Peak.

"So now this military genius is a workin for the railroad?" Willikers said, drinking the brew again. "Laying track?"

"Just in a fashion, yes. It's some sort of security," Major Twenty said.

"Uh-huh. Well, I've never been to Pikes Peak. Be a first for me."

"Me too, Gee," Major Twenty said. "You know what to do, go on down there ahead and 'scout' things out. I am told the telephone and telegraph system works very well back and forth. Tell us what you find. We'll be standing by at a day's notice."

"Scissors around here?" Willikers asked, spying the stack of wanted posters on the table.

"Ahh, yes. Hold on. Here," Lt. Bernes said. Willikers peeled about 20 copies of the wanted posters off the pile, sat down and five or so at a time, cut off the top and bottom of the posters, leaving only the portrait of Swellen from the middle to remain.

"Can't show a full wanted poster around Pikes Peak and Manitou Springs. Can't have everyone see a $1000 re-ward! They'll be trying to geet on him before I do. This ways I just have the face."

Major Twenty nodded.

"They say he is using the name Archie Turner," Major Twenty said.

"Archie Turner. Okay."

"Anything else?"

"No. But, the woman that told us all this, a 'Catty Corners,' went back to Manitou Springs before we could question her," Major Twenty said.

"Catty Corners? That's a tootin of a name. She must be a show girl?"

"Don't know, sir. Lt. Tembers who met her here said she was a looker. And he said she was madder than an old mule chewing on bumblebees. Apparently, she'd just discovered he was a wanted man an hour before."

"Humm. Probably wronged her is some fashion," Wil-likers said, "like a dalliance. If she has any salt and pepper, she'll try to shoot this bastard and get the money her own self. If she's a looker AND a hooker, she might be a tough enough. I'll have to find her first, I think. What exactly she look like?"

"Corporal!" Twenty shouted out. "Ask Lt. Tembers to come in."

Timbers entered.

"This Catty Corners. What does she look like?" Major Twenty asked.

"Tall. 5 foot 10. Pretty face. Good shape. Long brown

hair. Dressed well enough. In her 30s. 35? 37?"

"Okay. Hooker maybe?" Willikers asked.

"I wouldn't say so, sir. Not off hand. She didn't appear run-ragged, but she'll dill your pickle."

"Okay, sonny. Nonetheless, I will vamoose as immediately as possible. I will eat first, and…"

"We will finish preparing a small wagon for you, as to your usual specifications. Maps. Food. Ammo."

"Canvas for a body wrap?"

"That too." Major Twenty said.

Later that night in Manitou Springs Cliff House…

Cross off Carlo Greco.

Catty Corners was coming for Swoop.

Gee Willikers was coming for Swoop.

Tabby Stallmouth was coming for Swoop.

An Army platoon was coming for Swoop.

Meanwhile Swoop was in a hot bath in his hotel room, a glass of beer within reach on a windowsill.

But his guns were hanging on a stool nearby…

Chapter 28: Fernando's Reckoning
Zapello Compound

"Oooh, Good morning!" Zapello declared. He and Fernando stood up from the lobby conference table as Swoop walked in the front cabin doors, stomping his snow-covered boots on the welcome mat.

"I have heard both good and sad news. You have finally killed Greco. This is such good news in a way. Sad in a way, but is good."

But, Zapello did not seem too sad about it.

"You defeated him with a sword! How? How could you beat such a known master?"

"I didn't play his sword game, I reckon. You ever play tennis, Zap?"

"Yes-a. Some."

"Sometimes tennis experts like to play around. Do 1, 2, 3 set-ups. Work an opponent into their routine. Like boxing."

"Yes-a."

"I did not do this. I did not let him do this. I charged in like a madman."

"I heard that you asked him about God, like he always did with his victims. Ha! He said he still like-a God still. And you told him he was going to Hell anyway."

"That I did, and that he will."

And a conversation ensued when Zapello wanted to know all the small details of the fight.

Fernando Bosco finally impatiently, interrupted, "Zap wants to go to Manitou Springs. Even with Greco gone, it is not safe, I think."

"I will-a be fine!" Zapello demanded. "I do this all the time. Greco is dead."

Zapello explained and insisted on returning to Manitou Springs where he spent a lot of time shopping and eating every Monday. He refused to let his company problems interfere with his life's routine. Swoop protested too, but Zapello would not listen. Finally, they gave up.

"Well, I need to go to the city library," Swoop said, "I am sure I read something about somebody named Tabby-something in the Denver newspaper. He just done something in the last three weeks worthy of the news. I...I could be wrong, but need to try and look this up."

"Well, I want to go this morning. To my favorite stores. My chef-a will come along, and the head cooks for all the boys and Fernando will come. We have to buy some food and I always like to go too, look over the food. See the butchers. We go to the butchers and the grocery store. We will take the big wagon. I will have my *pistole* and so will Fernando. The cooks too - I will give the cooks some *pistole* too. They will not bother me in broad daylight. And who knows of this plan?"

Swoop and Fernando grimaced while considering.

"Zap, everyone knows this plan," Fernando said. "Everyone knows that every Monday morning you do this, you make this trip to town."

"If Deming gets rid of you, with Greco gone, Deming can

pretty much take over," Swoop said.

"Yes!" Fernando said, "And…maybe…one of Greco's friends will have plans to step up and take his place?"

"That would be very fast for them to design!" Zapello said.

Fernando added, "Yes, Archie is right. With Greco gone, if Deming and Tabby kill you? There's no one left to fight for your train company. Your patents. And they just…they will just quietly take it all over. Your partner in Ohio may or may not care anymore after all this trouble."

"I know! I go!" Zapello demanded. "I will not change my life and become the *ermita* because of them."

"Hermit," Fernando translated to Swoop.

"Okay," Swoop said. "The most dangerous part is the roadway to and from Manitou Springs. Isolated stretches. I will be with you for those parts. I guess being inside the town itself, daytime, lots of witnesses, might be safe."

And go they did. Zapello and Fernando sat up front with Fernando at the reins. The Italian chef and the main cooks were in the open back, all anticipating the purchase of a wagon full of food stuffs and gear. Swoop was on his horse at times running up front to scout the road ahead. Thus far, it was a clear, cold day. When they touched the city limits, Swoop rode beside the wagon.

"You are here. I'll be off for the library," Swoop said. "I don't know how long this will take. When I'm done. I'll go by the grocery store and butchers. If you are gone? I'll head back to the compound. But I wish you would wait for me."

"We will be okay. No matter. We have five guns here. See you later, my friend," Zapello said.

Swoop took the side streets to the library that he'd seen before while walking around the small town, as the supply wagon trundled off in their direction through the packed snow to the main streets. The volunteer city library was a small, ramshackle single-story place, only open a few hours a day, a few days a week. Fortunately for Swoop it was open. He slapped the reins around the wooden rail, and they whipped into a tie-off for his horse. He stepped inside.

"Hello, ma'am, may I presume that this library collects the local newspapers? From Denver?"

"Yes, sir, you may presume such a thing. Colorado Springs papers too."

"Is there any chance I can 'presume' the last three weeks of just the Denver ones then? Well, maybe make that the last four weeks?"

She smiled and guided him to a table and from nearby pulled a stack of newspapers from a shelf. Judging from the overloaded shelves, it looked like they'd collected every local newspaper for years and years, the bottoms of each pile looking crusty yellow.

"Presume away," she said.

The newspapers were familiar as he had little else of the news to study each day but these very periodicals. He started at the beginning and scanned the information. They were full of local business news and events, important and unimportant. A new restaurant. A fishing tournament. International news. A downtown bar fight that turned into a stabbing. The Denver Grizzlies baseball team went on a winning streak, then a losing streak. There were follow-up news stories about the Wounded Knee Massacre – more than half of the Lakota killed were women and children. Liliuokalani was proclaimed Queen of Hawaii, and…

"Hummm-dinger!" Swoop proclaimed. And there it was two weeks back in the sports section. A photo of several track and field runners, taken in southern New Mexico. A Tabby Stallmouth from Denver, Colorado had won a marathon race by a wide margin. One of many wins. The Denver newspaper did a short feature on the local track and field star. He was from Memphis, Tennessee, a former U.S. Marine with duty in the States and in Panama. He was a law student and an advisor and stockbroker to several Denver-area businesses, which they did not name. The feature went on to report that he was a proud member of the Rocky Mountains Gentlemen's Club, where he spends many dedicated hours, in the rain, snow or shine running vast distances on the Curtis Park Trail behind the club, where he might run 25 miles or more in a single trip every day, in any kind of weather. Next to the story was an advertisement for the club.

"Mister Tabby Stallmouth," Swoop said aloud. "Runner. Rocky Mountains Gentlemen's Club. Curtis Park Trail."

After two hours of shopping, the Zapello wagon was full of supplies, almost crushing the chef and cooks into a far corner of the wagon bed. Fernando guided the team back home. Zapello juggled with his ornate pipe, lighting it up amid all the shifting and bouncing, despite the four wagon wheels wrestling amid the frozen ruts and juts of the roadway. Some snow fell, creating almost a white fog.

Just past the unofficial city limits, the two men up front hypnotically watched other sporadic riders coming and going ahead, slowly appearing and disappearing on the turnpike. But one manifested ahead from an opening in the trees and approached them. The man was well dressed and given the weather they thought nothing of the neckerchief-scarf wrapped around half his face. Closing in, they noticed that the horse was beautiful, muscular, an expensive racehorse in build. Zapello had seen that horse before? The tack impeccable, along with the man's clothing. And the hat! That hat…

it…

"Tabby," Zapello blurted out.

With that announcement, the man and horse closed in the final few feet, and the rider pulled a pistol from his big side pocket. He aimed right at Zapello!

"Noooo," Fernando yelled.

The man fired!

Fernando let loose of the reins and in a gawky motion, reflexively dove in front of his lifelong friend. Tabby's bullet hit not his target Zapello, but rather the round plunged into Fernando's chest.

The close explosion instantly threw the wagon's two-horse team into a frenzy. Both geldings reared back on their hind legs in as much as the wagon tongue allowed. Then in an odd move, perhaps due to the narrow road and the inability to move backwards, the horses once full afoot again, charged forward at the lone rider!

The cooks scrambled to their knees, then feet, struggling with their balance and trying to pull their pistols from under their thick jackets. One of the cooks fell right off the back of the wagon!

Tabby, with pistol still in hand, yanked his reins to the right and had to escape from the appearance of pistols and the crazed horses. His horse leapt into the snowbank, struggling with its depths at first, until it could dash away into the bordering tree line. Not a shot was fired from the wagon. The shootist was quickly gone, out of sight in the pine trees. Fernando lay across Zapello, on his lap, gurgling and gasping. Zapello lunged for the reins and yanked them back. This stopped the horses.

"Fern! Fernando!" Zapello yelled, then ordered "turn this wagon around!" Zapello shouted to the cooks in the rear.

His emotions couldn't wait a second for the tedious turn-around process. Zap somehow climbed out from under his friend, got on the ground below, then impulsively hauled Fernando into his arms and began carrying him back into the city, since the city was north and the wagon faced south. The main chef got one leg, then the other over up front and into the wagon seat, got the reins and started the back-and-forth steps of turning the wagon around. The other cook that fell from the bed, got up on his feet.

Fernando was almost as big as Zapello! Zapello gasped and began to sob. He stumbled with almost every step, still driven by a force of desperation. He could see the north side of Main Street and spotted just a few, distant citizens looking his way after hearing the gunshot.

Swoop Swellen was on his horse, leaving the library when he heard the muffled bang filtered through the snow-covered pine trees bordering the town. It echoed through the buildings and crooked streets. He winced at the sound trying to decipher its meaning, its origin, then he heel-kicked his steed toward the Pike's Peak road.

Swoop rounded some street corners, running his steed as fast as the grounds would permit.

"Oh, no," he said aloud as he closed in.

In the distance, a man lay on his back on the ground, with another man sitting next to him, leaning over him. Who was what? He got closer. The man down on the snow was Fernando. The man over him, crying and howling, was Zapello. Swoop dismounted and walked up to them. Some inquisitive people from the town now approached them too. The wagon, now righted and northbound, drove up nearby and stopped. The cooks, the ones in front and on the ground, drew near. Zapello rocked his upper body back and forth like an uncontrollable child. He looked up at Swoop.

"He come from the trees. A surprise. He shoot. Fern…he jump-a in front of me. He take the bullet meant for me! His chest. Into his chest."

Swoop knelt down too, knees into the snow. Fernando Bosco was dead. Stricken by this, Swoop just sat back on the ground. Two of the cooks also kneeled down by them.

"Who?" Swoop asked.

"Tabby," Zapello answered. "It was this Tabby. His evil eyes. His hat. His clothes. His body. His-a face shape. His rich horse he rode at the compound the other day. I try to carry Fern to the hospital, while the wagon turned around. It was a crazy idea. Here, this is as far as I could go."

Swoop nodded. He got up, gathered up his horse's reins and motioned for the main chef to walk to the wagon.

"Where'd he go?"

"Follow me, I show you," the chef said.

"Okay," Swoop said, then he told the other cook, "Get Fernando in the wagon and to the funeral home. Get the sheriff. It's a murder and we have to report it. Too many witnesses not to report."

"The sheriff-a. He won't do anything?" The cook said. "He no like us."

"Yeah, I imagine so."
The chef pointed to the break in the trees and the escape route.

Swoop walked back to Zapello and knelt again beside him.

"Zap, there are too many witnesses to this," he whispered.

Some citizens were around them even closer now, gawking and talking.

"We have to tell the sheriff something," Swoop said. "Listen, do NOT tell the sheriff it was Tabby. Tell him it was a stranger who, I don't know, got mad that the wagon took up too much of the road and he couldn't pass. Or, or say it was a highway robber."

"Highway robber man," Zapello repeated.

"Tell the sheriff that. Give me a day or two. I found out at the library who Tabby is now and I know where he lives and visits."

"You take care of this for me too?" Zapello asked, within sniffles.

"I will take care of this. Tell the cooks what I just said. That is the story, A robber. A highwayman."

"Yes-a. Robber."

"I will see you today maybe. Tomorrow maybe," Swoop said.

"May God help-a you."

"I don't think God's gonna have much to do with this," Swoop said and mounted his horse.

"He go there. He went that way. Our horses reared at him, and we tried to pull our guns. They were under our jackets. Hard-a to do. Poor Manuel, he fell out of the wagon. All that scared the shooter off into the woods. There."

"Okay. And he was alone?"

"Si."

"Okay. Take care of Zap. I'll just see where these tracks go."

Horse and rider jumped into the roadside drift and after just a few steps, it started snowing heavily. What tracks he could see led to trees and other drifts, He followed what he could, but it soon became futile. He stopped at a clearing and scanned the landscape. There were many wild-woods-ways with intersecting trails to get back to Denver. And anyway, Swoop already had a lot of trackable information from the newspaper to work with.

He decided to return to the Cliff House Inn. He would rather not get involved with or be seen by the sheriff anyway. In his room he packed up a few items to make ready for a snowy trip to Denver. He would stop by Zap's train yard and pick up the best horse for the snow they suggested, and also some…dynamite.

Chapter 29: Tabby's Reckoning. Deming's Reckoning.
Curtis Trail Park

Tabby Stallmouth would never let a snow gale interfere with a morning or afternoon run. His physical constitution, his psychology would fall unbalanced, a bad day without a routine run.

Wrapped up where he could like a mummy with his eyes and nose open between upper and lower scarves, he jogged his favorite trail outside the Rocky Mountains Gentlemen's Club. He ran through the white and gray landscape, his mind free, the cold air in his lungs a wonderous cold, his sinuses fully clear and almost painfully raw.

As he trudged along, aspects of the Curtis Trail scenery came into view, flashes and parts of familiar rocks, trees, resting-point benches and directional signs peaking above the snow. The further out he dashed the less civilization surrounded him. His plan this white-out, blustery day? He'd run about 10 miles out, then back for a late lunch with Deming, where he would have to explain how his gunshot at Zapello missed, hitting another Italian who actually, foolishly, leapt right in front of his friend to save his life. Who does that, anyway, he wondered.

He would have to explain why he couldn't stay for a second shot among the wild-acting horses and Zapello's passengers who looked like they were all pulling pistols. He would have to tell Deming he would try again to assassinate Zapello, but it would be a bit harder the next time, maybe involving his mountain hunting rifle for a long-range shot?

"What's…that?" He thought.

A grey figure. Afoot, emerged from the snowy trailside. Someone lost? Who would be way out here in weather like this?   He had never seen anyone else in this sort of weather out there.

Swoop Swellen, wrapped in a grey blanket stepped up on the path. Tabby kept running but then stopped about 10 feet away.

"Swwwwwooo…"

"And…in…" Swoop said, and with an outstretched arm at eye level to aim – he shot Tabby in the forehead… "one second," he finished.

Tabby dropped, instantly and lifelessly in the snow. Swoop walked up to the body. The hole was small in the forehead and the round did not exit out the back, therefore scrambling around inside that cantankerous, twisted, conspiring brain and skull. He grabbed Tabby's ankles and dragged him off the trail. The snow was already settling in atop the corpse! He pulled Tabby near and under some trees and dropped him there.

Footprints and drag marks in the snow diagramed the event but would soon fill up from the fresh falling snow. Swoop turned and left on foot, on the route he came in on, to find his waiting horse further in. Tabby has had his reckoning as Swoop had promised, if they ever met again? The meeting would last but one second.

Lighter snow in Denver proper. Swoop was aboard his brown Zapello "snow" horse. Across his legs stretched a double gusset saddlebag set with the strap flaps undone. He'd rode from the Curtis Trail to the business and factory edge of town, and then drew reins across the street and up from Portland Manufacturing.

There he rested for a few seconds and looked the brick building over. Some people, mostly workers passed him walking, or on horseback or by wagon, ignoring him within the paces of their own life. All the Portland garage doors were open like last time, to let the invisible machinery heat and smells escape, wafting along with the visible smoke.

Inside the third garage door, just inside, there stood as last time, a few days earlier, their stolen, Zapello train engine replica, with its odd, track-gripping canted shape. It appeared to be complete but for some paint.

Swoop knew what he was about to do would be very, very dangerous, but not as perilous as many of the army missions of his past. He pulled the soft black neckerchief up over his face.

He pulled a cigar from a jacket pocket, lit it and lifted the cloth to stick the cheroot in his mouth. He pulled and puffed a few times to ensure the cigar's foot was burning well. Both saddlebag flaps were untied but he pulled the flaps back and folded them behind the bags. Quick access. He opened his jacket to expose his double Thunderers, the holsters not strapped to his legs but free to slant down. Quick access while on horseback.

He heel-tapped the horse forward toward the third open door. About 10 feet away he trotted the horse into the noisy factory. He stopped near the engine. He drew his lefthanded pistol, aimed at the ceiling and fired once.

"Run! Run!" He yelled to all the employes who were shocked by the gun blast and turned to him wearing expressions of dismay.

Swoop holstered the pistol, took a three-piece, tied stack of dynamite out of a bag and lit the fuse with his cigar. He tossed the bomb into the cab of the engine. He took the second stack out, this one with four sticks, lit it and chunked it under the engine, all the while astride the horse stutter-stepping horse and somewhat panicked from the gunshots and the riot-like flight of the employees. The runners spotted the burning fuses of dynamite sparking through the air!

Swoop turned the horse and galloped out and off down the street. Within a few seconds he heard the two explosions, and he hoped all the workers had time to find shelter.

The horse as promised was fast and surefooted in both the light and heavy snow, but he soon turned the steed toward the shoveled streets of downtown to confound any trackers. There, mask down, he calmly walked the avenues until he saw 11th Street - the one he'd designated for his eventual escape into the fields and woods. He turned into it, for a very roundabout path back to Manitou Springs.

So much could have gone wrong, but it hadn't, he thought. Deming's reckoning worked. Sure, he still had the stolen engine plans. Sure, they could start building another engine. But it would be quite a setback. And now for another setback, Deming had lost his gangster henchman, Tabby Stallmouth.

The snow started falling heavier again, swallowing up his tracks as he trotted off-road to the south.

Back at the factory, workers scrambled to put out the fires. As much of the engine's cab was wooden, it burned quickly. The train engine was toppled on its side and indeed ruptured, wrangled, its intricacies ruined totally. That second blast under the engine blew out the sides, and also knocked everything around it over and scattered.

Some of the men and women had dashed out the open bay doors into the winter winds. They watched the rider become just a blurry dot in the falling snow.

Deming and his assistant bolted into the warehouse.

"What the…what happened?" he asked to all aloud.

"Sir, a man on a horse, in a mask rode in here, he…he fired his pistol in the air and told us all to run, then he dynamited the engine," one replied.

"Turner!" Deming growled.

He turned to his assistant and ordered, "Get Tabby over here!"

The man spun for the lobby.

"Turner," he repeated in a growl, "I'm either gonna kill him or hire him."

Chapter 30: Subsequent Reckonings
The Cliff House, the next morning...

Bound for the Zapello compound with the good news that Tabby had been revenged and Deming's train engine destroyed, Swoop walked out the back doors of the Cliff House bound for the stables. The world was crisp, clear and frigid, but a mighty row of grey clouds was inching in from the west. Sometimes it was hard to tell the clouds from the snowy Rocky Mountain range tops.

"Mr. Turner!" The teenager said, "ready to go again?"

"Yes, Bobby."

"Horse or wagon?"

"Let's pick the wagon."

The teen turned off and away to hook a horse to the Zapello wagon Swoop used. Swoop waited, admiring once again the large, well-kept, Cliff House stables and operation. It even smelled good in there.

Then, his eyes fell upon another open wagon nearby. This wagon, this grain of wood, the hinges, the wheels and axles, the brown leather padded seat on springs, the buckboard, the tongue, the yoke, the sideboard and the metal bracings, the jockey box, all were a U.S. Army grade-purchase and issue.

Swoop had seen them as well as ordered them a plenty. It had everything but U.S. Army engraved on the metal or burned into the wood. It was so obvious, it might as well be so marked, but such wagon-branding was not standard.

"Bobby? Bobby who rode this wagon in?" Swoop asked.

"Oh, a real big, old feller. Crusty."

"What's he look like?"

"In buckskin clothes. Ho! Hairy and cranky."

"What's his name?" Swoop asked.

Bobby walked over to a big book on a wooden stand, by the office door.

"Ahh, he signed his initials only…G.W. He shoulda signed his whole name, but he didn't. My fault, sir."

"G.W." Swoop repeated. Gee Willikers. The Army's special bounty hunter.

"He checkin in the hotel?"

"He didn't say, sir," Bobby said, "just caretaking the horse and wagon for now."

"He say how long?"

"Bout a day maybe, sir, is what he said."

"Alone?"

"All alone."

Swoop looked into the back of the buckboard and that sealed his assumption, there were wooden, obvious U.S. Army boxes in the back and army blankets.

"Can I see the horse?"

"Well, sure," Booby said and guided Swoop to a stall.

The horse poked its head out of his stall and Swoop saw on the left shoulder, the brand "U.S.". The army had branded all of their horses like this since the 1850s.

"How long ago he stable this wagon?"

"One hour. Bouts."

Bobby had the Zapello wagon ready, and Swoop climbed aboard. He gave Bobby a whole quarter tip and the boy about gagged with excitement at the amount.

"This 'G. W.' feller. He's my crazy uncle. He thinks I owe him money. If this feller asks you about me, or someone who looks like me anyway, don't tell him a thing, okay?" Swoop said with a wink. He looked at the wall phone and pointed to it. "I may call you from time to time and ask if his wagon is still here."

"Yes, sir. Bad ol relatives, huh sir?"

"Bad ol something, yeah."

Swoop and transport went out the back, open doors and onto the rear field of the hotel grounds. He remembered what a ruthless sniper ol Willikers was and took a deep breath with the chance of being suddenly hit from nowhere? He remembered a back road off the property and off the main road. He pulled up the furry collar of his jacket, pulled down his hat and steered off for that older, less traveled, road.

Gee Willikers! He knew that Gee Willikers was their main manhunter and good for such a track down. They only used Willikers for vendettas. Dead or alive was not an option. He made it across the clearing, thinking about being shot from a distance? Now, he had to leave the area, the region. Right now. He knew it was getting around time to leave Manitou Springs for good anyway.

The sheriff had been called in after Tabby shot Fernando and he might start nosing around, questioning people about him too. But how in the world would the U.S. Army guess he was there, so damn fast? Just weeks. He thought a coincidence unlikely, but rather, just good, dogged manhunting.

For the first time since riding away from his Dakota post months ago, a blanket of depression fell over him. He really felt hunted now, not just lost and forgotten by the Army, but now hotly pursued. He knew that Willikers was often called upon for assassinations. He always knew he would be captured if stumbled upon someday, but chased this fast and furiously? And now, a known and very vicious bounty hunter was close at hand. He thought he knew what that tail would feel like, but it was just a guess. The real feeling, this new anxiety was much worse.

This back road connected to the main Pike's Peak roadway, further east, then he headed to a cut off for the Zapello compound. He made his way successfully and once inside the gates he stopped and examined the grounds. This opening layout of the compound was another wide space from which to be sniped. The men were all busy, and he couldn't spot any new visitors, horses or wagons at or near the main house. He could see no suspicious activity on the hillside behind the cabin where he and Zapello waited the other night. But Willikers would be impossible to spot anyway.

He rode around the cabin first, looking everywhere, eyeing where he would park if on an ambush mission. It all seemed clear as could be and then he stopped around by the front porch of the cabin and dismounted.

Zapello was at the main conference table again, looking over some ledgers when Swoop walked in.

"How are you doing, Zap?" He asked.

"I don't know. And now I have lost my best friend Fernando. I feel bad. He saved my life."

"Zap," Swoop said, sitting at the table, "and now I will tell you that Tabby is gone."

"He is?"

"He is."

"How did…"

"You do not need to know Zap. Better you don't, but it is done. And the train engine Deming is building? Gone. Blown up. That will at least stall him. Listen Zap, now I need to go."

"Blown up! But...you? Go?"

"Get?"

"Get go, you mean leave here?" Zapello said.

"Yup," Swoop said. "Listen, I was in the army as you presumed, and I never told you what happened as to why I left. But I left it. I walked away and now the Army is looking for me. They are getting close, too close and I have to go. Now. Right now." He stood.

"I…I see. Well, in the matter of two weeks, you have solved my biggest problems. I would be happy for you to stay. To oversee things here. Can my Denver lawyers help you?"

"No."

"Oh, no. I don't know what to say," Zapello said.

"I am…way beyond help. I need to get paid up and go."

"Of course. And I want to give you the wagon and the horse you are using."

"Oh?" And Swoop pondered that for a few seconds. The wagon would be great, and in this weather, it had a canvas cover to install over the bed that he could sleep under in the snow and rain. But it would also slow him down if he needed to make a fast run. But then, he could just make a quick escape with the wagon's horse.

"Can I buy a saddle from you?" Swoop asked.

"No! You cannot buy one. I can give you a saddle, and all the tack. Because you have done so much for me, you have saved my life, and you have saved the future of this company. And…and saved my romance life, too."

Swoop grunted at the mention of romance and a thought of Catty Corners, along with a smiling smirk.

"Okay," Swoop said, "I'll throw the tack in the bed. Yes."

"Breakfast?" Zapello asked.

"Actually, my friend, I'd really best be going."

"Now? Right now? Momento nel tempo?"

"I think so. Yes," Swoop said.

"It is this bad-a, eh?"

"Yes. So bad, I cannot go back to the Cliff House. I have a favor to ask you. I have money in the hotel safe, the army may or may not find out about it. It is my life savings and I have a feeling that I should not go back to the hotel, or to town to get it. There may be an ambush for me."

"Oh, no!"

"Someday, don't know when, can I send a telegram to the hotel and get them to release the money to you. Maybe then you can send it to me? To a bank somewhere where I can get it fast and run. It is my life savings."

"Of course. Yes-a," Zapello walked over to an enormous rolltop desk and shuffled through some drawers. He pulled out a stack of money, dealt through it quickly like a deck of cards and handed Swoop 50, 10 dollar bills.

Swoop's eyes widened and said, "Thank you sir."

"Thank YOU!" Zapello said.

Zapello walked to a telephone and called the kitchen, telling the chef to pack up enough food for a camping trip and met him at the big service barn.

"Okay, come on," Zapello said, slipping on a coat.

The duo left the cabin and Zapello trudged in the snow to a covered shelter of gear. Swoop lead the wagon horse to its open doors. Following Zapello's instructions, a worker tossed a new horse blanket, new saddle and halter and reins into the bed of the wagon.

The chef walked in with a canvass bag of food.

"Thank you, signore," Swoop said.

"And here-a, you need fire-a *partite*," the chef said, handing him a box of matches. Swoop tossed them into the bag and hoisted it in the wagon.

"I reckon I'll head southeast," Swoop said, after the worker left.

"Better flat land. There are roads there well into New Mexico," Zapello said.

"That telephone work?" Swoop asked, pointing to one on the wall near the barn.

"Yes. It should."

Swoop walked over and cranking the handle. Heard a dispatcher respond and he asked for the Cliff House Inn Stables. In a moment, stable boy Bobby Crisp answered. The connection was terrible.

"Bobby, this is Archie Turner. Is that wagon we talked about still there?"

"No sir, it…after…you…"

Swoop pressed the earpiece tighter to his ear and said, "So, it's gone now?" He yelled into the phone.

"Yes, sir, on the…same back…. they…so I…" the connection got even worse. So bad, Swoop gave up on it.

"Okay, okay, goodbye."

"Zap, I am leaving. Can you do me another favor? If people come and ask about me, tell them I went to Colorado

Springs. I will head south instead."

"I will, my *aimco.*"

"I wish you all the luck with your train business. You must sue Deming."

"I willa. I will!"

They shook hands.

"They like to say-a, you never see a Sicilian cry. You saw me cry over Fernando. But not again. So, you must hurry and go. Goodbye my friend."

Swoop jumped into the wagon bound for the compound exit. But wait…did he think he heard Bobby on the bad phone call say the word, "they" about leaving the stable, and not "he" left the stable? "They" left the stable? Two, not one? Or more?

Swoop's blood began to boil. He stopped at the gate. A "he" or a "they," he refused to run away with that damn mountain man maybe a half day, a day or just two days right behind him. The sudden gut feeling, the fist-clenching thought squeezed the reins and made him sneer. He stopped the wagon.

He did not turn right for a flight on the southern escape route, but instead headed left and back to Manitou Springs, with a crazed idea. A plan. He'd eyed the long rectangular wooden supply box in the back bed.

One quarter of the way back to the city, the road was wide enough to turn the wagon around. He did. Once again facing south, he pulled the brake. He climbed back and emptied the big, long box. He peeled off his jacket and hat…

In about 10 minutes, through a fresh, new snowfall, that very Army wagon from the stable approached on the road. There was indeed a "they," not just a "he," as two people sat in the wagon seat front seat. None other than Catty Corners sat next to Gee Willikers.

"That's him," Catty said.

"Sure?" Willikers asked.

"Yes. The wagon. The hat. That coat. That's him. Just sitting there."

"Looks like him…why's he stopped?" Willikers asked aloud, trying to discern movement within the slow, falling flakes.

The snow muffled the sound of their approaching wagon down to nothing. As soon as the Swoop wagon was in full sight and close, just some 100 feet away, Catty Corners impulsively pulled Greco's Italian revolver from her purse, took aim and shot at Swoop's figure on the driver seat ahead.

"Hells bells, woman!" Willikers cried out at the obviously missed, long distance shot. "You are…"

Catty turned the pistol on Willikers!

But on the slow wagon approach, Willikers had already drawn back his buckskin coat, and he was ready to pull his Colt out. He grabbed her gun arm with his left hand, pulled the pistol and hit her with the barrel hard in the face. Severely stunned, she almost fell off the high wagon seat.

"You have become useless to me!" Willikers said.

He shot her in the chest. She tumbled right off the wagon. Willikers immediately looked ahead at the Swoop Swellen rig. The snow had also really muffled the gunshots, but how much? He reached back and pulled up his rifle from the bed, took a "veteran" steady aim and shot the seated Swoop in the upper back. His bullet hit and flapped Swoop's jacket.

"What the…" he quickly worked the lever action and shot again. This time the force knocked the brown hat right off of the high jacket's collar. And Swoop was now…was he…sitting there headless?

"What the…" he said, squinting and working the lever action again, he was calculating the situation, realizing that…

Then Willikers was hit. Twice in his chest from the right side and from ground level. One round struck his hand on the stock and trigger finger on the rifle, busting through it, shrapnel tearing into him. The other round thumped him high in the chest. He felt the hot metal burn through him. He looked around, looked at his rifle, felt of his chest.

"Who…?"

Catty Corners had fallen hard and fast, but into the deep snow, and she still had that pistol in her hand throughout the fall! And, she had a line of fire straight to Willikers as he stood in the wagon. She'd crawled back a few inches away on the frosted road until she saw enough of …to shoot him twice and try to kill him.

"You monster!" She yelled.

"You witch!" He yelled back.

Willikers cursed.

Catty cursed.

Willikers now suddenly dizzy, with blood filling up his mouth, lost his balance and dropped to the roadside on the other side of the wagon. Their short, doomed, temporary and sinister partnership had come to a bloody end. They could still see each other, now on either side and under the wagon and grounded. But neither had the strength or the mind to try another shot.

Swoop Swellen, wrapped in the dull, grey blanket, emerged from the pine trees near Willikers wagon, his rifle aimed in the direction of his two downed pursuers. He glanced back at his wagon down the road and the wooden box he'd wrapped his coat around and the upturned collar he'd stuffed his hat on. His horse at the far end was fine and unhit, patiently waiting.

"Can, can you help me, Archie?" Catty Corners mumbled.

Swoop picked up her pistol. The falling snow thickened. He knelt, to better see her and glance at Willikers every few seconds.

"You have tried to kill me twice now," Swoop said.

"Lt. General Swellen," she said his name and rank, "there is a $1,000 bounty on you. I had to do this…"

"One! Thousand dollars!" Swoop said. "Impossible."

"Look…in…my purse."

He did. He reached over and unhooked her purse from her shoulder. He pulled out a folded piece of paper. He saw the drawing of his face, his name, and across the top, the words "traitor," "AWOL" and above that at the very top, the phrase - "Renegade General."

"What…did you do?" She asked between painful gasps.

"It's what I didn't do," Swoop said.

"That's a lot of money, and I wanted it, and this hillbilly turd had a wagon to cart you off in and…and help me catch you…"

"And cart my dead body off," Swoop said.

"Your dead body, and he…he needed local help to find you fast. He asked around the Springs and found me."

"Cat. Cat. Cat. You should have stayed in Denver like I told you, girl."

"Looks like it. Yes. We…we play pretended we would split the money. But I knew he wouldn't. He knew I wouldn't. I knew he would kill me. I just…I just got too excited and shot at you too soon."

"You knew he needed to kill you, and you knew, you needed kill him."

"It was a…" and she stopped talking. Her head rolled to the side. Her red lipstick touched the snow.

Swoop kicked her hard in the leg. Nothing. He dropped her pistol near her on the ground. He circled the wagon's horse and looked at Willikers.

His eyes were open, his chin flapping wind. He coughed, more like vomited a few ounces of blood and guts. The blood left a stream from his mouth onto the snow.

"Kilt down by a damn hussy," he muttered, "lung shot to shit. Gun hand punctured."

"Yup."

"Why you leave the Army?" Willikers asked. "Walk… walk away like that. You were some kinda got-dang hero once."

"Tired of killing, Gee. And this time, you two did it for me, killing each other off. I had a plan to stop y'all, but not with this ending."

"You'd a kilt us…huh?"

"Yup," Swoop said.

"Hey, trooper, if so? (he gasped) Why not put a bullet in me, anyway, huh? And end this slow, slippin off, will ya? Ima hurtin, Swoop. Ima dizzy and on-fire in my chest, sick to my stomach."

"Nope."

"Nope?"

"Nope," Swoop said again, "because I want only y'all's bullets in each other and none of my bullets for when the army comes and finds ya."

"Well then, geeeet my pistol and shoot me."

"Nope.:"

"Yer conniving won't matter a wit. Yer a wanted man, already dead or alive for one thousand dollars. A 'Renegade General,' an AWOL traitor. They can't have an AWOL general runnin abouts with a bad story about Wounded Knee. You'll never have a moment's peace in your whole life. Shootin me into peace, er not. But it's the right thing to do. You know it. You KNOW it!"

"You've still got a pistol in your holster, mountain man, shoot cha own damn self."

"Can't. Arms…arms don't seem to work. I don't even feel em. Dizzy, I say! This bullet done cracked my chest right in the center. And anyway, I ain't got the, the gumption, the fortitude lcft in me to do in my own self in, I…"

"Ain't? You've killed a lot of people," Swoop said in a low tone.

"I know. So have you." Willikers said just as low.

"I know," Swoop whispered.

And Willikers died. Swoop kicked him in the leg. Nothing. He walked back to his wagon down the road, high stepping through the snow. He moved the upright, "wounded" wooden box of himself off the front seat and back into the bed. He inspected the hole in the back of his jacket, then put it on. He picked up his shot hat, with its new hole, already half covered in fresh snow.

He climbed aboard and giddy upped back to the front gates of the Zapello compound about one mile away.

Once back at the front gates, he shouted out to a worker nearby.

"Hey! Hey there!"

"What? Yess-a?" The worker responded.

"Hey, looky here, can you tell somebody at the cabin to call the county sheriff? A man and a woman shot each other to death up the road to Manitou."

"Oh, no! I willa, sir. Yes," the Sicilian said.

"They're both dead, but I also worry more for the horse left out there attached to the wagon," Swoop said. "Somebody has to go get the horse."

"I compredere."

Then, Swoop Swellen took the south road, bound for "points unknown," New Mexico? Arizona? A new sense of empty, dread fell over him again.

The first few days, the first few weeks after Fort Shannon, he felt a sense of relief, of escape. Then that passed over when thrust into Zapello's problems and into a whole other world. But that was now over too. Now, hired killers would be after him.

His world, his past was really, truly over. He was anew. Reborn as a devil. Now totally new and alone, any and all achievements erased.

His body rocked with the ruts in the unseen iced road under the snow. The road ahead fogged white with little visibility. Little hope. There have been many reckonings these three weeks. This very day, Swoop had finally met with his own sort of reckoning – his future. His punishment for the things he did do, and the things he didn't.

Chapter 31: Tricked and Succumbed

Two days later, Major Twenty's small, makeshift army fugitive platoon appeared in Manitou Springs. At first, they heard no word from Gee Willikers for days. What did that mean? Did he need a few more quiet days "breaking ground" before they amassed? Then Fort Logan received a telegram from the region's sheriff's office that a man and woman were shot and killed on an Army issue wagon. The horse had the standard "U.S." brand on the left shoulder. And there was a Fort Logan regiment brand on the left hip. That had to be Williker's issued horse and wagon.
Also, the initial description of the dead man matched that of Gee Willikers, and the dead woman could have been Catty Corners.

Major Twenty and the other officers thought it best to pack up and head right out for the Springs. Sheriff Gene Martins promised to 'freeze' the scene for them to look over, as the bodies were already frozen solid in place from the weather since the shooting.

Major Twenty replied by another telegram to the local sheriff's office about their plans upon their arrival and Sheriff Gene Martins himself volunteered to meet them at the hotel.

They gathered at the Cliff House, the last known location of Swoop Swellen. They learned from the hotel crew that Swoop was absent for several days now and they quickly heard even more gossip about the shooting on the road to Pikes Peak and how a local known, "gal-about-town," Catty Corners was shot and killed by a mountain man.

After the Army officers heard about the events of the last few weeks, the three piled into Swoop's hotel room for a search. Sheriff Martins stood in the doorway beside hotel manager Howard Holden.

"He's been nothing but the most pleasant guest," Howard Holden said.

"A pleasant guest? One that buried a cavalry sword into someone's head out there on Main Street?" Major Twenty commented while he tossed the room.

"There is a long story behind that duel Sir, and the cretin what had his head plunged, deserved it," Holden said. "He was a murdering cutthroat. Mr. Turner, or as you would call him, Mr. Swellen, was a gentlemen's gentleman."

Major Twenty's eyes cut over to the sheriff, hunting an opionion on all that.

"These were duels and *CON*-senting parties can duel here-abouts in the Rockies," Sheriff Martins said. "There's a few new laws about using guns in duels, but there's nothin on the books about…about knife duels or certainly sword duels."

"Look, he even left his suitcase behind. What calm traveler leaves a suitcase?" Lt. Bernes commented. "Mr. Holden, do you have a hotel safe? Does he have anything in the hotel safe?"

"No, he does not," Holden lied.
"What do you discern from all this, Major?" Lt. Tembers asked Major Twenty.

"He left in a hurry. Look what he left," Major Twenty said. Twenty picked up Swoop's swagger stick and turned it in his hands. "Like this. This was an important memento to him.

Then these books. Look around. Clothes. He left, he ran like an escapee."

The search was fast and simple. No clues were found more than a too-much-left-behind, fast getaway.

"Well then sheriff, let's get out to the shooting scene on the road, if you will," Major Twenty said.

"Let's," the sheriff said.

Twenty kept the swagger stick.

Out on the roadway all the soldiers trudged around in the snow, intermingling with the sheriff and a few deputies, mentally and physically scratching their heads. Their Army horses and their wagons were parked about 20 feet away to keep the unusual scene clear. The day before the deputies roped off the wagon and bodies, steering passersbys off to the side of the road until the Army could have their look-see.

"I don't know," Major Twenty said, "what do you think, Sheriff?"

"Other than the horse, which we rescued two days ago, hey, I reckon it's for sure an Army horse, Major?"

"It is."

"We have em stabled for ya. Anywho, this is how we found them," the sheriff continued, "wagon. Bodies. Spread out like this. I thought it best to leave em all frozen like this for you to look at. No harm done leavin em in these positions with this cold ass shine we got this week." The sheriff took a dip of tobacco and continued. "It could be, looks like to me, that this man and this here woman...they shot each other. Could be your fugitive shot them? Could be. Ain't seeing how just yet."

"Maybe someone else shot them to steal the body for the bounty?" Lt. Tembers suggested.

"In such case," the sheriff continued, "then somebody will be turning Swellen's body in somewhere for the $1,000 reward. Not happened yet that we can tell. Not around here anyway. I mean, they could sneak the body down to Phoenix and try cashing it in there. We wouldn't know around here.

Army would eventually. But anyways, we'll have to turn our doctor loose on em in Colorado Springs to pull the bullets. We got the guns. See what he determines."

"I am fairly sure my General will want a military autopsy doctor in on that autopsy," Major Twenty said.

"Oh, sure, yeah, that can happen for sure. Do you know how well these two folks knew each other?"

"That is the woman, Catty Corners," Lt. Tembers said, "that marched into our headquarters last week with a wanted poster in her hand, claiming she knew where Swellen was and she wanted the $1,000 right then, right there."

"And that is our army scout Gee Willikers," Lt. Bernes said.

"I think they got to know each other," Major Twenty said, "only the day before yesterday! Real fast, to bounty hunt our renegade general. Willikers probably hunted her down first in town because she knew where Swellen was. I reckon from what I hear of the lady, and what I know of Willikers, they both wanted all the money and I think maybe you are right, sheriff. They may well have killed off each other, whence closing in on the prey."

"But where is the prey? Where's Swellen? Maybe he's laying out here dead too? Shot and crawled off?" Lt. Bernes said.

"Could be, could be," the Sheriff said.

"Men!" Major Twenty turned to his ten-man team waiting south of them. "Get afoot and search this whole area. Bullet distance. Look for Swellen's body or anything interesting out there."

"Rifle or pistol distance, sir?" one troop asked.

"Both."

"With this snow, it'll cover over a lot. Many layers. Spring-melt might turn up something," the sheriff added.

The troop dismounted and walked off, scanning the grounds.

"Now here's a bit of twitch ya need to know," Sheriff Martins said. "You told me your fugitive worked for the Zapello Train Company. Well sirs, just four days ago, just before lunchtime, someone tried to kill Zapello just outside of Manitou Springs. On this very road here, but way closer in, to town."

"That sounds like something," Major Twenty said.

"Zapello told me that a stranger rode up on horseback to their wagon to rob them and shot right at him, but Zapello's old friend jumped in the way and his amigo took the bullet in his gizzard. And the poor bastard died in a minute or two. Zapello said the stranger rode off lickety-split because he was afraid of being shot by the other men in the wagon. Oh, and the shooter was not Swoop Swellen, he's a sure of that. Swellen was not there. We don't know who the shooter was or why. Secret train business maybe? Robbery maybe."

"Just a few days ago!" Lt. Bernes said, astonished.

"This is a real mess," Major Twenty said, "could that somehow be involved in all this here?"

"Hell, if I know," the sheriff said.

Major Twenty walked up close to the once rangy, cantankerous, Gee Willikers, now just a gray, ice block of a figure, ever so preserved in the frosty wind chill. His eyes were iced open. Despite Twenty's war veteran, army officer constitution, it was an odd, hellish sight for him, and brought to his mind the recent dead, frozen bodies of Wounded Knee, of which he was a big part. A shooting part. He saw the corpse's shattered right hand and leaned in for a tighter look.

"Hard to believe this rough old son of a bitch would be tricked by anybody and succumbed by anything. He himself was the quintessential ambusher," Major Twenty said.

"Well, we'll be riding out there to see Zapello next," Lt. Bernes said. "We'll find out what he knows about Swellen."

"With all this commotion," the sheriff said and spit, "I'll bet Swellen's a long-gone daddy. I'll just give ya a head start on that Zapello bit of business. I spoke with Zapello. He said he hired Swellen for security awhile back and Swellen left middle of last week for Colorado Springs." He spit tobacco again. "So, if that's true? He wasn't here for this here shoot-em-up mess either."

"Zapello could be lying," Major Twenty said, but he knew Swoop left in a bit of a hurry, leaving much behind in his hotel room. Twenty held that very swagger stick in his hand now.

"He could be lying," the sheriff repeated.

Major Twenty bent down and studied the gun in Willikers' holster. Gee was in a gunfight? But his pistol was still holstered? But the leather strap was unhooked from the hammer. What to make from that? He moved the strap with the swagger stick. It too was frozen.

Lt. Tembers was thinking the same thoughts about Willikers' gun. On the ground near the front of wagon by the tongue was a rifle, the stock smashed as though by a bullet. He picked it up.

"This his rifle?" Lt. Tembers asked Major Twenty.

"Looks like it," Major Twenty answered, stepping closer.

"Huh! Shattered. Shot at the workings."

"Right where we found it," the sheriff added.

"Matches up with Willikers' exploded gun hand," Major Twenty noted.

"How did this…?" Lt. Tembers mumbled aloud.

"This Catty Corner's woman is over there with a gun out," the sheriff said. "He's over there with a holstered pistol and the rifle's been shot, his rifle. Yer scout's trigger hand shot and the rifle dropped off the front of the wagon. They's side-by-side," the sheriff pointed his finger around punctuating his narration.

"There's a strong idea for me that they shot each other. My report will say as I think, they shot each other. We'll pick them up and get these frozen bodies over to the doc's, get yer trooper doctor, see what they all sez about it. Nothin carved in stone yet mind ya. But it looks that way."

"Nothing…carved…in…stone," Major Twenty slowly repeated, mindlessly tapping Swellen's swagger stick against his thigh. "Sergeant, you stay here," Twenty continued. "Put one of your horse's on this wagon. Get the bodies and their guns in the bed. Then, wait for us here, we'll go see this Mr.

Zapello. We'll be back when we can."

"Yes, sir."

"Sir, should we make a fire? Get some coffee going?" another soldier asked with a tone of desperation.

Major Twenty looked at the sheriff, trying to get a read on how long a meeting with Zapello might take. The sheriff spit, scrunched up his face and shook it side-to-side with a meaning of "no, not long."

"Don't think so Johnny, just button up, son," Major Twenty answered.

Twenty climbed aboard his horse and took one last look around and said just above a whisper, "I just can't imagine that Swellen had nothing to do with all this. He's a clever bastard."

Thirty minutes later, Zapello welcomed Sheriff Martins, Major Twenty, Lt. Bernes and Lt. Tembers into his cabin. They all sat at the conference table while the butler Pepino poured coffee and laid a tray of cheeses down within their reach.

"So, you hired Mordecai Swellen, our fugitive," Major Twenty asked. "Why?"

"Yes-a, he come as Archie Turner. I have some business problems here. Theft…ah..ah…you know, just usual business problems. And I recognized him as a…a military man when I first saw him in Manitou Springs. Very stout man. Smart. We started a conversation because he was reading a book on stoics. Very good."

"I see."

"He is a good man, and he also became a good friend. Very helpful to me."

"When did he leave?" Lt. Bernes asked.

"About a week ago?"

"Why did he leave?" Lt. Tembers asked.

"He just said my problems here were solved."

"Were they solved?" Major Twenty asked.

"Very much so. Many solved. Yes. And he wanted to

travel on again. This time to Colorado Springs. He had a horse. He just left. So I say goodbye to him."

"There was a man killed in a sword duel with him almost a week ago now," Major Twenty said, "did this involve you? Why did Swellen fight him?"

"Well-a, yes-a, the dead man was my employee, so yes in this regard it did involve me. But the dead man? He was crazy. Crazy for the sword, you know. He was always challenging anyone to fight, back in Europe too and here too. All the time. I am told a teenager wanted to fight my employee, in a revenge for my man killing his father, a month ago? Or so. And your Mr. Swellen, he step-a in and saved the boy's life by taking his place. Swellen, he is a good man, as I said-a."

"A good man," Major Twenty repeated. "And the man who tried to shoot you and killed your friend instead the other day, did Swellen have anything to do with this?"

"Oh, poor Fernando Bosco! No. How? This attack was very strange. Maybe the killer was a robber? As you say here, a highwayman? Eh? They call this place - the wild, wild west. The skunk-a ran away when my men in the wagon pulled their guns."

"What will he do in Colorado Springs?" Lt. Bernes asked. "Why there?"

"Oh, I don't know. How could I know? So tell-a me, I see that you have my friend's stick."

Swoop's swagger stick was on the table where Major Twenty set it down."

"Yes, Swellen left it in his room."

"You steal-a?"

"No," Major Twenty said, "it was abandoned."

"Ahhh, *abbandonata*. I see. I see. I would not like to be around when my friend catches you with his stick," Zapello said with a very serious expression.

"Okay then, sir. We will take your leave," Major Twenty said and stood. The others followed suit. The cheese untouched. The coffee barely sipped.

"I would like to say good luck to you gentlemen," Zapello said, "buuuut, may you never catch this Mr. Swellen. He is a very good man."

The three soldiers and the sheriff stared at him for a second, then left. Through the front windows, Zapello and the butler watched them button up their coats and pull on their gloves as they joined the few uniformed men and deputies waiting outside.

"I will give them the Sicilian evil eye, not the jealousy one, oh no. But the other kind. I wish them great misfortune. The baddest of luck," Zapello said, and he squinted, his eyes emitting the magic.

Chapter 32: 1903! The Return of Swoop Swellen
Chinatown, San Francisco, California, 1903

After the long overseas boat trip from China, Swoop Swellen felt immediately comfortable in Chinatown, for all the obvious reasons. One reason? He already missed Peking. He'd bought a suitcase and some typical American clothes in a clothing store on the ship and walked the streets with his luggage.

The whole San Francisco area had just been besieged by the Black Plague according to the newspapers aboard ship, but the disease seemed to be diminishing, he hoped.

His first day back in the United States, he wandered the Chinatown streets and bought a San Francisco Chronicle newspaper. Next, by way of asking directions in fluent Chinese, he found a local photography studio.

"Hello, sir!" the oriental proprietor said in perfect English.

"Hello, sir," he said back in Chinese.

"What can we do for you today, sir?" the man said.

"I need four photographs. Each one of me, my face, holding up this newspaper near my face. With today's paper."

"Oh?"

"I know this might sound unusual, but I need to send some letters to four old friends that I have arrived safely back in San Francisco from overseas after a long trip. Thus, the newspaper, documenting this day."

"Ohhh, I see sir. They see your face and the headlines. If you put your face up next to the newspaper sir, you and the paper will not be too, too blurry, sir. I will work on it. I see what I can do."

The man set up the photo shoot in a backroom studio. Once ready, Swoop posed, his face expressionless in front of the large camera, newspaper in hand and up. Four brilliant flashes followed and soon four photos were quickly under development in yet another back room.

Meanwhile, the photographer supplied Swoop with a pencil and pieces of paper while they waited for the processing and the drying. Swoop wrote the same message four times on four pages:

"I am back in the United States. I am no longer in China. Pat Weeps and the other two Ditch Diggers that you sent after me are dead. They were killed in the self-defense of myself and the innocent people they took hostage trying to catch me. I am back in America, maybe bound for Canada or Mexico, or maybe up in the tree just outside your back door." – Swoop Swellen.

He knew he should not be threatening. He knew not to get too angry, but he ended with a threat anyway. He couldn't help himself. He knew that even if he killed all the Ditch Diggers, there would still be others hunting him down like a dog. The $1,000 bounty remained the same after all these long years, but it was still a fortune in 1903 as it was back in 1892.

The photos turned out to be as planned. You could see Swoop's face and at least the newspaper photos and head-lines on the front page. They were a little blurry but legible.

Swoop still had the addresses of Pat Weeps, and the other two men, as well and their leader Jerry Pickwirth in Wichita, Kansas, all from information and identifications he'd collected from the three wallets of the dead men after the Peking, street shoot-out.

Once the photos were sufficiently dry, he left the shop. Swoop walked to a post office, sheepishly entering, worried that, as he knew from the past, these offices often had wanted posters.

There were indeed some on a wall, but he noted there was no wanted poster of him hanging there. Now, most of the posters had photographic pictures of the wanted men and a few women, not many drawings, and the fugitive alerts were surrounded by requests for help locating runaways and army, navy and marine enlistment ads.

Swoop bought 4 big envelopes and shoved a handwritten page and a photo in each one. When he filled out the addresses, he placed, "Jerry Pickwirth" atop each one, with "In Care Of," so there would be four chances Pickwirth would get the message through all the four addresses. He used the return address of the post office, further proving he was back in the U.S. He mailed them off at the counter.

"This will take just about five days," the clerk bragged on the short delivery time.

Five days, he thought. How far could he get in 5 days? Swoop stepped outside the post office and looked around. Last month, he once thought he might live his life out in Peking with the Bellmonts, surrounded by friends, comrades and maybe even eventually living with that Chinese woman he grew closer and closer too. She was so full of grace and peace. Now, he was once again lost and alone. He would once again stay on the move, as he had from the winter of 1891 when he left Manitou Springs, Colorado.

He would leave tomorrow morning, by boat? Or train? Or by these new, popular mechanical buses? Or stagecoach? Or horse? In the American newspapers delivered to Peking and the newspapers collected from ships, there was growing news about gold in Alaska. Should he go up there? Where? He did not know.

Soon, walking the streets, bound for the train station, he stopped in front of the San Francisco National Bank, the place, the account Johann Gunther and Dr. Bellmont's father had set up to pay him for his protection work. He stood outside the stone edifice.

Should he collect all the money? Did the Ditch Diggers know about the account already? They knew he was in Peking, China! Walking in, getting the money right then might trigger local bounty hunters he was there, giving him no safe time to escape.

With the mailed letters he had about a 5-day head start. In his account was about $800 or $900. He'd been drawing small amounts of this every few months via the Legation's American Embassy. Was that how they found him in China? Tracking this account?

He walked inside, identified himself as Robert Small to a bank teller and reported the passwords needed. He collected $840 in ten-dollar bills, stuffed the full envelope into his large piece of new luggage. This money and the money Dr. Bellmont gave him would last a while. Traveling money. Again.

And now, his life as a hunted fugitive begins again...

An office phone rang in Wichita, Kansas.

"Captain Jerry Pickwirth, Ditchdiggers Bail Bonds, Incorporated."

"Mr. Pickwirth?"

"Yes."

"Mr. Pickwirth, this is Miles Shelly, one of the vice-presidents at the San Francisco National bank?" We spoke about a certain account 6 months ago?"

"Yes. Yes, sir."

"That man we discussed, he was in one of our branches yesterday in San Francisco and he emptied out the account."

"In p-p-person?" Pickwirth said, struggling with his stuttering.

"Yes, sir,"

"San Francisco. P-p-positively identified?"

"Positively, sir."

"Anything said in the transaction about where he was bound?"

"I asked the teller, and the teller said the man said almost nothing during the transaction."

"Okay, Mr. Shelly. Thank you. Be expecting something in the m-m-mail from me very soon," Pickwirth said.

Pickwirth stood and looked out his office window. Downtown Wichita, Kansas sprawled out before his purview, but he paid no attention to it. This was why he'd not heard from Pat Weeps and the other men for almost three weeks past. Swoop Swellen must have killed them and escaped. Yet…yet again.

Epilogue
Boer War, 1903, British Military Headquarters,
Johannesburg, South Africa

A British soldier walked into the officers' quarters den, scanning all those in the big, plush room. His eyes finally alit upon the only two in United States Army uniforms.

"Aha!" the corporal declared. "Major Gunther! Mail!"

Major Gunther and Lt. Jefe Cocoy looked quizzically at the source of the letter.

"Mail? Like...U.S. mail?" Gunther asked.

They had been sending numerous newsworthy dispatches back and forth as official observers for the White House. President Roosevelt himself sent them there to personally report to him directly on the progress and details of the Boer War. But those were dispatches by diplomatic courier, yes. Regular mail? No. They never got any regular mail.

"Good morning, sir," the Brit said, "Apparently you have

a letter, from China by way of the Americas, sir."

"China? Okay," Gunther said.

Gunther took the worn, dirty letter. It was indeed addressed to:

"Major Johann Gunther, United States Army, Washington D.C., United States of America."

The writer must not have known where Gunther was and addressed the correspondence so vaguely. He took a look at the many postmarking's from the U.S. Embassy in Peking to the United States, to the Department of the Army, and now by some miracle? It was shuffled into South Africa. Then he saw the return address.

"It's from Dr. Bellmont. Peking," he told Jefe. "It took four months to get here, to track us down."

They wandered over to a large conference table and sat down. Gunther tore open the envelope. He read aloud...

Dear Major Gunther,

I hope this letter finds you and Jefe well. I hope this letter can even find you at all, as I know not where you are! I am writing in an emergency because I bring you news of our mutual friend Robert Small, otherwise known as Swoop Swellen. (Gunther and Jefe exchanged glances.)

Since your rescue of us from the Boxer Rebellion, I have settled in, married here now in Peking to a beautiful Chinese woman, and we now have a baby boy. My happiness here, my work, my family is all thanks to you and Jefe, and the situation you negotiated for me with my California parents to remain here in China with the legations here. Things are very peaceful here in China for now. I have a doctor's office in Peking just outside the legations compound gates and treat the legations from all the countries here as well as the local Chinese.

Robert Small has been like an uncle to us, perhaps even a father at times, watching over us, and working at the legations as an advisor and security. His questionable military past that was once whispered years ago, was all but forgotten.

He had become totally accepted by all as a veteran of the Boxer Rebellion and a hero."

The key word being...was. Gunther looked at Jefe and repeated, "Was." He continued,

"However, last month, three American cowboys you might call them by their attitude and appearance, showed up at my medical office. They took me and my wife prisoner at pistol-point, and demanded Robert show up at the office. They were determined to capture or even kill him using us as bait. We were not beaten, they were not savages, but were threatening. All they wanted was Robert.

As is Robert's way, he quickly showed up and killed the three men in such an efficient way, as was Robert's way. But in doing so, he had to confess to us his full, prior transgressions in the U.S. Army. He told us that therefore, he would forever be hunted there in China since his whereabouts were now known, somehow, by these bounty hunters and their company. This endangered our lives, which was exactly the opposite of his mission to provide us safety and security.

That very afternoon of the confrontation, he fled Peking, bound for the United States to announce to his bounty-hunting, pursuers that he was no longer in China and that further seeking him in China would be futile. He assured us he would somehow convey this message to them, and we would again be safe here in Peking.

I wanted to alert you of these events and to tell you that our old friend, your old comrade in arms from our "China Alamo," Mr. "Robert Small" is once again stateside. And hunted. He swore to me that he would never tell you, see you or bother you, as such would endanger even you and perhaps your military reputation. But I wanted you to know, in case someday, in some dire emergency, Mr. "Swoop" Swellen might appear at your door.

Sincerely yours,
Dr. John Bellmont
Peking, China

Page 257

"Swellen," Gunther said to Jefe, "Swoop...Swellen," and he handed Jefe the letter.

Jefe read it over again even after Gunther's narration. He folded it up and laid it on the table.

"There's nothing we can do," Jefe said.

"No there isn't. He will remain a fugitive, until...until he isn't."

"He will not show up somewhere, someday to surprise us," Jefe said.

"Probably not. Unless...unless there is a mighty, mighty big reason to," Gunther added.

"Yes. Unless..." Jefe said.

Swoop Swellen, the Renegade general returns in "Swellen's Orphans." It's 1894, and the wanted fugitive Swoop Swellen escapes from bounty hunters in a race and shootouts across an Arizona desert. His horse is killed. Desperate for food and water, when on the horizon, he sees an old church and compound. It's an orphanage, and he wanders in asking for help. Staffed by nuns and priests they welcome him in. But once there, he is quickly surrounded by male and female children and teenagers, and these orphans begin secretly, hauntingly, whispering, pleading and begging him for help from a coming, shocking, horror. These nuns and priests are not what they seem...

A JUMPIN' JACK KELLOG POLICE THRILLER
KILL THEM BACK
"THEY JUST TRIED TO KILL ME."
"WHAT'S IN THE BAG?"
"STUFF TO KILL THEM BACK."
HOCK HOCHHEIM

WHEN YOU FACE YOUR WORST ENEMY...
FACE THE MUZAK
WHEN AN OBSESSED KELLOG CHASES HIS LIFELONG ARCH ENEMY JOHN MUZAK, A PSYCHO CRIMINAL IN A MURDEROUS TEXAS CRIME SPREE, WHO WILL LIVE OR DIE?
HOCK HOCHHEIM
A JUMPIN' JACK KELLOG POLICE THRILLER

JUMPIN' JACK KELLOG IS BACK IN
TAKEDOWN THE TAKE
A TEXAS DRUG TASK FORCE RUNS WILD AND BECOMES A CORRUPT CARTEL OF DEATH AND DESTRUCTION. CAN STATE SPECIAL AGENT KELLOG TAKE THEM DOWN?
W. HOCK HOCHHEIM

JUMPIN' JACK KELLOG IS BACK. AND THAT MEANS TROUBLE... FOR EVERYONE.
DEPARTMENT OF PUBLIC SAFETY
SPECIAL AGENT
CRIMINAL INVESTIGATIONS DIVISION

TRUTH IS DEADLIER THAN FICTION
DON'T EVEN THINK ABOUT IT
BOOK 1
TRUE STORIES OF CRIME AND JUSTICE IN THE ARMY AND ON THE STREETS OF TEXAS
HOCK HOCHHEIM

TRUTH IS DEADLIER THAN FICTION
DEAD RIGHT THERE
BOOK 2
TRUE STORIES OF CRIME AND JUSTICE IN THE ARMY AND ON THE STREETS OF TEXAS
HOCK HOCHHEIM

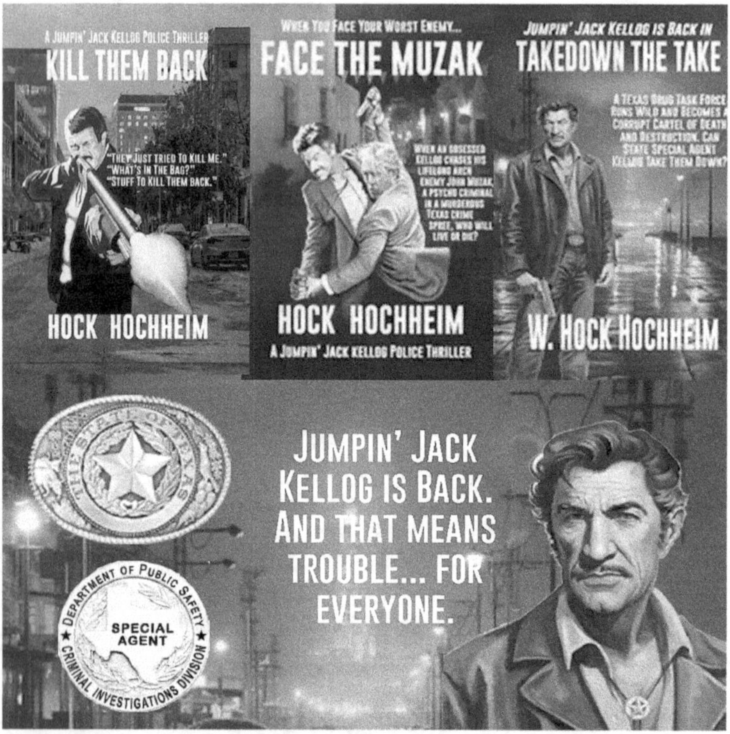

The Johann Gunther Western Hero Adventure Series. Ebooks, Paperback, Audio.

"The Horse Killers will be released Winter of 2026.